JEDBURGHS

JEDBURGHS

Set Europe Ablaze

Book 2

COLONEL RICHARD CAMP

CASEMATE

Philadelphia & Oxford

Published in the United States of America and Great Britain in 2022 by
CASEMATE PUBLISHERS
1950 Lawrence Road, Havertown, PA 19083, USA
and
The Old Music Hall, 106–108 Cowley Road, Oxford OX4 1JE, UK

Paperback Edition: ISBN 978-1-63624-174-6
Digital Edition: ISBN 978-1-63624-175-3

A CIP record for this book is available from the British Library

Printed and bound in the United States of America by Integrated Books International

Typeset in India by Lapiz Digital Services, Chennai.

For a complete list of Casemate titles, please contact:

CASEMATE PUBLISHERS (US)
Telephone (610) 853-9131
Fax (610) 853-9146
Email: casemate@casematepublishers.com
www.casematepublishers.com

CASEMATE PUBLISHERS (UK)
Telephone (01865) 241249
Email: casemate-uk@casematepublishers.co.uk
www.casematepublishers.co.uk

"And now set Europe ablaze."
Winston Churchill

Prologue

Headquarters, Office of Strategic Services (OSS), 71/72 Grosvenor Street, Mayfair District, London, England, 0930, 9 September 1942—U.S. Marine Captain Jim Cain marched purposefully down Grosvenor Street, past the looming American Embassy into the heart of "little America," so called because the surrounding square was flanked by buildings housing the huge American military buildup in London. The massive U.S. Army and Navy headquarters sat diagonally across the square. Smaller buildings fronting the quadrangle housed the overflow from the congested offices. The once beautiful park in the center of the square was dug up with rows of sandbagged trenches. Low wooden Quonset huts housing antiaircraft guns and the Women's Auxiliary Air Force barrage balloon crews were tucked in against the palatial neo-Georgian mansions that dotted the street. One of the barrage balloon wagons was sitting in the center of the park, its steel cables stretched upward above the trees to an elephantine-like silver-grey blimp filled with hydrogen. Designated the Low Zone Kite Balloon, its function was to support the steel guy wires that hung underneath it. Cain had been told that the balloon was supposed to keep German planes from swooping in low. *Hitting those cables could ruin your whole day*, he thought.

An American soldier saluted the Marine officer as he passed by. Cain winced as he returned the salute. His arm was still a little stiff and sore from the shrapnel wound in his right shoulder, compliments of a 20mm shell splinter from a German E-boat during the withdrawal aboard a British motor torpedo boat from a commando raid he had led against a radar site. He was lucky the projectile had broken up when it hit the metal ring of a .50-caliber gun mount or he'd be called "lefty." The image of that tracer round hurtling out of the darkness and the sudden pain of the shrapnel strike would never leave him. He'd spent five days in the Haslar Royal Naval Hospital trying to convince the medicos that he was "back in battery." The doctor finally relented after he swore that he wouldn't do anything strenuous. Actually, the wound had healed nicely, but it would probably be a couple more weeks before he had a full range of motion.

Halfway down the street Cain spotted his destination—a nondescript, bland, seven-story brick office building that housed the secretive Office of Strategic Services European Headquarters, America's newly formed national intelligence agency. It was just down the street from the U.S. Embassy. Drab and unpainted, the structure betrayed four years of wartime neglect, much as the other buildings on the square. *At least they're in one piece*, he reminded himself. Parts of London were in ruins, the result of the night-time German bombing. He was told that over 60 percent of the city's homes had been destroyed and over 200,000 inhabitants were left homeless by the Blitz. Despite the devastation, British morale seemed to be holding up, which Cain attributed to the Brits' signature "stiff upper lip and all that!"

Cain glanced at his watch and quickened his pace. His appointment was scheduled for 1000 and he didn't want to be late. He entered the building through the plain street-level entranceway and came face to face with the same belligerent security guards he'd confronted on his first visit. The two thought of themselves as tough guys who enjoyed throwing their weight around—literally.

"What's your business?" the pudgy one demanded brusquely. The second overweight guard stepped in front of him, blocking his way.

Unmoved by their attempt at intimidation, Cain replied politely, "I'm Captain James Cain and I have an appointment to see Mr. Kelly." One of the guerrillas checked a roster, found his name, and pointed to a circular staircase.

"Third floor, fourth door on the right," he growled.

"Thanks," Cain replied amicably, determined to ignore their hostility. He stepped around the guard blocking his path and started to walk toward the stairs. As he passed by the asshole, as Cain thought of him, the guy deliberately bumped him with his shoulder and smiled as if to say, "Soldier boys don't mean shit to me."

Acting purely on instinct—and commando training—Cain struck the miscreant in the throat with the calloused edge of his right hand. He pulled the blow at the last second, but the strike was powerful enough to send the man crashing to the floor clasping his throat and gasping for breath. The asshole's partner rushed forward. Cain side stepped, and using the man's forward momentum, grabbed him by the scruff of the neck and slammed him head first into the wall. The man went down for the count. "Oh shit," Cain exclaimed, suddenly realizing what he had done. The scuffle had happened so fast that he hadn't had time to think, only react. *How many years in prison will I get for roughing up the guards?* he wondered apprehensively. Just then a familiar voice called out in French-accented English, "Dangerous Dan would be proud of you."

Cain looked up at the top of the stairs and saw Lieutenant Colonel Henry, the French Special Operations Executive liaison officer, taking in the scene. He was greatly relieved; Henry had been with him on the raid to destroy the German radar site in the Channel Islands. The French officer was a tough son-of-a-bitch ... and he looked the part. At a brawny 16 stone (220 pounds), packed on a 6-foot-2-inch frame, the man was clearly not one to mess with. A face that was deeply scarred and a black patch over his left eye did nothing to diminish the fearsome impression.

"I'm not so sure Dangerous Dan would approve of me thumping the guards," Cain admitted. "Dangerous Dan"—the nickname for Major William Fairbairn—was the former assistant commissioner of the Shanghai Municipal Police and a renowned close combat expert, who had taught "gutter fighting" to Cain during commando training.

"Don't worry, I saw what happened," Henry replied. "Those two had it coming. I'll make sure they don't cause you any trouble. Now you better hurry; you don't want to be late for your appointment." Cain offered his heartfelt thanks and made his way up the stairs. Halfway to the top he stopped. *How did he know I had an appointment?* He looked back over his shoulder to ask Henry, but he was busy slapping one of the unconscious guards on the face—and none too gently. "Wakey, wakey," he heard Henry say, "time to rise and shine." With a smile, Cain continued to the third floor and found Mr. Kelly's office.

"Good morning, Captain Cain," the pretty female receptionist said politely as he opened the door and walked into the office. Her courteous greeting helped to soothe some of his anger over the encounter with the animal act at the security desk.

"Hello miss," he replied cordially. "I have an appointment to see Mr. Kelly."

"Yes sir, I have it on the schedule," she said, adding, "He will be right with you. Please have a seat."

Cain had hardly settled into a chair before the inner office door opened and Jack Kelly, the head of the London Special Operations Branch of the Office of Strategic Services, walked out to meet him. "Come in," he said, shaking hands. "I'm sorry to have kept you waiting." Cain was impressed. He expected to wait a minimum of half an hour just to remind him that he was a lowly captain.

Cain followed the older man into the office and took the proffered chair in front of a wooden government-issue desk, whose top was stacked with blue pasteboard files with a crimson stripe stamped SECRET across the top of the file.

"Have you made up your mind to join our team of warriors?" Kelly asked as he settled into a chair behind the desk. Kelly was referring to an offer he'd made to Cain to join a special OSS and SOE mission to work with the French Resistance. "The British are hot to have you come on board," he added. "They were impressed with the way you handled the raid." For his efforts, Cain had been awarded the British Distinguished Service Order for gallantry in action. "The equipment your commando team captured enabled the Brits to come up with a way to jam the German coastal radar network." It flashed through Cain's mind that Lieutenant Colonel Henry, who had been the second in command on the raid, must have played a large part in the request for his service on this mission. *That's how Henry knew about the appointment*, Cain realized.

Kelly leaned forward across the desk. "Let me also point out that the OSS relationship with the SOE has suffered from what I call 'the new guy on the block syndrome.' The Brits consider us to be neophytes in Special Operations, and their request for your service may indicate a thaw in our relationship. It might be just the sort of operation to prove that we're as good as they are." Kelly leaned back in his chair and fell silent. "So, what say you?" he finally asked.

"Sir, I'm your man," Cain replied excitedly. It was an easy decision to make; the promise of action was too good to pass up.

Kelly stood up and came around the desk. "Welcome aboard," he said, gripping Cain's hand tightly. "How's the shoulder, by the way?" he asked.

"Fine sir," Cain lied. "Couldn't be better," he added, trying hard not to grimace.

"Excellent," Kelly replied, "because you're scheduled to go through the SOE parachute course at the end of the week."

1

Victory Services Club, 63–79 Seymour Street, London W2 2HF, 1115, 9 September 1942—Cain lucked out and was able to snag a taxi back to the four-story Victory Services Club, a facility offering servicemen room and board, located on the prestigious Seymour Street in the heart of London. Normally he would have walked—he needed the exercise—but today he was in a hurry. He had a luncheon date with Loreena McNeal, a beautiful woman he had fallen head over heels in love with—the daughter of a retired Scottish officer whom he had met while attending the Commando Basic Training Centre at Achnacarry in Scotland. Cain had been billeted in the McNeals' home during the training and, lo and behold, the two young people developed a romantic relationship, albeit one that had been interrupted by their respective duties. Immediately after the commando course, Cain had been picked to lead a raid on a German radar station in the Channel Islands. Loreena, an officer in the Women's Auxiliary Air Force (WAAF), was stationed in the operations center of Churchill's Cabinet War Rooms and was seldom off duty. In fact, she was billeted in "the dock," a stuffy dormitory that was little more than a cave curtained off from one of the many corridors beneath the New Public Office Building in London's Whitehall area.

Cain hit the entranceway steps two at a time, brushing by the doorman, who muttered knowingly, "Yanks, always in a hurry." The small lobby was filled with chattering lunchtime diners waiting to be seated. He spotted Loreena in a circle of admiring servicemen, each of whom was trying his best to impress the young woman. Cain could not blame them; with her flawless skin, sparkling green eyes, rich auburn hair framing a strikingly pale face, and shapely figure, she was a Scottish beauty. A hint of freckles on her cheeks added to her attractiveness.

He watched Loreena's reaction to the attention. She was having none of it and it showed by the bored look on her face. Cain sidled up to the circle, spotted an opening, and stepped inside the male perimeter. "The Marines have landed," he exclaimed, taking Loreena's arm and steering her toward the dining room before anyone could object.

"Bloody Yank," a Brit officer muttered and turned to his mate. "Let's head to the pub for a pint."

Cain and Loreena snatched an uncleared tiny table for two in a back corner. They pushed the used dishes aside and hoped no one would notice they jumped the line. "I've missed you," he said ardently, holding her hand and staring intently into her green eyes. She squeezed his hand in return.

"I've missed you too, James," she said, leaning over and kissing him chastely on the cheek. Open displays of affection were simply not done in the club, although both young people were willing to chuck the formalities, given half a chance. *After all, there's a war on*, was the implicit understanding. An adept waiter swiftly appeared and cleared the table, taking their order as the handsome couple settled back to enjoy each other's company.

Cain soon learned that Loreena's father, "the brigadier," was back in trace, working for the government in some sort of hush-hush assignment that kept him in London a great deal of the time. Cain knew that she was also involved in government work in the city, but when he asked her about it, she became vague. "Kind of a clerk," she said, and quickly shifted the conversation back to his assignment. Cain had been warned not to talk about the OSS, so he merely stated that he was between assignments—and turned the exchange to less sensitive topics. Lunch passed all too quickly. Before they knew it, Loreena glanced at her watch and said, "James, I'm so very sorry. I have to get back to work. My boss has me on a short leash."

Cain was taken aback. He'd planned on spending the entire day with her and couldn't understand why she had to leave. "What is so all-fired important about being a clerk?" he grumbled.

Loreena could not explain that she was on the staff of the Special Operations Executive. Her assignment was classified "most secret," and she fell under the strict guidelines of the "Official Secrets Act," Britain's all-encompassing high-level government classification. A violation could mean an extended stay in the notorious Dartmoor Prison. "I must get back," she repeated, which only served to upset him even more.

"All right," he said testily, "I'm sure your job is vital to the war effort." Hurt and angry, he sullenly escorted her out of the building.

"I'm sorry James," she said, close to tears.

"That's all right, I understand," he replied stiffly, refusing to accept her apology. He hailed a cab and she got in, fresh tears glistening on her cheeks.

Cain's anger faded. "What a grouch I am," he mumbled suddenly and pulled the startled Loreena from the cab. "I love you," he stammered, burying his face in her hair. "Can you forgive me?" She answered by hugging him tightly and raising her face to be kissed.

The cabbie, an impatient old salt who had seen this scene enacted a thousand times, called out, "Come on mate, don't you know there's a war on?" The spell broken, the two lovers broke apart and Loreena got back in the cab.

"I love you too," she said through the open window as the car sped away.

2

Special Operations Executive Secret Training School 51 (STS-51), Dunham House, Altrincham, England, 0930, 12 September 1942—The Bedford QLD lorry jerked to a stop and Cain slowly got to his feet. The lorry's heavy-duty suspension system left a lot to be desired in terms of comfort, and he was stiff and sore after the four-hour drive from London. He stood hunched over, beneath the stiff canvas top, and waited for the other seven men and three women trainees to climb down from the lorry's bed. When his turn came, he quickly alighted and found that the truck was parked in front of a spectacular three-story red-brick manor house. The huge chateau was like something out of a child's fairy tale. Turrets and battlements ran the length of the roof line, reminding Cain of a medieval castle, while white-framed mullioned windows and Dutch gables gave it an air of wealth and status.

Cain shouldered his seabag and followed the line of trainees along a crushed stone pathway toward a waist-high brick wall covered with red and green ivy. A beautifully hewn granite staircase led to a wide terrace and a magnificent wooden entranceway. The intricately carved oak door looked like it had been there for centuries. As they approached, the door was opened by a casually dressed officer wearing uniform trousers, a khaki shirt, and a white silk scarf

4

carefully knotted around his neck. "Come in, we've been expecting you," he said in a clipped British accent. The group followed the officer along an oak-beamed corridor lined with antique weapons and armor, to a beautifully appointed library filled with hundreds of books neatly arranged on floor-to-ceiling shelves that stretched around the room. *My God*, Cain exclaimed to himself, *this place is a museum.*

The officer walked over to a massive stone fireplace and pulled a red cord that dangled alongside it. A batman appeared almost immediately with a tray of drinks. Cain was dazed by the reception. This was not the usual welcome aboard. Normally a mob of frenzied staff would descend on the new students shouting orders and generally harassing them. "I'm going to like this place," he mumbled as he took a glass.

As the batman served the drinks, Cain took the opportunity to scrutinize the other trainees. Most were in their early twenties, except for two older men and one of the women, who appeared to be in their mid to late thirties. All the trainees appeared to be fit, although the woman seemed an unlikely candidate for parachute training. She was tall and slim, with delicate features and fair hair. *She will never be able to stand the stress of rugged training*, Cain decided. *The shock of the parachute opening would probably crack her ribs.*

When everyone had been served, the major motioned for them to gather around him. "Welcome to Dunham House," he began. "I'm Major Parke-Hyde and I'll be in charge of your training." He paused to make sure he had everyone's attention and then continued. "I warn you that the course is difficult. It will require a high standard of physical fitness and mental toughness." The major studied the group as he talked. One of the older men shifted uncomfortably, but the others simply stared at the speaker, taking it all in. "The course lasts five days. During that time, you will make two parachute jumps from a stationary balloon and three from an aircraft, one of which will be a night jump. Are there any questions so far?" Dead silence answered him—not that there weren't questions, but nobody felt brave enough to ask them.

"I cannot emphasize enough the importance of security," Parke-Hyde continued. "During the time you are here you will not use your real names or talk about your personal lives. The men will call themselves 'Joes', and the women will be known as 'Josephines'. This is necessary in case you are captured. You will not be able to reveal the names of other agents and any personal information." The comment was not lost on the group; they had heard stories of how the Gestapo used torture to extract information from captured agents. The older "Joe" raised his hand. *Here it comes*, Cain thought. *He's going to quit.* "Major," the man said, rising from his chair, "I don't mind telling you that I'm scared, but I lost my boy at Dunkirk so I'm going to give this parachuting business a bloody go." He sat down. His statement brought an approving smile to Parke-Hyde's face. "Anyone else like to add anything?" He scanned the room, but there were no takers.

"Right, that's it then," the major barked. "I suggest you turn in after dinner. Tomorrow promises to be a busy day." With that he marched out of the room, leaving the group wondering what the next day would bring.

Dinner in the great hall was a subdued affair as the diners talked quietly about Major Parke-Hyde's welcome aboard speech. Cain found a seat at a table for four that included the delicate-looking Josephine and two Joes. The woman didn't say much at first, but after a glass of wine she joined in the conversation. She spoke with a noticeable French accent, and Cain guessed that English was her second language. One of the men innocently asked her where she was from.

"I would rather not say," she replied bluntly. "The major cautioned us that we should not talk about our backgrounds."

"Right," the embarrassed man spluttered, "I guess I better get used to keeping my mouth shut." The two men finished their meals, excused themselves, and left the room without another word.

"I'm afraid I offended them," she said to Cain.

"Tough," he replied strongly. "The sooner they learn that we're not playing games, the better off they'll be."

"You're absolutely right," she said and then added defiantly, "and to tell you the truth I don't care whether I offended them or not." Cain sat back in his chair and looked at her more closely. Her bluntness captured his attention. There was toughness in her voice. Maybe he had misjudged her based on her delicate appearance. She saw the way he was looking at her and broke the silence. "A penny for your thoughts," she prodded.

Caught off guard by her directness, he blurted out, "Why are you here?" And then, realizing he may have breached security, he quickly added, "Sorry, I didn't mean to pry."

She remained silent for a long moment and then leaned forward. "I hate the Nazis," she replied vehemently and pushed away from the table. She stood up and said, "Now, if you'll excuse me, I'm going to get a good night's sleep."

"Jeez," Cain mumbled to himself as she walked away, "she's tough as nails."

3

No. 1 Parachute Training School, RAF Ringway, Manchester, England, Special Training Site 51, 0830, 13 September 1942—Just after breakfast the group piled into the back of a metal-sided Fordson WOT1 crew bus for the short trip to Ringway airfield, the Royal Air Force base near Manchester, for their initial parachute training. They reached the outskirts of the base just as two Whitley bombers took off carrying a load of parachutists on a training jump. Their engine noise was so loud that it made talking impossible, forcing the trainees sit quietly on the benches, lost in thought. Cain happened to be looking out a side window when the bus reached the gated entrance to the base. Several armed sentries clustered around the vehicle, and he watched as the driver handed the route ticket to a tough-looking Royal Marine sergeant. The NCO scrutinized it carefully before handing it back without comment. At his signal, two men pushed the steel barrier out of the road. The bus lurched forward with a mashing of gears, much to the amusement of the NCO and the embarrassment of the driver.

A four-gun battery of quick-fire 3.7-inch antiaircraft concrete gun emplacements was located just inside the perimeter of the base. As they passed by, Cain did a double take. The tracking equipment was manned by Auxiliary Territorial Service women wearing shapeless battle dress uniforms and helmets that barely covered their hairstyles. He knew that England had called up all unmarried women between 20 and 30 years of age to serve in one of the auxiliary services, but this was the first time that he had seen women alongside the male artillerymen. The scene brought to mind Churchill's powerful "We shall fight them on the beaches" speech. He felt a stir of emotion as he watched the young women prepare to fight the Germans, "in the fields and on the landing grounds," as the Prime Minister had promised.

The bus drove across the northeast corner of the airfield, past two large hangars, several workshops, and a block of wooden barracks covered with irregular patterns of black, green, and brown paint. *Camouflage*, Cain thought, trying to envision what the buildings must look like from the air. The runway itself was textured with fine pre-colored slag chippings to reduce the "shine" of its concrete surface and make it blend in with the surrounding terrain. The bus stopped, the door opened, and the apprehensive trainees exited. They hurriedly got into formation just as Major Parke-Hyde appeared.

"Today we're going to practice how to land safely—one of the most important facets of parachute training," he said with a smile and pointed to an instructor standing on the edge of a 6-foot-high wooden platform overlooking a sand-filled pit. "Please watch the instructor. He will demonstrate a proper parachute landing fall—also known as a PLF." The instructor stood with his arms over his head, legs slightly bent at the knees, and chin tucked in. At a nod from Parke-Hyde, he stepped off the platform. As the instructor's toes touched the sand, he instantly tumbled sideways, taking the landing shock on the balls of his feet and then successively the side of his calf, thigh, hip, and ending up on the side of his back, all in one fluid motion. He quickly stood up and brushed himself off.

"See how easy it is?" Parke-Hyde said, smiling in encouragement. "The idea is to distribute the landing shock sequentially along five points of body contact to prevent injury to your feet, ankles, hips, and upper body. Are there any questions?" The trainees had none—seemed easy enough, Cain mused—and were instructed to mount the platform. One by one they moved confidently to the edge of the stand and prepared to step off. It was then that things started to fall apart. The 6-foot height was intimidating, nothing like what it seemed from ground level. The end result was that the trainees' first attempts left most of them crumpled in the sand nursing bruises. By the fourth "jump" they had gotten the hang of it, although one man who lightly sprained his ankle was forced to watch from the sidelines. Cain was surprised to see that the woman, now designated "Josephine One," was one of the first to master the landing technique and seemed to enjoy the experience.

The entire morning was taken up with practicing falls from different directions—left front, left side, left rear, right front, right side, and right rear—in the event that terrain, wind direction or the oscillation of the parachute changed the jumper's landing position. After a quick cold meat sandwich and a mug of tea, the trainees were marched to another platform for the afternoon session. This platform was mounted 12 feet off the ground and had a 4-foot-square hole cut in the center of the floor. A thick coconut mat had been placed beneath the hole to break the impact of the fall. Parke-Hyde explained that the hole simulated the bottom hatch of a Whitley MK II bomber, the aircraft that would be used for the training jumps.

Cain climbed the ladder onto the platform and stood on the edge of the "Whitley" hole. "Remember to keep your head up, arch your back, and drop straight through the hole, like a gentleman," the sergeant instructor directed, "or you'll hit your head on the opposite edge." Cain stepped off and dropped, barely missing the other side of the hole. Unfortunately, he concentrated so hard on not hitting his head that he messed up the landing and ended up crumpled on the mat. "Nicely done," Parke-Hyde barked mockingly. "Now if you would move out of the way, another trainee would like to try."

Cain stepped off the mat just as Josephine One took his place on the platform. She looked out of place with her "Victory Red" lipstick, blush, and blond hair sticking out from her crash helmet. At the command "Go," she stepped off without hesitation and executed a textbook drop and roll, much to Cain's embarrassment. "So much for delicate," he muttered. The next man couldn't resist bending forward slightly as he dropped and struck his head on the edge of the hole. Fortunately, he was wearing a Sorbo rubber training helmet that protected his head and, other than bruised pride, he survived "ringing the bell," as hitting the hole's edge was known. Parke-Hyde used the incident as a teaching moment. "Let this be a lesson," he emphasized. "A jumper can easily knock himself out or break his neck in an actual jump. Be alert!"

The remainder of the afternoon was spent in practicing PLFs. By the time the crew bus arrived, the trainees were exhausted, battered, and bruised, but they could execute a PLF like it was second nature.

4

Tatton Park Drop Zone, 0900, 14 September 1942—Cain lined up with the others in front of the parachute packing room window, where specially trained female members of the Women's Auxiliary Air Force carefully packed the chutes. The girls had been chosen because of their strong wrists and hands. They were paid a small stipend in addition to their regular pay because of the critical nature of the assignment. An attractive young WAAF slid a parachute across the counter to him. "If this doesn't open when you jump, please bring it back and I'll issue you another," she said, smiling sweetly. Cain acknowledged her comment, signed the logbook, and started to step away before he realized what she had just said. And then he broke out laughing, realizing it was her way of breaking the tension of his first parachute jump. He noticed that the next man in line didn't think the joke was funny. He turned pale and struggled to hold down his breakfast. "Blimey," he managed to say, "I've never been higher than the top rung of a stepladder."

The trainees shrugged into their parachute harness—leg straps, main lifts, chest buckles, and belly bands—and buckled them up. "Mind your leg straps," the WAAF counseled sternly, "or you could end up speaking with a high-pitched voice."

An instructor carefully inspected each trainee's harness before marching them to the drop zone. The morning fog was just light enough to allow them to see a hydrogen-filled barrage balloon, nicknamed "Bessie," flying high overhead. Bessie was famous for having escaped twice in strong winds before being lassoed and recaptured. The huge silver-gray balloon had a soft-topped wicker basket suspended underneath her. Suddenly, a man dropped from the basket. After an eternity, a parachute blossomed open and the man gently floated to earth. "See how easy it is— just like falling off a log," the instructor taunted. Three others followed the first parachutist. All of them landed safely. Cain noticed one of his colleagues had a wet stain in the crotch of his trousers ... but the man continued to move forward in the queue, overcoming his fear by force of will.

A diesel engine on the back of the blue Fordson "Sussex" six-wheeled lorry coughed into life and a winch started reeling in the heavy steel cable attached to the balloon. When it reached the ground, Cain and three others were told to climb into the 8-foot-square wicker basket with an instructor who was tethered to the gondola for safety. A panicked trainee had once grabbed an instructor's leg on his way out of the hole and pulled the parachute-less victim with him. The instructor was able to hug the trainee all the way to the ground and landed unhurt, which could not be said for the trainee. He was evacuated to the aid station with a broken nose, after the thoroughly pissed off instructor punched him in the face.

The four trainees automatically pushed themselves as far from the hole as possible. It was much more frightening to jump from a balloon than an airplane because there was nothing to think about except the height, the dead silence, and the gradually receding ground. Cain noticed teeth marks in the side of the hole, made by jumpers who hadn't kept their backs straight. The gas bag rose steadily until it jerked to a stop at the end of the cable, some 800 feet over the jump zone. It was an eerie feeling watching the ground recede. No one talked as the basket swayed gently in the light breeze. The four jumpers glanced at each other with a sickly grin of assumed assurance, as if to say, "There's nothing to it." The height gave Cain an opportunity to see the sprawling city of Manchester in the distance, while directly below he could make out the large white X of the landing zone. A good-sized pond shimmered in the morning sunlight just to the north. The instructor was careful to point it out because several jumpers had landed in its waters and drowned before they could be rescued.

"All right, sir, hook up," the instructor ordered. Cain reached up and snapped the end of his static line to an iron bar that ran across the top of the basket. The 15-foot static line was designed to pull the parachute out of the container. The instructor tugged the line twice to make sure it was fully locked. "Sometimes the student doesn't connect it properly," he said with a straight face. "You'll notice it if you don't." At the command "Action station number one," Cain sat down with his legs in the hole, placed his hands on the edge, and tilted his head back. He looked down at the ground out of the corner of his eye and, for the first time, he experienced fear with a sense of terrific excitement. The instructor cautioned him one more time. "Careful not to ring the bell, sir," he warned. "Drop straight out, like you were at attention."

At the command "GO!" Cain pushed off, lightly brushed the wooden edge of the hole, and plummeted downward, his heart in his mouth.

"One-one thousand," he said to himself. A buddy who had gone through jump training in the States told him to count to three-one thousand, and by that time he should feel the hard jerk of the parachute opening.

"Two-one thousand."

"Three-one thousand."

"Four-one thousand."

"Five-one thousand."

The ground rushed up to meet him. He was still dropping like a stone. *Jesus Christ, what's gone wrong?* his mind screamed. *The chute should have opened by now.* No one had told him that in parachuting from a balloon there was no slip stream to open the chute and the jumper had to plummet 240 feet before it opened.

Suddenly, the shoulder straps jerked tight and Cain slowed dramatically. He looked up at the beautifully blossoming 28-foot nylon canopy. "Thank you, Lord," he mumbled, and felt a tremendous sense of exhilaration as he gently floated earthward. An instructor with a loud hailer brought him out of his reverie.

"Get your head out of your arse!" he shouted. "Get your bloody feet together, point your toes, and roll into the landing." Cain hit the ground on the balls of his feet and fell on his side and back in a rough approximation of a PLF, although the instructor was quick to point out that he had "landed like a sack of you know what, sir."

Cain had no sooner collapsed his chute than Josephine One landed 20 feet from him. Her PLF was perfect. She bounced to her feet, hit the harness quick release, and began gathering in her parachute. "Marvelous," she shouted to him. "I can't wait to jump again!" Cain shook his head in amazement. *I sure misjudged her,* he thought to himself, as he watched her effortlessly carry the rolled-up parachute to the side of the drop zone. "How's your head?" she teased, but before he could reply, she cried out, "Look out! Roman Candle!" and pointed upward.

Cain glanced up. A jumper was plunging to earth. His shroud lines had twisted, keeping the parachute from opening and leaving him helpless, with nothing more than a long white "flame," instead of a lifesaving canopy. The jumper's body shook the ground as it slammed into the landing zone with a horrifying thud. Cain ran over and dragged the canopy off the motionless figure. It was the trainee who'd lost his son at Dunkirk. He lay in a grotesque concertina-like position. It was clear he was dead and there was nothing Cain could do, except stare sympathetically. *Poor bastard*, he thought. Several instructors ran up and hustled Cain away. The body was quickly loaded aboard an ambulance.

Despite the tragedy, training did not stop, and Cain soon found himself preparing for his second jump of the day. He watched the first jumper slide to the edge of the hole. "GO!" the instructor shouted. The man pushed off but at the last moment reached out and grabbed the lip of the basket. He hung from the side with both hands, a desperate plea in his eyes. The terrified jumper begged for help. "Don't worry," the instructor said soothingly, "just give me your hands and I'll pull you back in." The panicked trainee offered his hands to the unruffled instructor, who immediately released them and watched as the man fell away. "Silly bugger," was all he said. Another trainee lost his balance when the basket was tilted by an unexpected wind gust, causing the man to fall out before the instructor had given him the command. As the trainee fell, he shouted out, "I'm sorry!" The instructor calmly replied, "That's all right chap, don't bother to come back."

Cain's second jump was not much better than the first, but at least he didn't embarrass himself. The rest of the group finished satisfactorily and then were marched off to board the crew bus for transportation to Dunham House, having crossed the first difficult bridge in their training. The next day would be their second stage of training—jumping from an aircraft.

16

5

RAF Ringway, Number 1 Parachute Training School, Tatton Park Drop Zone, 0900, 15 September 1942—The nine trainees and an instructor were crammed into the narrow fuselage of the twin-engine Armstrong Whitworth Whitley MK II bomber, affectionately known as the "flying coffin" by those who flew it. The heavy, unwieldy, and cumbersome aircraft had been stripped of its bomb racks and armament so it could carry a stick of ten jumpers. A wooden trapdoor, called a "Joe hole," had been fitted over the opening in the fuselage where the belly turret had originally been fitted. Even with everything removed there was not a lot of space. The jumpers sat on the deck alternately facing each other, knees drawn up and backs against the side of the aircraft. The tight harness straps and the parachute packs on their backs, coupled with little headroom, made the ride extremely uncomfortable. One of the trainees remarked that it was made that way to prod the jumpers to get out as quickly as possible.

The deafening roar of the engines filled the fuselage as the aircraft slowly taxied down the runway, straining to gain take-off speed. The old bird shuddered and vibrated, making the trainees wonder if it would come apart on the ground. Just as the nauseating smell of the chemically treated lacquer fuselage made several of them gag, the pilot pulled back on the yoke and the bomber was airborne, much to the relief of the trapped passengers. A crewman removed the cover on the "Joe hole" and cold air swept into the fuselage, flushing out the stench of the lacquer. When the bomber reached an altitude of 1,000 feet, it circled the Tatton drop zone. The pilot checked the wind direction and speed. Satisfied that the conditions were right for the jump, he thumbed a switch.

A red light came on above the "Joe hole" and Josephine One slid into position. The staff had designated her to be the first out of the plane, believing that no man would then dare refuse to jump. She could see the mansion and its patchwork of fields and woods rushing by like a miniature terrain model. At the flash of the green light, she pushed off without hesitation. Cain took her place, hooked his static line to the bar, and leaped into space. The prop blast hit him, and he momentarily felt its full surge before falling away. His static line played out, pulling the rigging lines and the canopy out of its confining bag. Cain felt the welcoming jolt as the canopy filled with air, slowing his descent from 125 miles per hour to a landing speed of 15 miles per hour. Without the sound of the aircraft engines, Cain was struck by how quiet it was as he gently swung from the shroud lines.

The ground rushed up with alarming speed and he readied himself to land. Much to his relief, his reflexes kicked in and he hit the ground in what he thought was a skillfully executed PLF. "Well done lad," an instructor shouted over a loud hailer. "You managed to land without killing yourself. Next time you may want to do a PLF." Chastened, Cain spilled the air from his parachute canopy and quickly gathered it up. He joined Josephine One, who stood nonchalantly watching the rest of the group come down. One after another they landed without mishap. "All right, lads and lassies; don't stand around with your thumb up your bum," an instructor shouted. "Get in the bus. You're going to make another jump."

———◆———

Tatton Park Drop Zone, 2100, 16 September 1942—The Whitley fuselage was less crowded for their last qualifying jump, a night drop on the Tatton Park drop zone. Two members of the group had suffered injuries that sidelined them, and one other had been returned to his unit after refusing to make the night jump. "Parachuting in the daylight is bad enough," he grumbled, "but I absolutely refuse to jump at night." His intransigence left the instructors with no choice but to wash him out of the school and return him to his unit.

The bomber took off into a night sky illuminated by a quarter moon. Inside the windowless fuselage it was so dark that the jumpers could not see one another, and the noise from the engines made it impossible to talk. Each was left alone with their thoughts and fears. Cain sat next to Josephine One and could feel her trembling slightly. He couldn't tell whether it was from fear or from the cold wind that was washing over them from the open "Joe hole." Suddenly, the red warning light flashed. She slid over to the cold, whistling maw of the opening, her feet dangling in space. Cain saw her face in the light's reflection. There was no sign of fear, only determination. The green light came on, and without hesitation she plunged into the inky blackness.

Cain slid across the vibrating deck and took her place. The crewman tapped him on the helmet and he dropped into the black void, the slipstream hitting him like the blow of a club against the shoulders. With a familiar elastic boom, the dark-cream-colored chute opened and he checked it against the moonlit night sky to make sure it had deployed correctly. He then looked down, trying to gauge how close he was to the ground, but no lights were visible due to the strict enforced blackout because of the German bombing threat. A shimmering patch of color caught his eye and he suddenly realized that he was over the pond. *Jesus*, he thought, *I'm going into the water!*

He reached up desperately, grasped the risers, and yanked down hard, trying to steer his chute away from the pond. There was no hope; he was just too damn close. He took a deep breath just as his feet splashed into the water. He held his breath, expecting to sink over his head. Instead, he hit bottom and collapsed onto his side in a muddy spray of foul-smelling water. To make matters worse, his parachute collapsed on top of him in a welter of shroud lines and wet nylon. He struggled to his feet and tried to free himself from the tangled mess. After several minutes, he finally resorted to cutting his way out with his commando dagger. He waded ashore, cussing mightily, dragging the waterlogged remnants of his parachute behind him. To add insult to injury, Josephine One stood on the bank waiting for him.

"Coo," she uttered, "you are one lucky man. If you had landed 20 feet further out, you might have drowned."

Cain sloshed up to the packing room window and slid the sodden remnants of his parachute across the counter to the WAAF attendant. "This one needs a little mending," he deadpanned.

The attendant eyed the shredded rayon canopy and then looked Cain up and down, taking in his soaked battle dress, and shook her head. "Bit late for a plunge, isn't it, sir?"

6

Special Operations Executive Secret Training School 51 (STS-51), Dunham House, Altrincham, England, 0800, 17 September 1942—The five surviving members of the class stood at attention on the flagstone walkway in the mansion's garden. For once the air was clear and filled with the promise of autumn warmth. The class had returned just before daybreak, leaving just enough time to pack up and prepare for graduation. The ceremony was to be a simple affair presided over by their training officer. Parke-Hyde stepped in front of each graduate, shook their hand, and presented them with a maroon beret and the cloth insignia of the SOE parachute badge they were now authorized to wear on the left shoulder of their uniforms. He stepped back and congratulated them on successfully completing the course and wished them well—short and sweet. When the blue crew bus pulled up, they quickly loaded their baggage on board. The newly minted parachutists had been given two days' liberty in London before reporting to Milton Hall for deployment, and they didn't want to waste a second of it.

Victory Services Club, 63–79 Seymour Street, London W2 2HF, 1130, 17 September 1942—The crew bus pulled up in front of the Victory Services Club. Three of the men spilled out and made a beeline to the front desk, anxious to check in, drop their gear, and hit the town. Cain and Josephine One brought up the rear. "This is where I leave you," she said. "I'll see you in two days. I'm off to Cambridge to see my sister." And with that she turned and marched off, leaving Cain open-mouthed and flabbergasted at her abrupt departure.

"I guess I'm on my own," he mumbled. Just then a voice called out, "James! James!" He looked across the street and spotted the most beautiful woman in the world waving frantically to get his attention.

"Loreena!" he bellowed, impetuously stepping into the street and weaving his way through the lines of vehicles that had stopped for a traffic signal.

A bobby blew his whistle and shouted, "Hey Yank, use the crossing England needs every man for the war effort!" Cain saluted in acknowledgement of the reprimand and stepped onto the curb, just as Loreena threw herself into his arms.

"I can't believe it's you," he breathed into her ear. The two finally broke apart, slightly embarrassed by their embrace in the midst of the lunchtime crowd. Passersby simply took the hug in stride and smiled good-naturedly.

A conveniently located bench gave them a place to sit and talk. "How did you know I was going to be here?" Cain asked, quite bowled over by Loreena's presence.

"I have my ways," she responded evasively, brushing aside his question. For his part, Cain was content to admire the gorgeous woman beside him. "I've missed you, James," she said, gripping his hand tightly. "How long do you have?"

"I've got a day's leave before I have to report back," he replied.

"Then let's not waste a minute of it," she replied shyly, taking his hand and leading him to the club's entrance.

Cain made his way to the front desk, while Loreena went to "freshen up" in the ladies' room. The clerk told him that the last two rooms had just been taken by three graduates of parachute school. "And I must say they were terribly anxious to check in," the clerk smiled knowingly.

Cain swore under his breath then regained his composure. "Where can I find a room?" he asked. Before the clerk could answer, Loreena stepped up.

"I have reservations," she stated dramatically, holding up a room key.

"Will you need help with your luggage?" the clerk asked innocently.

Red-faced, Cain replied, "I believe we can handle it ourselves."

The two made their way up the stairs, pausing long enough for a quick kiss before reaching their room on the third floor. Cain opened the door and they stepped in. They embraced. Loreena whispered, "I've missed you terribly," before passionately kissing him.

Later that afternoon the two made their way to the tiny pub in the basement where several British service members were enjoying a pint of ale. The place was crowded, but they were able to snag a table when two servicemen left. Loreena ordered the house brew and brought two bottles of Victory Ale back to the table. Cain raised an eyebrow when he saw the label.

"Does everything in Britain have a patriotic theme?" he asked.

"Absolutely," Loreena chuckled. "This ale was originally made by a Belgian company to commemorate the end of World War I. Now it will honor victory over the Nazis."

The two made small talk until the beer was gone, each wondering who would be the first to suggest going upstairs. Cain finally worked up the courage.

"Shall we adjourn to our room?"

Loreena turned red. "I'm really tired," she answered, and then laughed in embarrassment.

They left the pub hand in hand. As they passed the registration desk, the clerk on duty stopped them. "I'm afraid everyone has to leave the hotel," he said. "There's a big air raid coming in. You'll have to go to the shelter down the street." The two couldn't believe it. Their big night ruined by the damn Nazis!

The night clerk handed them blankets and gave them directions to the shelter. Seymore Street was pitch black, but fortunately they ran into a friendly Fire Warden who assisted them in locating the entrance to the Tube. There was a queue already at the entranceway. Cain was surprised to see people in various stages of dress and undress, showing little concern for what others were wearing. A little boy trundled by in his nappy—Loreena's word for diaper—and no one gave him a second glance.

They were finally able to squeeze onto the stairs and make their way down to the tracks. Cain could not believe the number of people that were crammed into every inch of space—the walkways were full of people lying down or leaning against the walls and even in the space between the rails. Hundreds and hundreds of people. Their discomfort did not seem to tamp down their good humor. There was a palpable spirit of comradery among the crowd.

A family took pity on the two latecomers and shuffled closer together to make room for them. They spent the rest of the night catnapping, interspaced with periods of conversation and people-watching. At one point everyone joined a four-person group in singing patriotic songs. Vera Lynn's "We'll Meet Again" seemed to be everyone's favorite.

Early the next morning the exhausted couple emerged from the shelter and enjoyed some toast, a couple rashers of bacon, and a pot of tea in the club's dining room before Josephine's scheduled pickup. Their parting was emotional and tearful, but typical of the times. Those who saw it merely shrugged.

Josephine was already in the car when it pulled up outside the club. She caught the love birds' sad goodbye but she let it pass when she saw the stricken look on Cain's face. The Wren driver decided that discretion was the better part of valor.

7

Milton Hall, Military Establishment 65 (ME 65), Peterborough, Northamptonshire, 1400, 18 September 1942—As their car motored down a narrow dirt road with sheep and cattle grazing in the pastures on either side, the two newly minted parachutists admired the scenery that was remarkably untouched by the war. It seemed a far cry from the bombed-out streets of London. The car passed through an open stone gate and along a tree-lined boulevard before pulling up in front of an enormous, ivy-covered limestone 17th-century manor house. As they took in the landscape, they were reminded of the reason for their visit. Rows of Nissen huts marred the pristine grounds, lining the lawn along the north front of the mansion, and a large climbing wall clung to one corner of the building.

"My God, do all Brits live like this?" Cain jested.

"Of course," Josephine replied with a straight face. "This is just the servants' quarters. You should see the main house."

Cain laughed. It was not the first time she had shown a quick sense of humor. He had been the brunt of it on more than one occasion. She had impressed him. Throughout the entire week of tough parachute training, he had never seen her exhibit anything but a positive attitude.

During the 100-mile car ride, the two had gotten to know each other better, and despite the warning not to share personal information, they'd broken the rule. Cain found the young woman easy to talk to, and he enjoyed listening to her. He already knew that she had attended the SOE's communications school and that she was a highly skilled radio operator. But he was surprised to learn that she had escaped from France after the surrender by bribing a fisherman to take her to England in his boat. "A dozen of us were jammed in the hold," she related. "We had to stay out of sight because of the German patrol boats. The Channel was rough and everyone got *mal de mer*," she explained disgustedly. "I thought I would die."

Cain sympathized with her. "My buddies call me the 'fastest flash' in the fleet, because every time I go on board a ship and they yell 'cast off,' I get deathly seasick," he said humorously. Josephine laughed and then turned serious.

"My parents were not able to escape. They live in the 'free' part of France," she said sarcastically.

"I don't understand," Cain said. "I thought the Germans had captured the whole country?"

"No, there are two countries: one is under Nazi control and the other is headed by Marshal Pétain, their lapdog," she spat. She continued to rave about the occupation and how the Germans really controlled everything by holding thousands of French soldiers as hostages. They spent the rest of the time in the car talking about conditions in the subjugated country.

The two picked up their baggage and followed the other trainees into the administrative office in the main house where they were assigned rooms and given training schedules for the next several days. Cain looked at the document and noted that the schedule ended on Day 5 with the notation "Briefing." *At least we know something's going to happen soon*, he thought. After they stashed their gear, a staff member appeared and led them to the main first-floor lecture hall through the dark oak-beamed hallways lined with Cromwellian suits of armor. Large family portraits and paintings from a bygone era hung from ornate wood-paneled walls. The lecture hall was filled with over a hundred Allied soldiers—British, American, Belgian, Dutch, Norwegian, Danish—and French officers who had escaped from the continent and joined De Gaulle's Free French Forces. The French were initially standoffish, careful not to reveal anything that might endanger their families back home. A scattering of women stood out against the crowd of men. The different nationalities clustered in groups, talking and smoking incessantly while they waited for someone to tell them what was going on.

Cain was heading for the American group when a voice boomed out, "About time you got here, old boy." He smiled, recognizing the voice of Lieutenant Colonel Henry. The two shook hands warmly.

"What are you doing here?" Cain asked.

"We're going to be a team," Henry replied. Before he could ask what the hell he was talking about, a tall, whip-cord thin French lieutenant colonel wearing a winged arm patch—spread white wings with a red circle with the letters SF in light blue on his upper sleeve—appeared and asked everyone to sit down.

"Ladies and gentlemen," the colonel began without preamble, "welcome to the Milton Hall holiday camp." His opening sally was greeted with scattered laughter. "I am Lieutenant Colonel de Gard, and I run this course." He paused for a long moment and then made a stunning announcement. "You have been selected to parachute into France to help organize, train, and lead French Resistance groups against the Germans."

My God, Cain thought, *he certainly doesn't mince words.*

"How many Germans is the Resistance up against?" one of the men asked.

"Not many—just over half a million," the officer responded nonchalantly. There was a long pause.

"Oh, that's all," one of the men quipped nervously, and the room erupted in laughter.

The news was electrifying. A rush of excitement surged through the crowd. The colonel had to wait for them to quiet down before continuing. "You will form three-man Jedburgh teams—"

"What the hell is a Jedburgh?" one of the brash Americans interrupted.

"It refers to a Scottish town in the Middle Ages," he replied, turning to a group of Brits, "where the locals played sports with the heads of the Englishmen they killed!" The room exploded with cheers and shouts. The colonel waited for the furor to die down then continued. "The team will consist of three agents known as Jeds: a British or French officer, an American officer, and a radio operator, who will maintain contact with us by short-wave wireless. You will be dropped by parachute in uniform at prearranged drop zones where the French Resistance will be waiting."

The audience eyed each other curiously, wondering who their teammates would be for the highly dangerous operation. The briefer answered the question for them. "Over the course of the next week, you chaps will make up your own teams from the men and women in this room." For a moment an uneasy silence descended. Even though they were allies, there were frictions that had to be overcome. The unconventional selection decision had been made by SOE to accomplish two things: force them to get to know one another, and forge bonds of trust and comradeship that would carry them through the days and weeks of training and deployment. There would inevitably be a few "divorces," but for the most part the pairings worked remarkably well.

"Your mission will be quite different from previous intelligence operatives that were infiltrated into France," the officer continued. "Your job will be to assist the resistance groups in taking the fight to the Nazis through sabotage and direct action." There was not a sound in the room as the audience hung onto every word.

"This school," he said, "is designed to train you to be experts in irregular warfare. You will learn how best to advise, arm, and aid members of the Resistance. It will be a three-stage training plan that will include preliminary, paramilitary, and finishing schools that will last several months." A loud chorus of angry shouts erupted from the Americans, including Cain, who had volunteered for SOE because he thought he would be sent immediately into combat. The thought of more training did not sit well with him. "Gentlemen," the colonel said forcefully, "Jerry is a tough seasoned fighter and unless you know what you're doing, he will hand you your arse on a platter." He paused for dramatic effect. "This school will teach you to hand Jerry *his* arse on a platter." The line brought laughter and then cheers. "And now, ladies and gentlemen, England is waiting for each of you to do his or her duty, so let's get at it."

———

Milton Hall, Military Establishment 65 (ME 65), Peterborough, Northamptonshire, 1800, 25 September 1942—"We need a competent wireless operator. He will be our only link with London," Henry declared.

"Not to worry," Cain replied, "I know just the person." He pointed to a petite woman in a smart-looking First Aid Nursing Yeomanry—or FANY—khaki uniform sipping tea.

"You can't mean *her*," Henry exclaimed. "Why, the woman can't weigh more than 100 pounds. She'll never survive the parachute drop." Cain smiled knowingly and told him she was intelligent and quick-witted and a graduate of parachute training at Tatton Park. He added that she was also a top graduate of radio operator and code school. Henry was not convinced she would make a good teammate but agreed to talk with her. That night at dinner, they invited her to sit at their table, which they made sure was set for three, not the normal foursome. The two men stood up as she approached, and Cain even held her chair.

The three sat down, and before the conversation could start, Josephine looked Henry in his one good eye and said, "Yes."

"Yes what?" he asked quizzically, taken aback by her one-word statement.

"Yes, I would like to be a member of your team," she replied evenly. "That's what this little *tête-à-tête* is all about, isn't it?" Henry sputtered, for once at a loss for words, and Cain broke out laughing. "It's no secret that you two have formed a team and are looking for a radio operator to fill it out," she continued shrewdly, "and I'm not only one of the best, but I'm French and I speak the language as only a true native can." She paused to catch her breath. "I am also an excellent pistol shot and I can jump out of an airplane without ringing the bell." She looked at Cain and smiled innocently.

"You certainly don't lack self-confidence, I'll give you that," Henry admitted.

Cain suggested they seal their "marriage" at the Fox and Hounds, a notorious watering hole a 20-minute hike from Milton Hall. The trainees had appropriated the pub as an after-hours hangout. While hard liquor was scarce, there seemed to be an unending supply of ale. The local bobbies turned a blind eye to the rowdy goings on there as long as the patrons maintained a semblance of good order and discipline.

As the three "betrothed" stepped into the pub, they were met by a raucous crowd in full cry, bellowing out a verse of "The Ball of Kerrymuir," a particularly profane and raunchy ditty that perfectly suited the mostly hyper-masculine throng. The British Jedburgh contingent had furnished an entire songbook filled with bawdy songs that had started this entertaining tradition.

In the middle of the pub a drunken Scot, in full regalia, balanced precariously on a tabletop swinging a battered shillelagh in time

31

with the foul lyrics. Several men, deep in their cups, bellowed out an offbeat chorus.

Cain fully expected Josephine to beat a hasty retreat. Instead, she joined in the chorus—"Four-and twenty-virgins came down from Inverness, and when the ball was over, there were four-and-twenty less"—surprising the hell out of her two compatriots. "The song is an old favorite," she said, laughing at their embarrassment. "This is not my first time in a servicemen's club."

Henry headed for the bar and ordered three mugs of beer, while the other two rescued a table. They had to shout to be heard above the uproar, making it almost impossible to carry on a conversation. "A toast," Henry barked when he returned with the mugs. "Success to our team and death to the Jerries." The Frenchman made a point to salute Josephine with his mug in a display of respect. Cain took in the gesture.

"*Semper Fi*," he shouted.

8

F Section, Special Operations Executive, Norgeby House, Site 69, 83 Baker Street, London, 1000, 27 September 1942—It was a typical morning in London—gray and overcast with the promise of more rain. The streets were wet and slick, posing a special challenge for the American chauffeur unaccustomed to driving on the "wrong" side of the road. He steered the black Chevrolet uncertainly through the heavy traffic desperately searching for his destination. It didn't help that the guy in the back seat fancied himself a skilled charioteer. "Turn left," Jack Kelly ordered the driver impatiently, "and take a right at the next intersection. Eighty-three Baker Street is on the west side." The flustered driver, whom Kelly referred to as "Wrong Way Corrigan" because he always seemed to get lost, pulled up in front of the inconspicuous six-story building known as Michael House. Kelly got out. "Don't wait for me," he said abruptly, adding, "I'll catch a cab back to the office"—much to the driver's relief. Anxious to get the meeting underway, Kelly dodged through the jam of uniformed personnel and civilians on the sidewalk and took the stone stairs two at a time to the heavily sandbagged entrance. He was surprised that there was no outward sign of security; after all, this was one of SOE's most important offices. A discreet metal plaque, inscribed with "Inter-Service Research Bureau," was affixed to the

33

brick wall beside the door. The innocuous title was the cover name for the SOE's French section, known simply as "F Section"—one of six sections that actively ran all the clandestine operations in France from the top three floors.

Kelly strode briskly through the entrance into a rather dark passageway, up a dreary set of stairs, to the first floor, where he was greeted by a muscular young man dressed in brown slacks, regimental tie, and dark blue sport jacket.

"Can I help you, sir?" he asked politely. The bulge under his left arm suggested something other than a pocket full of fountain pens.

"Yes, I'm Jack Kelly and I have an appointment to see Lieutenant Colonel Buckmaster." The man checked a roster.

"Sir, if you would follow me, I'll take you to the colonel's office." They rode up to the fifth floor in an ancient wheezing lift that had seen better days. It certainly wasn't an express because it stopped at every floor to let harried messengers in and out. By the time they reached their destination, Kelly decided that it would have been faster to walk.

The aide led Kelly down a dark narrow corridor to a door marked "F" and ushered him in. The office gatekeeper, a formidable-looking gray-haired woman, met them and politely steered the two men past several uniformed men and women hunched over desks quietly working. *Sure as hell isn't like Grosvenor Street*, Kelly thought. At times OSS headquarters looked and sounded like a Chinese fire drill.

The head of F Section, 41-year-old Lieutenant Colonel Maurice Buckmaster—a tall, rather thin man with round shoulders, a gaunt, almost emaciated face, and piercing blue eyes—shook Kelly's hand and escorted the three into his office. The aide quietly disappeared, but the gatekeeper stayed long enough to ask if they would like tea. The two men turned down the offer, secretly preferring something a hell'va lot stronger, and sat down. Buckmaster sat behind his desk, the seat of power, while Kelly took the chair facing him. Winston

Churchill's pugnacious, bulldog-like mug stared at him from a photograph hanging on the wall next to a window overlooking Baker Street.

This is going to be fun, Kelly thought. Buckmaster had a reputation as a no-nonsense officer who did not welcome American involvement in the Special Operations arena. A formidable personality, he had been hardened by combat in France with the British Expeditionary Force and was one of the lucky ones to be evacuated from Dunkirk. Upon his return to England, he'd been recruited into the SOE and appointed head of the French section. In this position he was responsible for selecting and controlling all undercover agents in France. It was reported that Hitler had said, "When I get to London, I'm not sure who I shall hang first—Churchill or that man Buckmaster." Undercover agents in France were an entirely British-run show ... and one that Buckmaster was keen to keep that way.

This was the first time the two had met, and neither one was sure how the meeting would go, so they remained wary of the other's intent. "Welcome to F Section," Buckmaster said, starting the conversation. "I'm looking forward to working with you." Kelly nodded politely but thought, *What bullshit! You have treated us like inexperienced amateurs. All you want is access to our equipment and planes. If truth be told, you would just as soon take the equipment, especially aircraft, and let us hold your coat while you carve out Europe for yourself. The British simply do not want us in their backyard.* It had finally taken the top command levels of the American army to force the Brits to cooperate more fully, and even then it was grudgingly provided. *I'm sure Buckmaster has been ordered to play nice,* he thought, *but his welcome is neither sincere nor an expression of closer cooperation.*

Kelly's boss had ordered him to "cool it," so he responded courteously. "Thank you for taking the time to see me, colonel. I've wanted to meet you for some time," he said, which was true.

He was determined to clear the air with the head of F Section and establish a professional working relationship between the two organizations. Kelly had asked for the get-together to confirm the inclusion of an American in the next mission into France. The mission was important to OSS headquarters, who wanted to know whether the Maquis was a viable force that could support an Allied invasion of the country—and if so, what it would need in terms of weapons and equipment. The issue was a touchy subject, because the Resistance movement was split into two camps, with Britain favoring General Charles de Gaulle's espionage service, called the *Bureau Central de Renseignements et d'Action*, while the United States supported his rival for power, General Henri Giraud, commander of the non-Gaullist French troops in North Africa.

"Colonel Buckmaster," Kelly began—no sense in beating around the bush—"my headquarters would like confirmation that an American will be included on the next inter-Allied mission to France."

"Mr. Kelly," Buckmaster replied tightly, his face red with anger, "I could take offense at your demand, but I have been ordered to cooperate with your organization. That said, however, I have no intention of sending an untrained American into France."

Kelly, ever mindful of his boss's guidance, kept his cool. "Colonel, I understand your position and I totally agree with you," he replied. He noted Buckmaster's confusion and added, "That's why I'm recommending an officer who recently completed the SOE commando and parachute courses and led a highly successful raid on a German radar station in the Channel Islands, for which he was decorated with the DSO."

Buckmaster was taken aback by the candidate's qualifications but he was not easily defeated. "Your man may be highly trained and combat experienced, but the next mission requires a three-person team," he responded, confident that his position was secure.

Kelly smiled. "Yes, I understand. That's why I'm also recommending the entire team. You may have heard about its leader, Lieutenant Colonel Andre Henry.

"Oh my God," Buckmaster exclaimed, "not that wild man!"

"So you've heard of him," Kelly chuckled. Henry was a legend in the SOE for numerous acts of derring-do. During the raid in the Channel Islands with Cain, Henry had threatened to kill a British scientist who had lost his nerve and didn't want to play anymore. After Henry fired a pistol close to his head, the frightened man quickly found his balls and finished the assignment.

Before Buckmaster could recover from the Henry surprise, Kelly added, "The third member of the team includes an honor graduate of your radio operator's school, Miss Olivia Harrison, known as Josephine by her teammates."

Buckmaster's shoulders sagged in defeat. There was no way he could hope to hold the line against the selection of that team. "The mission is slated in a fortnight," he harrumphed.

9

Secret Training Site 72, No. 6, Orchard Court, Portman Square, London, 1000, 5 October 1942—The team had been sent on a two-week field exercise, known as a "scheme," in England's wooded upland. They were to establish a secure base, open radio contact with headquarters, arrange parachute drops, move clandestinely from place to place, and organize and control simulated partisan groups, played by members of the Home Guard. The exercise was in essence a final examination and required them to put their guerrilla warfare lessons into practice—stealth, sabotage, clandestine communications, and ambush. Several days into the scheme, they suddenly received orders to return to Milton Hall. The messenger did not know the reason, only that he was to deliver the orders to Lieutenant Colonel Henry and stand by to drive them back.

"What the heck is going on?" Cain asked, but Henry just shrugged his shoulders.

"I haven't the slightest idea," he replied.

An hour later they arrived at Milton Hall, where they were told to gather all their clothing and equipment and prepare to join an exercise with the Special Air Service. The exercise was planned to last about five days but could go on longer. Transportation had been arranged to take them to London. The three looked at each other knowingly. There was no sensible explanation—except the possibility of a real mission. The exercise with the SAS was merely a cover story.

Twenty minutes later the team threw their gear on the back of a Dodge truck, climbed aboard, and began the two-hour drive to London. They hadn't even had time to clean up or change their filthy clothes and still wore the remnants of camouflage paint on their faces. Cain thought that even with a dirty face, Josephine seemed quite fetching. Henry, on the other hand, looked positively frightening. His gaunt, unshaven face and prominent hawk-like nose gave him the appearance of a predatory animal. The black eye patch added to his terrifying appearance. Cain himself was covered with mud from having fallen in a water-filled ditch the night before and smelled like a pigsty. All in all, it was safe to say that the three would not have been welcomed in polite society.

By mid-morning they reached the northern outskirts of the city, a residential area that seemed to have escaped the bombing. They pulled up in front of a nondescript red-brick 18th-century building on Orchard Court, just around the corner from the Baker Street Tube station on the eastern side of Portman Square in London's West End. The building's flats were used as temporary quarters and briefing rooms by Buckmaster's F Section headquarters staff for agents going on a mission. SOE's main headquarters on Baker Street was off limits to field agents because of the classified nature of the work being done there. If the agent were captured, he or she could not give the Nazis any information about headquarters.

The location for the secret organization seemed appropriate. As the home of the fictitious private detective Sherlock Holmes, Baker Street exerted a magnetic attraction for the cloak-and-dagger activities of the war. In fact, the wartime occupants of the street called themselves the "Baker Street Irregulars," after the gang of street urchins that Sherlock Holmes employed to "go everywhere, see everything, and overhear everyone."

The tight-lipped driver let slip that it would be their home for the next few days. The building was less than half a mile from Special Operations Executive headquarters on Baker Street and Special Force headquarters in nearby Montagu Mansions. The team's disheveled appearance did not seem to attract undue attention from the local residents. They knew that several of the flats and houses in the area had been taken over by the government for use as temporary quarters, but they were unaware that the men and women that used the premises were Special Operations agents being briefed on various missions. The residents assumed that the grubby soldiers were returning from some training exercise.

Cain rang the bell. An erect, tallish gentleman wearing World War I service ribbons on the lapel of his dark suit opened the door. "Welcome, I'm Arthur Park," he said cheerfully. "We've been expecting you. Please do come in." The three exchanged bemused smiles at the cordial welcome, having grown used to the usual severe treatment. Park continued. "I'll be your contact should you need anything during your stay." They found out later that Park was one of the longest serving members of the intelligence community—and knew every secret in the Empire, according to legend. With that introduction, Park led them through an archway into an inner courtyard which opened up to a lobby beneath an ornate crystal chandelier. He directed them to the gilded gates of an ancient lift that creaked to a halt on the third floor, where they found their respective rooms. The accommodation turned out to be first class. Nothing had been spared to make their short stay a comfortable one—clean sheets, luxurious beds, a fully stocked bar ... and most importantly for Josephine, scented shampoo, which was all but unobtainable in London. Finally, Park showed them the legendary black bathroom with its smooth jet-black-tiled bathtub, an onyx bidet, subdued pink lighting, thick carpeting, and peach-pink mirrors engraved with scantily clad maidens. It was difficult to tell who was more embarrassed, Josephine or the two men.

Park allowed them time to drop off their bags and then led them to an office on the second floor. After a quick knock on the door, he ushered the three Jeds inside. They were met by Major Maurice Buckmaster, a tall, slender, hard-eyed man with angular features and fair, thinning hair who was the head of the French Section, Special Operations Executive. He spoke evenly, precisely, carefully. "Welcome to F Section," he said, vigorously shaking each agent's hand before perching on the edge of his desk. "I won't take up too much of your time, because there is much to be done before you leave for France at the next full moon." At Buckmaster's casual confirmation of their mission, Cain cast a sideways glance at the other two. Josephine's face lit up and her eyes radiated excitement. She dreamed of returning to France. On the other hand, Henry's facial expression hardened at the thought of taking revenge on the Nazi bastards.

"In the next few days," Buckmaster continued, "you will receive briefings from my staff that will prepare you for your mission. I strongly encourage you to take full advantage of this information because it's based on hard-earned lessons gained from experience in the field." With that Buckmaster stood up, wished them well, and strode out of the room.

Henry was the first to speak. "Bugger doesn't waste words, does he?"

"Short and sweet," Cain echoed.

Josephine looked at her two teammates. "Let's get at it, shall we?" she said simply.

The atmosphere in Orchard Court was deliberately informal. Women smoked openly and men casually passed through, chatting in French. No one knew who anyone was, as they all had aliases. There was, however, an underlying feeling of tension. Conversations were guarded. Nobody spoke about their particular mission.

The team met Major Nigel Brook outside Buckmaster's office. He cheerfully introduced himself as their escort and conducting officer: "I'll be with you for the duration of your stay here." After ushering them into a small room on the second floor, he told them to take a seat at the conference table. An open Michelin road map spread out on the tabletop caught their attention. Henry immediately identified it as the Vercors region of southeast France, along the mountainous Italian border, an area he was intimately familiar with. He had served with the *13e Bataillon de Chasseurs Alpins*—13th Alpine Hunters Battalion—in the region before France's capitulation. "I know you're wondering why you're here," Brook said. "Suffice to say, your training days are over."

"Finally," Cain proclaimed enthusiastically, summing up the team's feelings. They had been preparing to go operational for weeks.

Brook merely nodded and pointed to a spot on the map that confirmed Henry's observation. "This is the Vercors massif," he said, using his finger to outline a section of the chart. "It's a remote, almost inaccessible upland 1,500 feet high, 30 miles long, and 12 miles wide, surrounded by mountains. The mountainous terrain makes the plateau almost impregnable. There are a few roads and only one or two narrow, ill-defined paths. Those that penetrate the remote plateau can be easily defended or blocked. The plateau has a maze of hiding places—cave networks, densely forested vales, and steep fields of scree or sheer rock faces which rise out of the upland.

"Before the war only a few dozen families lived on the plateau, but with the outbreak of hostilities, the inhabitants fled. Now hundreds of men have gathered there to escape the Germans and have formed guerrilla bands; the largest and best organized is De Gaulle's French Forces of the Interior or FFI, under the command of Monsieur François Hervieux, code name LeGrand. He has reported that he has 150 armed, highly disciplined men and 1,500 unarmed Maquis. Hervieux has been begging for arms and ammunition to fight the

Germans, but headquarters is hesitant to give him anything until we know more about his organization and what their needs are. He has specifically asked for a Jedburgh team. That is why your team is being sent in to assess their strength and determine what they need," Brook said. He studied their faces, gauging their reaction. None of the three so much as blinked. They stared back at him with a hard-eyed intensity.

"We're ready to go," Henry announced quietly.

Brook explained that in the next 24 hours they would be briefed on all aspects of the mission. And then he dropped the bombshell. "The operation is scheduled in three days during the next moon period."

"I don't understand what a 'moon period' is," Josephine said somewhat hesitantly, fearing that the term referred to a female's menstrual cycle.

Brook was quick on the uptake and immediately clarified. "The moon period, roughly speaking, refers to a period of ten nights on either side of a full moon when its brightness is 91 percent of its total light. This enables the pilots and parachutists to see the terrain features that they will be flying over and jumping into." He went on. "The remaining ten nights of the month are known as the 'no moon period,' when conditions are too dark for accurate parachuting or safe flying. As you can see, the moon is our goddess." Josephine nodded, relieved that the explanation wasn't embarrassing.

"What about the Krauts—what are they doing?" Cain asked.

"So far they haven't tried to attack the plateau, but it's only a matter of time before they do," Brook replied. "They're using two major roads to convoy troops and supplies through the area." He pointed to a road that ran in the shadow of the plateau's eastern wall and then to the other road that ran along the Rhone River valley on the highland's southwestern shoulder. "Headquarters believes that a guerrilla force might be able to interdict the road network and keep the Germans off balance. However, in all likelihood the raids will piss off the Germans and goad them into a full-scale attack on the plateau."

Henry interjected, "Yes, but the plateau is like a fortress. There are very few roads into the area, and those that are can be easily defended with the right type of weapons and enough manpower."

Brook showed the team an aerial photograph of a grassy field surrounded by heavily forested mountain slopes. "This is your drop zone," he said. "It's a high mountain pasture known as the Darbonouse and is some distance from any road or village. The only way to reach it is by a single cart track through the woods. The field is ideal for receiving a parachute drop—a rolling, pastoral stretch of countryside with no high-tension wires or other obstacles on the field itself or along the plane's approach route." Brook paused to let them examine the map and then briefed them on all aspects of the mission.

Late in the afternoon he stopped. "Before I proceed any further," Brook continued, "I want to assign each one of you a code name. Lieutenant Colonel Henry will be 'Adrien,' Captain Cain will be 'Pierre,' and Olivia will be 'Belle.' The team's code name will be 'Alexander.'" With that he opened his briefcase and handed each one a thick folder. "The packet contains documents that will enable you to pass a cursory inspection if you are stopped in civilian clothing. Memorize everything about your new identity."

10

No. 3 Group, Bomber Command, RAF Tempsford Station, Bedfordshire, 1900, 7 October 1942—The group intelligence officer was talking with his assistant when a clerk interrupted. "Sir, it's Air Ops," he announced, passing him the green scrambler telephone.

The officer glanced at his watch. "Right on time," he muttered. Every evening at this time, SOE Air Operations headquarters in London phoned him with the list of approved agent insertions and their mission numbers for the following night. "Good evening, sir," he said. "What's the program for tomorrow?"

"There's quite a lot on," the ops officer replied. "I've just got the details from the Air Ministry. We've got a number of parachute jobs." He then read off the missions in order of priority—indicating their degree of importance—while the group intelligence officer checked the master list of drop zones and made a notation beside the ones that had been designated. After reading back the names and numbers of the zones to verify them, he ended the conversation and walked over to the large-scale operational map of France that covered an entire wall of the office. The map scale, 1 to 500,000, or 10 miles to the inch, showed topographical features—elevations, rivers, and forests and any areas that Special Operations flights were prohibited.

As he read off the list, a FANY marked them with a tiny colored ticket marked in black indicating their priority.

"Looks like a busy night tomorrow," the intelligence officer declared.

Secret Training Site 72, Apartment 6, Orchard Court, Portman Square, London, 0800, 8 October 1942—Breakfast was a hurried affair—a rasher of bacon, a pot of jam, and a mug of weak tea.

"Much to do today," Flight Lieutenant James Bruce chided, waving the three Jeds into the conference room that looked like a schoolroom, with individual desks, tables, and a large blackboard, with the team's code name, individual names, and their operational name in large print.

Team Alexander

Lieutenant Colonel Henry Adrien

Captain Cain Pierre

Sergeant Harrison Belle

A rather pudgy figure, wearing a wrinkled prewar suit that looked like he'd slept in it, thick glasses, and a welcoming expression, greeted them. "Good morning," he said brightly, "nice day for coding, don't you think?" And then he made a great play of unlocking his beat-up leather briefcase, extracting three thick pads, and placing them on the conference table. The pad of 8-inch-square sheets provided a key for enciphering and deciphering messages and was matched by an identical pad in the receiving station. Each sheet, distinct from the rest, was used only once and then was destroyed, enabling the rendering of a brief message in a cipher that was unbreakable to anyone not possessing an identical pad.

"These are one-time pads," the instructor said. "It is the only cipher system that cannot be cracked by the Germans if used correctly." He emphasized "used correctly" and explained that each character of the text was encrypted by combining it with the corresponding character from the pad using modular addition.

Cain rolled his eyes. "What the hell is modular addition?" he grumbled.

"You don't have to know," the coder explained. "The one-time pad does it for you." Cain noticeably relaxed. Mathematics had never been his strong suit. "As long as the text is never reused and kept completely secret, the message is impossible to break." The man paused. "The use of the one-time pad is your lifeline," he emphasized. "Now let's get to work, shall we?"

The "coder," as Cain dubbed him, spent the rest of the morning explaining how to use the one-time pads. He had them write the alphabet on a blackboard and then place a number under each letter:

A B C D E F G H I J K L M N O P Q R S T U V W X Y Z
01 02 03 04 05 06 07 08 09 10 11 12 13 14 15 16 17 18 19 20 21 22 23 24 25 26

The coder created a key by breaking a series of random alphabet characters—HLMSEZRBHPSJOTDW—into blocks of two characters each—HL MS EZ RB HP SJ OT DW. He then showed them how to convert the alphabet characters into numbers: H=08, L=12, so the first block became 0812, followed by 1319, 0526, 1802, 1802, 0816, 1910, 1520, and 0423. This series of numbers, called the "Key," became the one-time pad. The key would then be given to the station monitoring the message traffic.

After creating the Key, the coder had them encrypt a message. Josephine's experience at the Code and Cyphers School enabled her to quickly code a message, which she handed to the instructor. By the time he finished deciphering it, his face was red with embarrassment. The message read, "Breathe there a man whose soul so dead, who never to his wife has said, come dear let's go to bed." He glanced at the virtuous-looking girl in front of him and wondered just how pious she actually was. When the two men turned in their messages, the coder immediately pointed out several mistakes and kept them at it until their product was perfect. Given her experience, Josephine took on the role of assistant trainer. Cain noticed that she was careful to conceal any hint of superiority, although he did catch her grimacing after he'd made a particularly stupid mistake.

The coder gave them a schedule for sending and receiving messages. During those times, the receiving station in England would monitor their frequency. For added security, Josephine was given a two-letter security code, which was to be inserted into the messages she sent to indicate whether she had been captured or was sending the message under duress. She was also given a 20-inch-square piece of silk—which would outlast paper in the field—printed with four-letter brevity codes designed to replace often-used phrases in all messages that would keep the sending time as brief as possible.

The session ended in the late afternoon, and the team was given time off to prepare for the insertion. A special courier from London brought word the mission was definitely on for the following day. They ate a last-minute dinner dressed in their battle dress uniforms with the winged patch on the upper sleeve. In the center of the patch's spread white wings was a red circle with the letters "SF," for Special Forces, in light blue. They were being deployed in uniform in the hope that, if they were captured, the Germans would deem them combatants and treat them as prisoners of war. What no one knew at the time was that Hitler had just issued the "Commando Order," which stated, "All enemies on so-called commando missions, even if they are to all appearances soldiers in uniform or demolition troops, whether armed or unarmed, in battle, or in flight, are to be slaughtered to the last man. No pardon is to be granted them."

The Jeds were just finishing dinner when Park escorted a tall, trim woman in her mid-thirties into the dining room and introduced her. "Everyone, I'd like you to meet Ms. Vera Atkins." The three got to their feet. They presumed she was a very senior woman in F Section—and they were right. The elegant blonde in front of them was their boss in a way, for she coordinated the preparation for all agents dispatched to France. She knew every secret mission, oversaw the handling of each agent in the field, and took personal responsibility for their affairs while deployed. It was said that she considered them as her friends. After offering her hand to each of them, she invited them to sit down for a "chat." The four of them talked about unimportant topics for several minutes before Park discreetly entered the room. He nodded to Atkins—time was short.

"I have something for each of you," she said, taking several items out of her purse and handing them out: to Josephine, an expensive silver compact, and to the men, silver hip flasks—all made in Paris. To avoid any hint of the gifts being a last memento before sending them on a suicide mission, Atkins quipped, "You can always hock it if you run out of money." With a final handshake, she said, "*Bonne chance*" and "*au revoir*," and walked out the room.

It was time to go. Arthur Park held the door open for them. "Good luck," he stated passionately. "Give them hell!" A large Ford estate car, nicknamed "the hearse" by the SOE headquarters staff, sat idling at the curb with an attractive, amiable FANY driver at the wheel. Henry took the front passenger seat; the other two sat quietly in the back. The driver asked them to pull the curtains over the windows, explaining that it was standard policy so that the agents would not be able to identify which airport they were flying out of, leaving unsaid, "in case you are captured." In any event, it would have been difficult to determine their route because all the road signs had been removed in the event of a German invasion.

11

Armstrong Whitworth Whitley Bomber No. DK 209, Dispersal site, RAF Tempsford Station, 0600, 9 October 1942—The airfield tractor tug slowly pulled the two-engine Whitley bomber to the remote dispersal site on the northern outskirts of the airfield. The Whitley had been specially modified to serve as the transport for the SOE. Its bomb bays had been altered to carry up to 7,000 pounds of containers; the lower gun turret was removed and replaced with a flapped trapdoor, and additional fuel tanks had been added, extending the plane's range to 850 miles.

The dispersal site was surrounded by an 8-foot double-strand barbed wire fence. For security reasons, the Special Operations aircraft were always positioned in isolated areas, out of sight of airfield operations and always loaded in secret. The Jeds were transported in vans so no one could see their faces.

A ground crew waited to pre-flight the bomber for the night's mission. Under the watchful eye of a grizzled old flight sergeant, the ground crew swarmed over the Whitley, preparing it for the evening's mission. Although the ground crew was often taken for granted by the pilots, "Flight"—as the sergeant was called—would not allow his lads to slack off. He insisted that they learn the intricacies of the aircraft, particularly the engine mechanics. The

Whitley's 14-cylinder Armstrong Tiger engines were less than reliable and rarely produced the designated power, but not if Flight could help it. He listened intently as a mechanic ran the engines up to full power. Their steady throb assured him that the synchronized engines were in tip top shape.

A Matador AEC 854 fuel bowser pulled alongside the Whitley. Two crewmen jumped out and unreeled a hose, struggling to lift it to the top of the wing to fill the main tank. A mechanic grabbed the nozzle and inserted it into the opening. At his signal, the refueling operator pressed a switch and the petrol started to flow. The mechanic watched closely. Flight would have his arse if he allowed the fuel to overflow onto the wing. While the ground crew went through their pre-flight checks, the ordnance section was busy offloading 12 6-foot-long tubular-shaped "C" containers from trailers and half a dozen large Sorbo wrapped packages containing delicate items. The packages, actually wire and sacking cages—about 3 feet by 2 feet by 2 feet and reinforced with horse hair, latex, and corrugated paper to absorb impact—were stacked in the forward section of the fuselage.

The containers were hung from racks in the bomb bay and from special clamps under the wings. They were made from stamped sheet metal, reinforced by ribs that were welded on the outside. Three latches held the two halves of the container together. Four handles were welded on the outside for ease of carrying.

A small compartment at one end of the container held a colored parachute—red for weapons, blue for food, white for medical supplies—attached to a static line that protruded from a hole in the compartment. The static line was fastened to a bar in the aircraft's interior; when the container left the aircraft, the line would pull out the parachute. Each "C" container consisted of three inner compartments that could be packed with approximately 200 pounds of weapons, ammunition, and supplies and was lined with sponge rubber to protect the contents from the jolt of landing. The containers were dropped at low speed and altitude to reduce dispersion and damage to the parachute, as the shock of opening was much less at slower speed.

The ground crew finished its check just as Flight Officer Pool appeared. "Evening, Flight," he said. "It looks as though we will need the old girl for service tonight. I hope she's ready to go."

"She's in absolutely top form, sir," the sergeant replied. "All systems are spot on."

Pool grinned. "I'll concentrate on getting this old girl back to you in one piece tonight."

"You have my very best wishes on that, sir," Flight answered with a salute.

No. 138 (Special Duties) Squadron, No. 3 Group, Bomber Command, Group Operations Room, RAF Tempsford, 1600, 9 October 1942—Squadron Leader Harry Scott-Nesbitt, DSO, the commander of "B" Flight, examined the colored flags that pinpointed the drop zones for the evening's show. He selected the targets for each aircrew by balancing the difficult with the comparatively easy, the distant with the near, and the abilities of his pilots. Scott-Nesbitt tried to even out the missions so that everyone received an equal share of the assignments. Tonight's mission to Vercors was a tough flight, requiring a skilled pilot and crew. After several moments he reached a decision and assigned the mission to Flight Officer Jimmy Pool's aircrew. Pool was one of his best pilots. He drove his crew hard, but they respected and trusted him. As testimony to his ability, the Royal Air Force had awarded him a Distinguished Flying Cross, the RAF's third-level military decoration for, "an act or acts of valour, courage, or devotion to duty whilst flying in active operations against the enemy."

Early that evening, after their pre-flight meal, Pool's crew gathered around a large map of Western Europe pinned to the wall at the far end of the squadron's Nissen hut briefing room. Their attention was focused on a long blue string that stretched across its surface. The string ran from England, across the Channel, into eastern France, charting their course to and from the objective. The navigator pointed to an area outlined in red where the string crossed the French coastline. It represented flak gun positions. "Here's where the Jerry ack-ack tagged us," he said. His comment brought back a flood of memories from their last mission, as they remembered the horrible feeling of nakedness when a German searchlight had illuminated their aircraft, blinding the pilots. They had to put their heads down inside the cockpit to see the instruments. Before they could escape its beam, an antiaircraft battery found the range. It was only Pool's quick reaction and skillful evasive maneuvers that saved them from being shot down. The navigator's comment sparked a lively discussion as everyone added their own account of the incident until Pool bellowed, "Attention!"

Squadron Leader Scott-Nesbitt entered the room. The crew stood quietly to attention as he marched briskly to the briefing platform, leading the briefing staff. "Please be seated," he said pleasantly. The crew took seats on one of the benches that lined both sides of the aisle. Scott-Nesbitt took his chair and told the squadron meteorological officer to commence the brief.

"Gentlemen," the warrant officer began, "moon's good tonight; it rises late but the weather to and from the drop zone will be good. You can expect light cloud cover over the Channel, but once you cross the coastline it will clear off." The crew heard this information with mixed blessings. It would make the cross-country navigation easier, but it would also make them easier to see by the Messerschmitt night fighters that prowled the airspace over France.

"What about wind velocity?" Pool chimed in.

"You will have a very strong tail wind on the outboard flight, which will give you a groundspeed of over 180 miles per hour," the met officer added.

Pool's co-pilot whistled in surprise. "That's a 60-mile-per-hour wind velocity!"

"Yes, it'll be a short flight out," the warrant officer replied, "but coming home you'll have that headwind to face."

"We're in for a long flight," Pool commented. The weather officer ended his portion of the brief by giving the crew a "time check" to synchronize their watches.

At a signal from Scott-Nesbitt, the squadron intelligence officer stepped up on the platform. A natural-born comic, he used that gift to lighten the tension before a mission. "I do not expect fighter opposition over the objective," he began, eliciting a sigh of relief from the men, but then added, "But I can't promise to and from." The men groaned. "Regarding the coastal flak, I have some good news. We received a report that the German antiaircraft battery that gave you so much trouble on your last mission got clobbered last night by the Yanks and suffered heavy damage." The aircrew cheered.

"I say, it couldn't happen to a nicer bunch of Krauts," the navigator added. He remembered the wind whistling through the flak holes in the fuselage, one pretty close to his head.

"The replacement battery is manned by reserve troops," the intelligence officer continued, "who are supposedly poor shots. Of course," he added quickly, "they might hit you accidently, but they wouldn't mean it." The crew booed him off the stage.

The squadron operations officer followed. He stressed the importance and secrecy of the mission before giving the precise details of the drop—the route, the load, exact latitude and longitude, the composition of, and means and height for dropping containers, and the recognition signal. He issued large-scale maps of the area and the general route and emphasized that all maps must be handed in on return and no reference made or record kept of the drop zone.

He finished his portion of the brief with the engine start-up and take-off times.

Finally, it was time for Squadron Leader Scott-Nesbitt to take the stage. "All right chaps," he began, "the mission tonight is important to the French Resistance. You're going to drop a Jedburgh team whose objective is to evaluate the potential of the locals to support guerrilla operations. It's a critical mission that may help to shorten the war." He paused for effect, wished them "good luck," and strode purposely out of the room.

After the briefing, Pool and Boskins—the bomb-aimer—sat down at a table to plan the flight. The operations officer had given them a briefing folder containing a recent vertical aerial photograph of the field and its immediate surroundings. The photograph showed a clear meadow surrounded by heavily forested high ground.

"What do you think, Harry?" Pool asked. "Is the field big enough?"

The bomb-aimer referred to the agent's description of the drop zone—a field 2 miles north of the town. The field was ideal for receiving a parachute drop of men and equipment—a rolling, pastoral stretch of countryside with no high-tension wires or other obstacles on the field itself or along the plane's approach route. They marked the maps with the latest intelligence on the flak defenses near the route and the distances along their flight path to the coast of France and to their objective.

Pool then made up his "gen"—information—card with basic navigational data for each leg of the flight and the latest meteorological information. He also noted the Morse letters to be flashed that night identifying them as friendly to the antiaircraft batteries on their return.

While Pool and the bomb-aimer worked on the flight plan, the rest of the crew went to the locker room and emptied their pockets of items that could be helpful to the Germans in the event they were shot down and captured. They changed into their flying kit—a laborious process that involved stripping down and adding several layers of clothing to help fight off the freezing temperatures at high altitudes. They started with long johns with full-length sleeves and high neck, adding a thick white polo neck jersey under their wool battledress, and then a long-sleeved vest made from a mixture of silk and wool. Most of the men wore heavy wool stockings under their sheepskin flying boots and three pairs of gloves—silk, wool, and leather. All the layers were needed. Lastly, they tugged on bomber jackets, which they topped off with flying helmet and goggles. If that wasn't enough, they wore a Mae West life vest and harness for a clip-on parachute, which they would carry on board. At this point it was difficult to move.

Before leaving the locker room, each man was issued a plastic escape kit containing two silk handkerchief maps—one of Western Europe and the other a large-scale reproduction of the localized area—a small compass, bar of soap, razor, fishing hooks and line, morphine injection, and some food tablets, as well as photographs of themselves in civilian clothes which could be used for a forged identity card if forced down. The kit fit snugly in a breast pocket. To a man, they hoped it would not be needed.

After kitting up, Pool led the crew out to a waiting bus for the trip to the aircraft dispersal point. A detachable three-step ladder allowed them to climb aboard the Whitley through the hatch on the port side of the fuselage—not an easy task bundled up with all their clothing—and check over their two-engine bomber, including running up the engines. First port, and then starboard, coughed and burst into life. He ran each engine up to take-off rpm and tested the magnetos, oil pressure and temperature, cylinder head temperature, and checked and set the gyro, cooling gills, and flaps.

Satisfied with the pre-flight check, Pool signed for the aircraft— regulations stated that the pilot-in-command had to verify the plane was acceptable with his signature on a standard form 50A. With everything in order, the crew disembarked and stood around waiting for the time to start engines and prepare for takeoff.

12

Chef d'escadron François Hervieux, Oradour-sur-Glane, 2030, 9 October 1942—For several nights running in the large market town of Oradour-sur-Glane, the police chief François Hervieux, code name LeGrand, and his two trusted officers had been glued to the illicit short-wave radio waiting for coded instructions through the nightly BBC foreign broadcast. After the announcer completed his news broadcast, the radios would emit the first four notes of Beethoven's Fifth Symphony—three dots and a dash—Morse code for the letter "V," symbolizing "Victory." The French Resistance segment would begin, "*Ici Londres. Et voici maintenant quelques messages personnels*"—and here are some personal messages. The first part of each seemingly nonsensical message was known as the reference phrase. It acted like a postal address and indicated that the forthcoming message was intended for a particular agent or Resistance leader. The second part of the message contained coded instructions telling the leaders what to do. The system was foolproof, for while the Germans knew the BBC messages contained orders for the Resistance, they had no way of knowing exactly what the contents meant.

LeGrand was just about to take a sip of coffee when he heard the English announcer's inflectionless voice say, "The bears are prowling tonight"—his coded instruction. "*Mon Dieu!*" the chief exclaimed. "It's us!" He jumped to his feet, spilling the hot cup of coffee on his assistant's pants.

"François," the assistant cried, sweeping burning liquid from his trousers, "what shall we do?"

"We must tell the others that tonight's the night and they are to assemble on the drop zone before midnight." With that the three men hurriedly left the small police station to alert the reception committee.

Chef d'escadron François Hervieux, code name LeGrand, Rayon Drop Zone, Massif du Vercors, 2100, 9 October 1942—The alert spread quickly through the town. Within minutes a dozen members of the reception committee were making their way along the secluded paths and tracks through the forest toward the mountain meadow that served as the drop zone. They had broken the six o'clock curfew and risked arrest if they were caught by the *Milice*, French Militia, or the *Feldgendarmerie*, the German military police, who might be out enforcing curfew or conducting spot-checks on identification papers. There was also a danger that a collaborator or an informant might betray them. The Germans offered a reward of ten thousand francs for such a denunciation—not an insignificant sum in wartime France. They had also decreed that anyone aiding or harboring Allied agents was to be summarily executed.

A few men armed with ancient shotguns were posted as sentries at strategic points around the area for security. As people approached them, they were required to give the password and their names. The full moon's rays provided enough light for the members to find their way through the rambling woods and canebrakes without too much trouble. Two horse-drawn carts were brought to the site for carrying supplies and weapons back to the safety of a cave known as the *Grotte de la Draye Blanche*. The light Comtois draft horses weren't too keen on tramping along the rutted track in the dark and showed their displeasure by snickering loudly. "Can't you keep them quiet?" LeGrand pleaded.

The committee assembled in a small natural amphitheater in front of an abandoned shepherd's hut, the drop zone spread out in front of them. The field ran southwest to northeast and was about 900 yards long and half as wide. Dense woods covered the slopes to the west, while a bocage of thick bushes and low scrub swathed the ridge to the east. LeGrand had paced its length and breadth and studied the entry and exit routes. He recorded the local landmarks and transmitted the information by code to London to help the pilots navigate.

After checking to make sure everyone was present, LeGrand turned to one of his assistants. "Take the men and show them where to stand." Each man was given an electric hand torch with red paper slipped over the bulb to reduce the amount of light it emitted. Three of the men were to stand in a row, along the direction of the wind. The fourth man was to stand so that the flare path looked from the air like a reversed capital "L."

"When you hear the aircraft, turn on your torch and beam it toward the sound," LeGrand instructed—for the umpteenth time. LeGrand himself would flash the agreed upon recognition code letter with a fifth torch. "Make sure you count the number of parachutes and where they land so we can pick them up quickly. Watch them closely so you don't catch one in the face! Now, off you go. *Bonne chance.*"

No. 138 Special Duty Squadron, No. 3 Group, Bomber Command, RAF Tempsford, Bedfordshire, 1800, 9 October 1942—It was a two-hour drive over a circuitous route through blacked-out roads

deep in the countryside. The car maneuvered down a narrow winding road marked "This road is closed to the public," past flat fields of beet and kale, and stopped at a closed railroad gate. Cain asked the FANY driver where they were and realized it was a foolish question when she politely told him, "It is the place you will be taking off from." After several minutes a train thundered past in a gush of billowing steam, and the gates raised up. They drove over the uneven tracks for another half-mile and pulled up to the airfield security checkpoint. They found out much later that the field was RAF Tempsford, known as Gibraltar Farm, the home of the RAF No. 138 Special Duties Squadron, often referred to as one of the "Moon Squadrons," because they inserted agents into France only on nights of the brightest moonlight—between the quarter wax to the quarter wane. The squadrons served as transport organizations for the SOE.

The airfield and the squadron were perhaps the most secret in Britain. Thus far the airfield had not been discovered, although a German spy had been caught in the vicinity. His swift trial and execution kept Tempsford from becoming known to the *Abwehr*, Germany's counter-espionage organization.

The airfield was not much of an RAF station—a rush job built over what had been a large area of marsh. Designed to fool German air reconnaissance into thinking it was not in use, all the hangars and domestic buildings were camouflaged to blend in with the surrounding farmland. The brick officers' mess, station headquarters, and squadron offices were covered with wood to give the impression they were farm buildings. The Nissen huts resembled pigsties. In some places, a thick black line was painted across the runway to make it look like a continuation of a hedge row. Patches of green and brown had been added to resemble clumps of grass. Farm animals were allowed to roam the fields during the day. Intelligence sources found out that aerial photographs taken by German pilots fooled analysts into interpreting them as a disused airfield.

An armed sentry meticulously checked the driver's authorization document and, using his shielded flashlight, looked over the passengers and closely scrutinized their papers before allowing them onto the airbase. They drove around the perimeter, crossing the end of the main runway. The vehicle finally stopped at a huddle of blacked-out buildings that looked like cowsheds, and they got out of the car. After wishing them a cheery "Good luck!" the driver sped off into the darkness. A sentry appeared and guided them to an entrance. To their surprise, what looked like a cowshed turned out to be the last station before their departure.

Once inside the three underwent a last, thorough security search by two ex-Scotland Yard intelligence agents. One was very tall and the other was very short. Cain immediately dubbed them "Mutt and Jeff." The Jeds had to appear separately before them to be searched. Despite the fact they were in uniform, they had to turn their pockets inside out to make sure they weren't carrying information of intelligence value. Even the linings of their uniforms were searched for identifying markings. The two men placed their wallets in a folder, while Josephine handed over her purse. The items were put in a sealed plastic bag with their code name printed on the front. "You can pick them up when you get back," the inspector told them cheerfully. Cain wondered how many agents actually retrieved them and then dispelled the thought. *We'll be the ones who make it*, he thought. They were allowed to keep the gifts Atkins had given them.

Next, a security officer inspected their expertly forged papers. It was said that the forgeries were better than the originals produced in France. The pictures on their ID cards had been taken in civilian clothes, in case they decided to wear them, and bore the name of a French studio. The ration and work cards had proper up-to-date stamps and were endorsed by genuine-appearing signatures of the local officials in the area, courtesy of recently escaped French patriots. The British forgers even went so far as to use paper and ink that perfectly matched that used in France. Each Jed was given a Swiss watch, French cigarettes, matches, and a map of the area printed on silk to carry in their pockets. Josephine was given lipstick and makeup that were all unmistakably French. Finally, each member of the team was quizzed on the information printed on their birth certificate and then asked questions about their background.

Satisfied that the team was ready, the security officer distributed canvas money belts, containing 100,000 used French francs—wouldn't do to have brand new notes—and 50 U.S. dollars, to wear around their waists under their battle jackets. He cautioned them to keep the large denomination bills in the belts, out of sight. "Be careful how you spend it. Remember you're just average folks. Live like one. Put the smaller bills in your wallets and purse for everyday expenses."

Finally, he gave each of them a set of pills. "The blue pills are Benzedrine Sulphate to keep you awake. The white ones are knockout drops that will put someone out for six hours. The last one is a cyanide 'L' pill. Bite hard on it before swallowing." He told them the poison would kill them in 15 seconds and assured them that the cyanide was painless.

"How do you know?" Cain asked dryly. "Have you tried one?"

The color drained out of Josephine's face as the security officer handed her the set, but she didn't say anything. Then, after wishing them "*Bonne chance*," he turned them over to the dressing crew.

An RAF sergeant and two assistants helped them step into their jump suits—a heavy canvas smock in a mottled dark green and mustard brown color. The padded outfits had a zipper down the front and extra wide arms and legs that made it easy to slip on over their clothing. Dozens of zip fasteners and large pockets had been sewn into the garment. They stuffed a flashlight, first aid kit, compass, emergency rations, a knife in case they landed in a tree and had to cut themselves out, and a short spade with a removable handle to bury their equipment, into a leg pocket. They wore holstered .45-caliber pistols and ammunition magazines around their waists. A lanyard was attached to the butt of the pistol and looped over their shoulders as a precaution in case it fell out of the holster. Extra ammunition magazines were packed in one of the breast pockets for easy access. Their American-made folding-stock M1 carbines and ammunition were placed in a rucksack, along with rations and a few extra items of clothing. Josephine's ruck was also packed with eight cipher books, a small black Bakelite box containing spare transmission crystals—two slices of quartz about the size of a postage stamp cut to precise wavelengths—and extra six-volt dry cell batteries for the receiver. A compartmented canvas backpack carrying her Type B3 Mark II "Jed Set" radio was packed in one of the "C" containers that would be dropped with her. The 30-pound Jed Set was a short-wave Morse transceiver—a transmitter and receiver combined. In addition to the transmitter, the set included a small, tripod-mounted hand-cranked generator to provide power. A second radio was packed in another container.

The bulky uniform was topped off with goggles, leather gloves, a British parachutist helmet that had sponge-rubber cushioning, and American jump boots. Because of the heavy load she was carrying, Josephine's ankles were tightly wrapped to prevent them from breaking on the impact of landing. It took two men to help them into their parachutes and pull all the straps tight and fasten them properly. Another man meticulously checked each strap and tested the release mechanism several times to make sure it worked—more than one parachutist had been dragged along the ground by the wind after landing. Both men strapped a special kit bag to his leg with a 20-foot length of rope tied to a waist belt. It was to be released during their descent. By this time all three were sweating heavily and barely able to hobble. The sergeant shook hands with them and then led them slowly out to a black RAF Armstrong Whitworth Whitley special mission bomber sitting on the tarmac.

Armstrong Whitworth A.W. 38 Whitley Bomber No. DK 209, 1900, 9 October 1942—The Whitley's five crewmembers were smoking quietly under the wing of the aircraft as the Jeds approached. They broke off and came forward to shake hands.

"I'm Flying Officer Jimmy Pool, the boss of this mob," the older-looking officer said, sticking out his hand. The others quickly introduced themselves: co-pilot/navigator, radio operator, bomb-aimer, and rear gunner/dispatcher.

"I'll be looking after you," the 20-year-old sergeant dispatcher declared. "If you need anything during the flight, please let me know." The man's genuine offer helped to dispel some of the anxiety they were carefully concealing.

With the introductions out of the way, Pool gave the Jeds a short brief. "We've got a tail wind, so the trip should take less than three hours. We'll be flying at low level to avoid the German radar, but we might pick up a little light flak as we pass over the coast. Don't be worried; Jerry can't hit the broad side of a barn."

"Yes, but he's not aiming at a barn," Cain muttered.

Pool chuckled and pointed to the nose art on the fuselage, the words "Flak Bait" emblazoned in yellow script just forward of the cockpit. A dozen miniature shell bursts representing antiaircraft hits were painted alongside. "The old girl has been hit so many times that we decided it was an appropriate name," Pool explained.

"Cute," Cain remarked, "Nothing like a little humor to liven up the mission."

The pilot continued. "We have a light load this evening, just the three of you and 18 containers. You'll be the first drop at 600 feet above the ground. We'll come around for a second pass and dump the containers. Any questions?" Seeing none, he glanced at his watch. "Well, if you're ready, let's get cracking."

The flight crew climbed awkwardly aboard the aircraft and struggled into their cramped positions. With all her gear on, Josephine had trouble climbing the metal ladder that extended from the rear of the aircraft. Cain unceremoniously reached up and shoved her rear end with his hands. "Don't get so pushy, Yank," she growled. Once inside, they crawled on hands and knees along the corridor-like hull to the center of the aircraft in the order they would jump—Henry, Josephine, and Cain. The "Joe hole" still had its folding plywood cover in place. They sat down on the uncomfortably hard deck, facing each other across the narrow fuselage, knees bent almost to their chest, with the parachute pack bunched up against their backs. The cabin smelled of a mixture of hydraulic fluid, high octane fuel, and chemically treated lacquer that made them feel slightly nauseous.

Even though the fuselage had been stripped of all unnecessary equipment, there was barely enough room because of the half-a-dozen packages that were arranged along the forward section of the fuselage, close to the "Joe hole," so the dispatcher could quickly push them out. Using a tiny pocket flashlight, the sergeant dispatcher squeezed past the rubber-coated packages, the tangle of legs and webbing, to hand out wool army blankets. "It'll be cold once we get in the air," he cautioned. "You may be sweating now, but shortly you'll be freezing your arse off." With that bit of guidance, he raised the ladder and locked the hatch just as the two Armstrong Tiger piston engines, which had been running softly, rose to a full-throated roar. The ground crew pulled the chocks and retreated from the swirling dust storm kicked up by the backwash.

Flying Officer Pool tightened his grip on the control yokes as he stared at the control tower waiting for the "clear for takeoff" signal. A yellow light pierced the darkness. "Here we go," he muttered and pushed the throttles to the wall. The engines rose to a screaming crescendo as they built up their revs and the entire aircraft shuddered. The propeller blades bit in, sending a hurricane of air that buffeted and rocked the fuselage. The bomber strained to take off.

Pool released the brakes and the Whitley picked up speed, the shielded runway lights shooting past the cockpit's window in a red blur. Flak Bait bounced two or three times as the end of the runway loomed up. Finally, the graceless bird pulled itself into the night sky. Pool eased back on the stick, climbed away, and turned onto his first heading. As checkerboard farm fields slid past in the ivory glow of the full moon, the team left England behind and headed for Nazi-held France.

The English Channel sparkled far below them as the plane reached its cruising altitude of 7,000 feet—just below the height that required oxygen—and it got cold very quickly. The dispatcher was not kidding. The floor was like ice, and the team was stiff, cramped, and freezing. Josephine lost feeling in her feet and worried that she would not be able to walk once she was on the ground. At that point the dispatcher came round and offered them a slug of *Grappa,* a fiery Italian grape spirit. It burned all the way down to their stomachs and helped to drive away the cold. The roar of the engines and the high-pitched wind whistling through openings in the fuselage was deafening, making it impossible to speak. The three huddled beneath the blankets in the darkened fuselage, lost in thought as the aircraft droned through the night out of British airspace and over the English Channel. The only glow on board was a dim green light in the navigator's compartment that allowed him to read his maps and charts. Tattered blackout curtains covered the fuselage's tiny windows so they could not see anything outside.

"Enemy coast coming up," Pool announced over the intercom as they neared the French coastline, which appeared as a darker gray than the light gray of the Channel. He turned onto the course that was designed to avoid German flak concentrations. "Here we go chaps; let's hope the intelligence was right about the new battery." Almost before the words were out of his mouth, exploding shells from an 88mm antiaircraft cannon and a machine-gun battery arched toward the aircraft from all directions, disappearing in front, behind, above, and below. The pilot and his co-pilot could look straight down at the machine-gun tracers coming up. Hundreds of what looked like red and yellow and green balls of fire hurtled past and around the Whitley: sometimes they were so close it felt like one could stretch out his hand and catch them.

The balls of fire seemed to be traveling very slowly, heading directly for the aircraft, and then just when it seemed that they couldn't miss, they veered off at an incredible speed and disappeared, quicker than the eye could follow. The cannon shells came close, spent shrapnel clattering along the fuselage. Explosions rocked the plane. Pool took drastic evasive maneuvers, throwing the three of them against the side of the aircraft. "I guess the intelligence report was wrong," the navigator muttered sarcastically.

The antiaircraft fire didn't faze the young dispatcher. Wedged tightly into his rear turret, he wasn't thrown around, although the maneuvers made him slightly nauseous. The Jedburghs held their breath, and after a few minutes the plane passed inland and into light cloud cover that screened it from the German spotters. The antiaircraft fire died away, and Pool put the nose down to lose height gently to 2,000 feet, a good altitude for map-reading. Henry had heard that the pilots in the special duty squadrons were among the very best in the RAF. He thought that it must take a special breed to fly the solitary night missions at very low level into the enemy's backyard just using terrain features to locate the drop zones.

In the cockpit, Pool and the navigator/bombardier poured over their creased 1:500,000 Michelin strip maps spread out on their knees, using the moonlight reflecting off landmarks to verify the plane's position. Their maps were folded so that their flight path was in the middle of each strip with about 50 miles on each side. The last strips were 1:250,000 to provide more detail around the target.

Peering out of the cockpit, all Pool saw was an occasional pinpoint of light; other than that, there was no color, just tones of bluish gray. He pressed on, referring to the navigational data on the "gen" card, compass headings, and airspeed. When he estimated they were 15 minutes from the drop zone, Pool began descending to a drop altitude of 600 feet above the ground. He stayed on course by following the moon's silvery light reflected off a river that flowed toward the target. Spotting the bend in the river he was looking for, he signaled the gunner/dispatcher—"Get ready, dropping in ten minutes, open the Joe hole"—and began the run into the drop zone.

The dispatcher pulled the 44-inch hinged plywood hatch off the "Joe hole" and carefully stowed the two halves out of the way. He then hooked the Jeds' static lines to a strong point that was built flush with the deck, tugging them twice to make sure they were securely fastened. "Running in! Action Stations, number one!" he shouted above the noise of the wind whipping through the hole. Henry scooted to the edge of the opening, dangling his feet in the buffeting slipstream. He gazed at the fields and roads and dark patches of woods as they flashed past the opening in the pale light of the moon and cleared his mind of everything but the jump.

———◼———

F Section, Special Operations Executive, Norgeby House, Site 69, 83 Baker Street, London, 1900, 9 October 1942—Loreena wound her way carefully along the cluttered hallway, dodging exposed light cords, ladders, and half-full paint cans waiting for the painters to resume covering the walls with the ubiquitous sickly green color so loved by the government bureaucrats. Section F had been forced to move in before the office spaces were ready after outgrowing its old haunts on Baker Street, a short distance away. Half in tears, she was mad at herself for wearing her heart on her sleeve. Her distress had been noticed by the boss, who expressed concern. It only added to Loreena's misery. She prided herself on being totally professional, but this time her emotions had gotten the best of her.

Earlier that afternoon she had attended a classified briefing in the operations room on the first floor where the inner circle officers discussed current operations. The duty officer had just finished posting the notice detailing the evening's operations on the section's status board when she noted that Jedburgh Team Alexander was being deployed that evening. A quick glance at the personnel roster showed that Captain James Cain was listed as the second in command. "Not again," she murmured, for the man who'd captured her heart. His going into action after being severely wounded in the raid on the German radar station, on top of the loss of her brother at Dunkirk, shattered her fragile emotions. "I hate this bloody war," she muttered angrily.

Vera Atkins, F Section intelligence officer, who was chairing the meeting, heard her remark and noted Loreena's distress. "Is everything all right?" she asked politely.

"Yes, Miss Atkins," she responded, but when the meeting broke up she quickly sought refuge in her office before anyone else noticed.

13

Reception Committee, Rayon Drop Zone, Massif du Vercors, 0100, 10 October 1942—The full moon slipped toward the horizon; time passed slowly in the cold. The reception committee strained to catch the first faint sounds of an aircraft engine and puffed their strong Gauloise cigarettes in cupped hands, swigged a little Armagnac, and grew restless. There was light cloud cover but not enough to interfere with the mission—still, everyone was nervous and doubt was beginning to set in. "Are they going to come?" was asked time and time again. "They will come," LeGrand assured them.

Finally, the faint drone of a multi-engine airplane reached them. The throb of the engines grew louder. The men turned on their torches. LeGrand pointed his light in the direction of the engines and flashed a series of dots and dashes in Morse code—three long flashes, two short ones, followed by three long ones—alerting the pilot that he was in the right place. Then, with a deafening roar and a trace of a fleeting shadow outlined against the moon, the plane faded into the darkness. Excited shouts broke out. The *résistants* pointed at the ghostly silhouettes floating to the ground. Unable to contain themselves, the excited men ran into the drop zone.

"I never thought it possible," LeGrand exclaimed, almost overcome with emotion.

———+———

Whitley DK 209, No. 138 Special Duty Squadron, No. 3 Group, Rayon Drop Zone, Massif du Vercors—The Whitley approached the drop zone from the southwest, and when the bomber crossed over a small ridge, the crew saw the faint glow of lights. The navigator/bombardier identified the correct ground signal and pressed the standby switch, illuminating the red warning light for the team. Pool lowered the landing gear, used half-flaps, reduced the throttle to slow the plane's speed, and leveled off at 600 feet. The airspeed indicator showed 120 knots, so he throttled back until it indicated 100 knots, or approximately 120 miles per hour. Spotting the fairly large cleared space on the hillside, he lined up the aircraft. The bomb-aimer switched on the green light. The dispatcher dropped his arm and shouted, "Go!" Henry did not hesitate. Head back, he launched himself into space.

Josephine immediately took his place and jumped. "*Bonjour France!*" she shouted. Cain was next. As soon as he disappeared through the hole, the dispatcher shoved out the rucksacks. The pilot began a gentle climb to the right, preparing for another pass to drop the packages. The tail gunner reported that all parachutes had opened.

Henry felt the slap of the prop wash against his face and the jolt of the opening shock and knew that his parachute had deployed. He played out the kit bag secured to his leg, but the darkness threw off his depth perception and he landed heavily, knocking the wind out of him. *Hell'va PLF*, he mused. *The instructors would give me hell.* He struggled to sit up, but the wind had caught the parachute canopy and it started dragging him along the ground. "Insult to injury," he swore.

A man suddenly appeared and collapsed the canopy, allowing him to stand up, albeit somewhat shakily. The hip he had landed on was sore as hell. "*Vive la France!*" the figure shouted, before enveloping him in a huge bear hug and planting a kiss on both cheeks. Others ran up, shouting jubilantly and pounding him on the back. It was an extraordinary moment as they welcomed "a French officer in uniform!"

Josephine landed perfectly and within seconds had shrugged out of her parachute harness. She had just started gathering in the canopy when she was swamped with sweaty bodies, all trying to kiss her on the cheeks and shouting joyfully. Cain, however, was not so fortunate. As the last man to jump, he was closer to the end of the drop zone and ended up heading toward the trees. He remembered the instructor at Ringway saying if you ever have to jump into trees, keep your blooming legs together; so he kept his legs together, his elbows tight against his side, and his chin tucked in. He crashed through the top of a pine tree, though layers of boughs until his parachute caught, leaving him hanging but uninjured. Swearing mightily, he retrieved his jump knife and started cutting the "goddamned" shroud lines. His thrashing only seemed to make it worse. He was concerned that if he cut any more lines, he would fall, and in the dark shadow of the tree he couldn't see how far he was from the ground.

Suddenly he heard movement and struggled to retrieve the .45-caliber pistol from the holster on his hip. Before he could draw it, Josephine's voice called out from the darkness, "You OK Yank?"

"Shit," he swore under his breath. Of all the people to come upon him in this predicament it had to be her. He was embarrassed as hell! But that wasn't the half of it. She came closer and he saw that she was only 4 feet below him. He could have stepped down from the tree. Within minutes, he was cut free and surrounded by jubilant Frenchmen kissing and hugging him.

Henry was appalled; the drop zone reminded him of Piccadilly Circus—absolute bedlam, security was a joke, noise and light discipline was nonexistent. He tried to restore some sort of order. During training the instructors had drilled into his head that the drop zone should be as quiet as a cemetery and evacuated quickly, as if the Germans were skulking around every tree. "*Silence, s'il vous plaît*," he hissed.

"*Ça ne risqué rien*," they replied. "Don't worry. The Germans are far away."

"How far?" Henry asked.

"About 2 miles," one said, which was far from reassuring. German troops had briefly occupied a town barely an hour away. The Frenchmen were treating the whole business as some sort of game. Suddenly, the roar of aircraft engines reminded him that the Whitley was returning to drop its load of "C" containers.

"*Attention!*" he shouted. "*Attention!*" and sprinted toward the edge of the drop zone. His actions finally alerted the reception committee to the danger. The aircraft swept over the drop zone. Shadowy parachutes blossomed. The heavy containers and packages smashed into the ground, fortunately missing everyone—but not by much.

As another wave of celebration broke out, Henry grabbed one of the men and asked him who was in charge. He pointed to a tall, slender figure standing on the edge of the field.

"Who the hell are you?" he shouted at him in French. The man explained calmly that he was the *Chef d'escadron* and the leader of the Maquis du Vercors. "You've got to clear the drop zone quickly before the Germans spot us," Henry declared urgently.

"Don't worry, they don't come this far," the police chief replied confidently. "Anyway, we'll soon be gone." Henry was not mollified, but after a few words from the police chief the joyous crowd settled down, collected the heavy containers and packages, and manhandled them onto the horse-drawn wagons.

Cain was in the process of burying the colored parachutes so the Germans wouldn't find any trace of the drop when the Resistance members stopped him.

"Give them to us," they said. "Our wives will use them to make underclothing."

Dismayed at their blasé attitude, Cain explained, "If the Germans discover the parachutes, you'll be shot."

"Ça ne risqué rien," they replied nonchalantly, shrugging their shoulders and walking away with the balled-up parachutes.

<hr />

Oberleutnant (lieutenant/flying officer) Max Rudolf, 3 Staffel, *Nachtjagdgeschwader* 1 (3/NJG1) (German Night Fighter Squadron), 5 miles west of Rayon Drop Zone, 0120, 10 October 1942—*Oberleutnant* Max Rudolf was piloting the black, twin-engine Messerschmitt BF 110 night fighter when his radio operator received a short burst of radio traffic from the ground controller. "Eagle 54 from Argonaut, adjust 280 degrees to your present course. Single aircraft approaching you at 30 to 35 degrees." Rudolf banked sharply 120 degrees and increased speed in an attempt to intercept the unknown aircraft. The onboard Lichtenstein FuG 202 B/C radar picked up a blip image on its cathode ray tubes only 2 kilometers away.

Rudolf couldn't visually spot the enemy aircraft in the night sky; however, the radar operator had it on his scope and provided him distance and course corrections. At 1 kilometer, he reduced speed so as not to overrun the plane. At 300 meters, Rudolf picked up the unmistakable outline of an aircraft just above the horizon, silhouetted against the night sky. He brought the BF 110 closer, positioning it below and to the left, so as to keep the enemy bomber in sight. "It's a Whitley, one of those 'specials' helping the terrorists," he declared over the intercom. The radar operator watched anxiously as Rudolf edged the Messerschmitt still closer. *Why doesn't he shoot?* he thought to himself. *Any nearer and I could reach out and touch it.*

Whitley DK 209, No. 138 Special Duty Squadron, No. 3 Group, Rayon Drop Zone, Massif du Vercors—The Whitley rear gunner intently scanned the night sky for the blurry shadow of an enemy fighter when he suddenly observed a small red glow below and to the right of his aircraft. He instantly recognized it as exhaust flames from a German night fighter. He had been trained to recognize aircraft by the number, type, and disposition of its exhaust flames and correctly identified the intruder as a Messerschmitt BF 110. He desperately swung the hydraulically operated gun turret in front of the enemy's nose and squeezed the triggers of the quad-mounted .303 Browning machine guns. The overwhelmingly bright yellow flashes from the muzzles of the guns as they fired temporarily blinded him, and he was unable to see where to aim after the initial burst of fire. "Night fighter below and behind!" he shouted over the intercom. Flight Officer Pool reacted instantly, throwing the Whitley into a sharp, diving turn.

Oberleutnant **Max Rudolf**—The startling lines of tracer fire that shot past Rudolf's windscreen and the unexpected violent maneuver caught him by surprise. Instinctively, he pushed the control column to the right to get out of the Whitley's cone of fire and then brought the night fighter back in position at the rear of the British aircraft. Rudolf fired a three-second burst at the fuselage and wing roots using the two 20mm cannon.

Whitley DK 209—The gunner's vision cleared but the night fighter was not in sight. *Maybe I hit him*, he thought, but just then the turret's Plexiglas exploded as the night fighter's shells shredded the flimsy resistance. The gunner did not stand a chance under the hail of cannon fire.

Pool felt a terrific jolt as cannon rounds tore through the aluminum fuselage in a hail of jagged metal fragments. Pieces of the port engine flew off and the engine burst into flame. The plane lurched violently and peeled over on its left wing despite Pool's desperate attempt to keep the Whitley level. Flames from ruptured fuel lines streamed back along the fuselage. The two pilots struggled mightily with the controls and managed to pull the plane out of its dive into level flight, but they realized it was only temporary. Flak Bait was done for. The crew had to get out quickly before it was too late.

Oberleutnant **Max Rudolf**—Rudolf saw fragments fly off the wing and flames shoot from the engine as the British aircraft suddenly fell off in what appeared to be an uncontrolled dive. *This one's finished*, he thought and broke off the attack. Better to save his remaining ammunition for another target.

"Chalk up another kill," he radioed Argonaut jubilantly.

"Congratulations, Eagle 54," the ground control station replied. "Stand by for another vector."

Whitley DK 209—"Bail out!" Pool declared over the intercom, "Bail out!" He turned to his co-pilot. "Get out Tom. I'll handle it until everyone gets out." The co-pilot unbuckled his seatbelt and climbed awkwardly out of his seat. He grabbed his parachute pack, frantically clipped it onto the chest clamps of his harness, and stepped down to the open forward escape hatch—the bomb-aimer, radio operator, and navigator had already bailed out. He swung his legs into the opening and was immediately sucked out into the slipstream.

Pool waited until he was sure the crew had bailed out and then put the plane on automatic pilot. He climbed out of his seat and jumped for the escape hatch just as the plane took a sudden lurch, sending him sprawling on the side of the aircraft. He spent the next two minutes bouncing around the cockpit as flames engulfed the Whitley. Smoke and lack of oxygen made breathing difficult, not to mention the stifling heat. Would he burn to death? he wondered. With a strength born out of desperation, he threw himself out of the escape hatch, grabbed the metal "D" ring on the parachute, and yanked. Nylon shroud lines streamed past his face.

The chute popped open with a sound like a bursting paper bag full of air. A terrific jolt racked his entire body as the fully deployed canopy suddenly braked his fall. Seconds later Flak Bait exploded. The force of the explosion partially collapsed his chute, sending him plunging toward the ground. He hit, hard, the wind knocked out of him. Before he could recover, the wind caught his parachute and started dragging him along the ground. He caught his breath and grabbed the shroud lines to collapse the canopy. He got shakily to his feet, shrugged out of the parachute harness, and took stock. Physically everything seemed to be OK, except that he ached all over. He had no idea what had happened to his crew or where he was.

Pool decided to stay put, rather than wander around in the dark; he just needed to find some way to conceal himself. A dark shape loomed in the darkness. As he inched closer, he discovered it was a mound of recently cut hay. He tunneled into the bottom of the pile and succeeded in completely concealing himself. Satisfied that he was safe for the moment, he let sleep overcome him; the next thing he knew, something was growling and tugging on his flight boots. Startled, he kicked out and his foot connected with a dog. The mutt let out a cry of pain and launched another attack. A voice called out and the dog stopped. *Shit*, Pool thought, *I've been discovered, no sense in lying doggo.* As he backed out of his hiding place, he came face to face with a teenage boy holding a pitchfork.

Pool held up his hands in a gesture of surrender. "I mean you no harm," he said. The teen stared at him for a long moment, taking in his uniform and pilot wings.

"*Pilote anglais?*" he asked.

"*Oui,*" Pool answered in schoolboy French. The boy nodded and gestured for him to follow him toward several farm buildings in the distance.

"It's about time you got here," Pool's co-pilot welcomed him as he entered the farmhouse. The kitchen was crowded with three of his crewmembers and a French family. The men enjoyed a hearty welcome, overjoyed that their pilot was safe. Pool looked around for the rear gunner.

"Where's Archie?" he asked.

"He didn't make it," the co-pilot responded. His comment put a damper on the reunion even as the farmer's wife announced breakfast.

The conversation around the table revolved around the crew's escape from the burning aircraft and their discovery by the Resistance escape network.

"This farmhouse is part of the Pat O'Leary Line," the co-pilot explained.

Pool almost choked. "You're kidding me," he quipped.

"No, sir," the navigator responded. "The farmer said the network was initially established by a Scottish soldier who recruited hundreds of volunteers to spirit airmen across the Pyrenees mountains to Spain. He indicated that we can expect local guides to accompany us along the route within the next few days. All we have to do is lie low and wait."

14

Les Berthonnets Farm, Oradour-sur-Glane, 0230, 10 October 1942—"*Allons*," the police chief ordered. "Let's go." The excited group retraced its steps along the same rutted track through the dense forest until they reached a spot in the trail where erosion had laid bare the side of a steep escarpment, exposing its limestone face. The base of the slope was covered with thick brush, which the men pushed aside to reveal a narrow fissure in the rock just large enough for a man to slip through. LeGrand squeezed through the opening and motioned the Jedburghs to follow him.

"This is our supply depot," he said, turning on his flashlight and shining it around the pitch-black space. The light barely penetrated the darkness, but it was sufficient for them to see that they were in a large, high-ceilinged room. "This is the beginning of an underground network of caverns that extend for more than a mile in different directions," LeGrand explained. "In ancient times the caves served as a refuge for the hunted. Now they serve as our storehouse and sanctuary from the Germans." He shined his light on the rough hand-made bricks that lined the walls. Bench-like shelves had been built to hold supplies, evidence that the space had been turned into a storage area.

The cave showed signs of recent use. The dirt floor was thick with footprints and strewn with scraps of paper from food packages. The police chief led them further into the cave. It smelled of decaying vegetation, dank soil, and stale air.

"Mind the steps," he cautioned, shining his light on slippery, rough-hewn steps that had been carved into the stone. Josephine shivered with the drop in temperature. "It stays about 60 degrees," LeGrand said, noticing her discomfort. "Before the war, the caves were used to store vegetables." He played the light over the ceiling. Something flitted past them and they all instinctively ducked. "Bats," he uttered disgustedly.

His flashlight swept over straw-like stalactites hanging from the dirty white limestone ceiling. Cone-shaped stalagmite towers reached the full height of the room, giving the space the appearance of a wondrous cathedral.

"Marvelous," Josephine exclaimed. "Such beauty. I would like to visit this place after the Germans are gone."

"Yes," LeGrand replied emphatically. "With your help we will soon make that happen."

The sound of rushing water caught their attention. "There is an underground stream that passes under the mountain," he explained. "It surfaces below the plateau and provides water for the farms in the lowlands." They continued along the central passageway. Several smaller passages angled off the central corridor.

"It would be easy to get lost in here," Cain said.

"Yes," LeGrand replied, "there are many stories of people disappearing in the caves and chambers that honeycomb the whole Vercors plateau." Another 25 meters and the passageway got noticeably smaller. They felt a rush of warm air. "This is the back entrance," LeGrand said, shining his light on an opening half-choked with brush. "Just outside there is a path that leads further up the mountain."

LeGrand led them back to the front entrance where they found the containers neatly stacked in a corner of the cave. "We'll come back tomorrow night to open them up and distribute the weapons," the police chief said. "Right now everyone needs to get home before dawn. We don't want to draw unwanted attention."

It was not to be. When they reached the farm, a large throng of boisterous locals filled the farmyard trying to get a good look at the newcomers—so much for operational security.

A celebration began, the three Jedburghs being hailed as heroes. Women, children, and old men laughed and cried with joy. Young girls kissed the Jeds and showered them with flowers and wine. It seemed that every Frenchman in the world wanted to welcome them and celebrate their arrival—truly a community event. The 140-proof Calvados flowed like water—only it was a potent apple brandy called "White Lightning" by the locals. Cain swore it could be used for lantern fuel. Before long the team was feeling the result of the brew and lack of sleep. They were finally able to force their way through the crowd and into the barn that served as the Resistance headquarters just as the first streaks of dawn appeared in the eastern sky.

LeGrand followed them inside and showed them the stable that had been prepared for them.

"At least the horse shit has been shoveled out," Cain remarked flippantly, eyeing the fresh straw.

"My first night in France, what a treat," Josephine said cheerfully. "I'm so tired I could sleep on a rock."

"I will post guards to make sure you are not disturbed," LeGrand promised, "and tomorrow you can talk to my commanders. They will be here by mid-morning."

The Jeds still had reservations about the lack of operational security, but at this stage there was nothing they could do but accept their host's hospitality. They spread blankets on the straw and collapsed, trusting the Maquisards to maintain security. It was full daylight before the local celebrants dispersed to make their way back to their homes in the surrounding farms and the village of La Chapelle-en-Vercors. Hervieux decided to spend the night at the farm and asked a neighbor to tell his wife that he wouldn't return home until the next afternoon.

***

SS-*Sturmbannführer* Helmut Krause, 1st Battalion, SS *Polizei Regiment 19, Geheime Staatspolizei* (Gestapo) Headquarters, Grenoble, 0715, 10 October 1942—The duty orderly hurried along the passageway of the headquarters building until he reached the commander's room. He took a deep breath to calm himself and knocked loudly on the door frame. No response. "Damn," he swore under his breath. "Why does it always happen to me?" The last time he'd woken the officer, he was threatened with orders to the Eastern Front. *The man is pure evil*, he thought to himself, and knocked again, louder.

"What the fuck do you want!" a voice shouted.

"Herr *Obersturmbannführer*," the frightened soldier replied, "the *Standartenführer* is waiting to talk to you on the radio."

Thirty seconds later, *Obersturmbannführer* Krause picked up the phone. "*Jawohl, Herr Standartenführer*," he answered respectfully. Before he could say anything more, the regimental commander informed him that the British had parachuted supplies and agents to the *Bandens*—criminal bands—near the small village of La Chapelle-en-Vercors, 80 kilometers south of Grenoble. Krause knew the area intimately, having run several *Bandenbekämpfung*—actions to eradicate French resistance—there in the past few months. The information he used to conduct the operations was provided by several French informers and the blue-uniformed *Milice française*,

Vichy paramilitary police who specialized in tracking down "internal enemies"—Resistance fighters, dissidents, escaped prisoners, Jews, and those evading the *Service du travail obligatoire*, the German Compulsory Work program or STO.

"I want you to take your battalion and the Grenoble *Milice*, and exterminate the terrorists in Oradour-sur-Glane," the regimental commander ordered.

"*Jawohl, Herr Standartenführer,*" Krause responded enthusiastically. Krause hung up the phone and turned to the orderly. "*Schütze,*" he barked, "find the officer of the day and tell him I want the battalion formed up on the road in 20 minutes with weapons and ammunition. Do you understand?"

"*Jawohl, Herr Obersturmbannführer,*" the soldier replied, coming to rigid attention.

"Then why the hell are you still standing here?" Krause shouted. "Get your ass in gear!" The curse propelled the soldier down the hallway, much to the amusement of the officer, who delighted in bullying his men.

Krause called Robert Bonnica, known as "*Capitaine* Bob," the district *Milice* chief himself. "The man is just like all the other French—haughty," he fussed. "You'd think they'd won the war." The only reason he tolerated the *Milice* chief at all was that his men were good at infiltrating the *Banden* organization and identifying its members, several of whom had been arrested and interrogated in the basement of his headquarters. The information they had given up had resulted in breaking up at least two terrorist rings and earned Krause a commendation from the regimental commander. He reached the *Milice* chief, who was still half asleep but came awake at the mention of action. Bonnica assured him that he would come with a detail of his best men. Almost as an afterthought, the chief mentioned that Colonel Maude would accompany him. Krause smiled as he hung up the telephone.

There was another, more personal, reason Krause tolerated the head of the *Milice*—his mistress, nicknamed "Colonel Maude" by the Resistance. The woman was extremely attractive and had a figure that turned heads, particularly *Capitaine* Bob's. Krause was anxious to form a closer "personal" relationship with the *Freudenmädchen*, but he had to be careful. *She is not a woman to screw with*, he thought, and then chuckled to himself with the double entendre. The woman had an appetite for cruelty and sadism that was well deserved. She often acted as prosecutor at the secret tribunals of terrorists and personally controlled the torture that was administered in the headquarters basement. Having observed her in action, he did not want to experience one of her interrogations.

Krause met with the key personnel of the force and read them the order of the day. "The regimental commander expects this undertaking to proceed with extreme severity and without any leniency. This constant trouble spot must finally be eradicated. Partial success is of no use. The forces of the Resistance are to be crushed by fast and all-out effort. For the restoration of law and order the most rigorous measures are to be taken to deter the inhabitants of this region from harboring terrorist groups. We must send them a warning. Ruthlessness and rigor at this critical time are indispensable if we are to eliminate the danger that lurks behind the backs of the fighting troops and prevent even greater bloodshed among our men in the future. I want to emphasize," Krause shouted, "no one is to be spared. The terrorist nest is to be burned to the ground."

Thirty minutes later, Krause's Volkswagen *Kübelwagen* led a convoy of Opel Blitz light trucks, two half-tracks, and three Gonio wireless-detector vehicles out of the headquarters compound and onto A49, the road to Oradour-sur-Glane. Krause estimated the convoy could be at the village in less than three hours, if all went well.

15

Les Berthonnets Farm, Oradour-sur-Glane, 0800, 10 October 1942—The smell of fresh coffee brought the Jeds out of a sound sleep. They awoke to find LeGrand standing over them holding a tray with three large steaming mugs.

"I thought you could use a little wakeup after last night's exertions," he said in accented English.

"You're damn right," Cain replied, sitting up and reaching for one of the mugs. He took the drink in both hands and blew on it to cool it before taking a sip. "*Merci beaucoup*," he ventured hesitantly, trying out his high school French.

"*De rien*, you're welcome," LeGrand responded, "but you don't have to speak French; I understand English very well." The chief of police, in his early 40s, had an air of supreme self-confidence that at first could be taken as arrogance. However, his easy smile and unpretentiousness soon put the Jedburghs at ease.

Henry and Josephine took the other mugs and thanked LeGrand for his kindness. LeGrand invited them to use the "necessary" and join him in the farmhouse to meet his officers. Washed and shaved, the three Jeds trooped into the warmth of the kitchen where the scent of breakfast wafted in the air. An older, heavy-set woman bustled about the room studiously ignoring them as she prepared

86

the food. Four men dressed in rough farm clothes sat around a heavy oak table smoking cigarettes. At the sight of Henry's French rank insignia they leaped to their feet, almost upsetting the table. He was the first senior French officer they had seen since the armistice and they were overcome with emotion.

"*Vive la France!*" they shouted. "We have not been forgotten!" Henry was positive proof that they weren't alone in the fight.

"These are my *Chefs de bataillon*," LeGrand said pridefully and introduced the four battalion commanders using their *noms de guerre*. "This is Commandant Maurice. He is responsible for the long, broad plain between Autrans and Meaudre in the northwestern sector of the Vercors. His headquarters is located at Ecouges farm."

Maurice executed a smart salute. "*Mon Colonel,*" he said respectfully.

LeGrand put his hand on the shoulder of the next man. "Commandant Phillippe," he said kindly. "He is our veteran of *La Premiere Guerre Mondiale*, World War I. He is in charge of our most vulnerable section, Saint-Nizier, under the very noses of the *Boche*." The veteran's eyes burned with patriotic zeal, and Henry did not doubt the man's dedication to the cause. LeGrand pointed to the next man, who looked to be in his early twenties. "Commandant Jean is our youngest commander. He is responsible for the Gresse-en-Vercors sector in the southeast. His headquarters is at Mandement farm." The man nodded humbly, and LeGrand introduced the last man. "The fourth member of the Maquis du Vercors is Commandant Alphonse. His command encompasses the southwestern sector. His headquarters is in the village of Vassieux-en-Vercors."

LeGrand paused and looked directly at Henry. "My plan," he emphasized, "is to harass the German supply lines. But first I need weapons and ammunition, more than what you brought with you." Before Henry could reply, Madam Berthonnet, the portly wife of the owner and the mistress of the house, interrupted.

"*Messieurs*, I must insist that you eat before the breakfast I fixed gets cold." She had been cooking since early that morning over a wood-burning cast iron stove and was in no mood to see her efforts go to waste. The frosty glare in the older woman's eyes and her stance—hands on hips, holding a large wooden spatula—indicated the issue was not up for discussion.

"*Pardon Madame*," the men apologized, "we are not used to such gracious service."

With a disdainful "Humph," she proceeded to serve breakfast—fresh eggs, bacon, French bread with butter and jam, and a pot of coffee—luxuries that were almost unheard of in England.

In between mouthfuls, Henry briefed the Resistance officers on the mission of the team. "We are here to determine what you need to fight the Germans," he declared forcefully. The men were silent for a long moment, and then they broke out in huge smiles and excited chatter, everyone talking at once. Henry's statement was exactly what they wanted to hear. He held up his hand, quieting them. "In order to properly determine what you need, Captain Cain and I will visit each of your units over the next two weeks."

LeGrand interrupted. "That won't be a problem," he assured him. "Each unit will provide guides." The commanders nodded agreement and pledged to show the Jedburghs anything they wanted to see.

"What about the weapons that were delivered last night?" Commander Jean asked. "When will they be distributed?"

"They will remain hidden until tonight," LeGrand replied. The discussion continued for the next hour until the travel details were worked out, and then the Jeds were bombarded with questions about England and the progress of the war.

Finally, Josephine and Henry excused themselves and went to the barn to send their first wireless message. Cain stayed behind. According to the pre-arranged schedule set up by SOE, the team should send a situation report twice a day—0830 and 2100. Henry checked to see that the 70-foot antenna was in place and then jotted down the brief report on a message pad: "Have arrived safely and made contact—impressed by organization—will commence visits immediately," signed "Adrien."

Using the lid of the open radio case as a book rest, Josephine quickly encoded the message using the one-time pad and prepared to send it on the B2 Jed Set wireless transmitter, which had been set up in one of the stalls. The antenna was strung to the top of the roof. Josephine plugged in the telegraph key, checked the power pack, and carefully tuned the transmitter to the five-megacycle band. "I'm ready," she said, and sent out her call sign, praying that the signal was strong enough to reach the intercept station and that someone was listening. Seconds later she heard a faint response. Grendon intercept station replied with the prearranged code: she could begin her transmission.

She switched the Mark II on. The high-pitched dit, dah of Morse code echoed through the stable as she transmitted the message in a blur of dots and dashes. The speed of her transmission was crucial; the faster she transmitted the message, the less likely the Germans would pick it up with their direction-finding equipment. After transmitting for 25 minutes, an operator would be heading into the danger zone. Headquarters estimated that it would take the Germans 30 minutes to discover where the transceiver was located. She signed off the transmission with "Love and kisses." Her instructor had drilled into her head, "Never end a message with 'Over and out' or 'Message Ends.' It's a cliché, and if you know it then the Germans do also, and they can use it to decipher the entire message."

Josephine switched to listening mode and heaved a sigh of relief when she heard, "Message received." She turned off the power switch and the voltage dial died back to zero. Henry patted her on the shoulder. "Well done lass."

Station 53A (Radio Intercept Station), Grendon Hall, Grendon Underwood England, SOE Signals Center, 0840, 10 October 1942—The high-pitched chatter of Morse code flooded the headset of the highly trained FANY yeoman at the top-secret monitoring station at Grendon Hall, a large, stately manor in the flat English countryside. Over 500 radio operators and code breakers were stationed in Nissen huts on the manor's grounds to maintain wireless contact with agents inside France and other occupied European countries. The radio operators were permanently on alert. Each switchboard operator was assigned a certain number of clandestine radio transmitters, and every agent in the field had their own operator who would be on duty when they were due to come up on the air. Known as a "godmother," the operator was familiar with the agent's wireless technique—or "fist," as it was called. The agent's fist was as individual as a fingerprint, and if it appeared to be different, the godmother would immediately notify her superior and special precautions would be established. As a security check, the FANY operator would ask for the wireless operator's password in the form of a question. For example, "How bright is the moon?" was to be answered by "The flowers are wilting."

It sometimes happened that a wireless operator was captured by the Germans and "turned," resulting in an entire network being compromised. An SOE operator working in the Netherlands had been captured and given the choice of execution or cooperation. He chose the latter but attempted to warn London by omitting his security check. Unfortunately, the omissions were not picked up. The Germans took complete control of the Netherlands operation. By the end of the war, 52 Allied agents were dropped straight into their hands and 350 resistance workers were arrested.

The specialist tapped a few times on her Morse key to confirm she was listening and then rapidly jotted down the indecipherable five-letter code groups on a message pad. She had to fine-tune the

Marconi 100 receiver because the signal was slightly off beam, but she was still able to receive the message. At the end of the transmission she acknowledged receipt and then tore the page off her pad and handed it to a clerk. The message was quickly decoded in another room at the secret monitoring station, where the decoder was under orders to decipher the message exactly as sent, regardless of any apparent "mistakes." The message was then passed in a sealed envelope to a motorcycle courier, who signed for it and transported it as fast as he could to an F Section signal officer at SOE headquarters, where it would be analyzed.

16

SS-*Sturmbannführer* Helmut Krause, 1st Battalion, SS *Polizei* Regiment 19, Oradour-sur-Glane, 0842, 10 October 1942—As the convoy neared Oradour-sur-Glane, one of the Gonio vehicles picked up wireless transmissions. The skilled operator had become adept at locating clandestine radio transmitters and only needed a short transmission to organize a hunt. He radioed the two other vehicle operators, who immediately spread out to triangulate the source of the signal. They slowly shifted their directional antennas round the compass to nose out the bearing of the communication.

Within minutes they located the source as emanating from a location approximately 1 mile east of the village. Krause looked at his map and saw that Les Berthonnets farm was located close to the source of the signal. "That son of a bitch!" he swore. The farmer had been questioned in the past, but the interrogators were unable to get anything out of him and he was released. "We'll see what you have to say this time," Krause muttered, vowing to squeeze the truth out of the man once and for all. He ordered the 2d Company to split off from the convoy and proceed to the farm, while he led the rest of the battalion to the village.

2d Company, 1st Battalion, SS *Polizei* Regiment 19, Les Berthonnets Farm, 0915, 10 October 1942—*Hauptsturmführer* (company commander) Gerhardt Unger had his men dismount about a half-mile from the farm—far enough away that the vehicle noise could not be heard. He deployed the company in a "V" formation—one platoon on each side of the farm lane and one platoon in reserve. This formation placed firepower up front, with the ability to maneuver the reserve platoon to either flank. Unger chose to move with the left flank platoon. Despite the brush and secondary growth, the men moved with minimum noise. They were seasoned veterans who had served on the Russian front and knew how to move in brush-covered terrain—no spoken order was given—hand and arm signals only.

The company had gone only a short distance when a soldier in the left flank platoon smelled the strong odor of tobacco. He took a few more cautious steps and spotted a terrorist sentry casually leaning back against the base of a tree smoking a cigarette only a few feet away, oblivious to the danger. Instantly reacting, the veteran German soldier charged through the brush, intending to bayonet the unsuspecting man to keep him from alerting the terrorist camp. The startled sentry half rose at the sudden appearance of the enemy soldier and instinctively threw his hands up in an awkward attempt to protect himself from being impaled. Putting his weight behind the 15-inch blade, the German plunged it into the man's ribcage. The powerful thrust sank the bayonet half its length into the Frenchman's chest cavity, piercing his heart and killing him instantly. The execution was over in a minute and was noiseless, except for the sudden thrashing in the underbrush.

The German soldier tried to recover his bayonet but it was proving difficult. Placing his foot on the body, he gave a final heave; the bayonet came free with a sucking sound as the flesh fell away from the blade. He wiped the bloody steel on the corpse and then searched the body. He found nothing of value, except half a packet of Gauloises, three shotgun shells, and a few francs, which he pocketed. An antiquated shotgun was propped up against a tree and a half-eaten sandwich lay in the grass. "Poor fodder to be killed for," the soldier muttered, and picked up the shotgun. Several other soldiers passed the Frenchman's body with hardly a glance. They had seen dead bodies before. "What kind of a sentry smokes on duty?" Unger sneered after spotting a half-smoked cigarette lying in the grass.

The SS soldiers filtered through the sparse undergrowth. The forest opened up, and the Germans spotted the farmhouse, a two-story stone building typical of the houses on the plateau. A collection of wooden outbuildings—a barn, sheds, and storage shelters—stood behind the farmhouse. The structures were surrounded by a waist-high stone wall. Harvested fields stretched from the wall to a thick stand of trees that extended into the distance.

Several armed terrorists were gathered around the main building, talking and smoking, completely unaware of the danger they were in. At Unger's signal, the men moved quickly into line and made their way toward the edge of the tree line. As the formation stepped into the open area, one of the terrorists spotted them.

"*Les Boches!*" the startled man cried out.

Unger immediately bellowed, "*Erschiesst!*"—the signal for the men to open fire—which they did, with a vengeance.

SS-*Sturmbannführer* Helmut Krause, 1st Battalion, SS *Polizei* Regiment 19, Oradour-sur-Glane, 0940, 10 October 1942—"The Germans are coming!" The cry raced through the small town, sending the inhabitants running for the uncertain safety of their homes. Krause's VW *Kübelwagen* led a long column of snub-nosed

Opel Blitz trucks grinding noisily along the hastily deserted Rue Emile Desourteaux, the town's main street, and stopped in the *Champ de Foire*, the little market square. Guttural commands echoed off the storefront facades. Heavily armed, camouflaged-smocked soldiers climbed off the trucks and quickly formed a cordon around the center of town. Machine-gun teams blocked both ends of the street, while others took positions overlooking possible escape routes with orders to shoot anyone who tried to flee. The villagers, who just a few hours before had welcomed the arrival of the Jedburghs, now peered anxiously from their windows, wondering what lay in store for them at the hands of the *Schutzstaffel*—SS. The residents knew things were going to go badly when Colonel Maude and a formation of blue-uniformed *Milice*, suddenly appeared. They were universally hated and feared, even more than the Gestapo, because of their cruel treatment of ordinary French civilians.

Under the direction of the district chief, the *Milice* quickly fanned out and broke into homes, brutally forcing the inhabitants into the street. "Everybody out!" they shouted. The SS troopers pushed and jostled families with their rifle butts through the streets into the *Champ de Foire.*

The mayor protested to Krause. "Why are we being treated like this?" he asked indignantly.

"Because you're harboring terrorists," the officer snarled, slapping the hapless man in the face. A soldier hauled the official away. Krause pointed to a man with muddy shoes. "Why are your shoes dirty?" he barked. "Because you were in the field last night helping the terrorists!" Others were deemed terrorists because they were dirty or unshaven. Any pretext was used to identify suspected terrorists and justify their actions.

It wasn't long before muffled shots were heard, as the *Milice* proceeded to shoot anyone in the houses who was infirm or unable to walk. There was to be no mercy. Colonel Maude held up a screaming child and snarled, "Stop crying or I'll kill you!" LeGrand's wife and two small children were forced from their home.

"Where is your husband?" a *Milice* screamed at her.

"He is on police business outside the village," she cried.

"You lie," the thug replied. "He is with the terrorists," he spat, and slapped her in the face. The terrified children screamed and he threatened to kill them if they didn't shut up. LeGrand's two assistant police officers and three members of the Maquis de Vercors and their families were singled out. It was obvious that someone in the village was a collaborator and had turned them in. After the men were taken out of sight, lined up against a wall, and shot execution-style, their distraught wives and children were driven into the *Champ de Foire*. Many of the others caught up in the sweep had only recently returned from the celebration at Les Berthonnets farm and were still bleary eyed from getting home so late.

In an attempt to keep the terrified villagers subdued a French-speaking SS storm trooper shouted, "There are concealed weapons and stocks of ammunition that have been hidden by terrorists. A house-to-house search will be conducted. While this is going on, you will be assembled in barns and garages to facilitate operations. When the search is completed, you will be allowed to return to your homes." The villagers' fear was palpable, but with a ring of heavily armed SS soldiers surrounding them there was nothing they could do.

———————

Les Berthonnets Farm, 1005, 10 October 1942—The group was enjoying the last of Madam Berthonnet's breakfast when a Resistance fighter suddenly burst into the room. "Germans!" he shouted, and ducked back out. For a fraction of a second everyone was frozen at the table—and then they exploded in a frenzy of action as shots erupted.

"What is that?" the old woman exclaimed, clutching an antique silver cross. Cain knew exactly what it was.

"Get down!" he yelled, and pushed the woman to the floor, upsetting the table and scattering plates in his haste. Commandant Maurice was slower. He had not been under fire before and was caught by a deluge of German bullets that tore through the windows and the door. Taking a bullet in the face, Maurice collapsed amidst blood and breakfast wreckage, dead before he hit the floor. The other three Frenchmen miraculously escaped injury. Commandant Phillippe, the combat experienced veteran, joined Cain. "Come on!" Cain shouted to him. "We've got to get out of here." Panicking, the terrified woman jumped to her feet and started to run. Several bullets ripped into her and she crumpled to the floor. Cain edged over to her but there was nothing he could do. He and the surviving men crawled to the back of the house, climbed out a window, and sprinted into the woods. They hurled themselves through the forest undergrowth, trying to put as much distance as possible between them and the Germans.

The attack came so suddenly that German bullets tore into the camp before any kind of defense could be organized. The untrained Maquis had no idea what they should do, and they panicked. Some ran, while others grabbed weapons and tried to hold off the onslaught. Automatic weapons raked the camp. Men were killed and wounded but they slowed the German assault long enough to enable Cain and his compatriots to reach the safety of the woods.

"Come on," he urged the three shocked Maquis commanders. "We've got to get further away before they surround us." LeGrand and Cain had to drag them deeper into the forest. As the adrenaline wore off, exhaustion set in, and they stopped to rest. "LeGrand, take them to the weapons cache," Cain ordered. "I'm going back to help any others that might have gotten away."

Startled by the sudden gunfire, Henry and Josephine quickly recovered and grabbed their weapons. Josephine started to pack up the Jed Set. The heavy volume of fire told Henry they'd better get the hell out of there.

"Leave it," he shouted, "there's no time!" She pulled her pistol and emptied the magazine into the transmitter and receiver.

"At least the Germans won't get them," she uttered. Henry grabbed her by the arm and pulled her away. "Wait," she demanded, and scooped up the one-time pad and the radio crystals before fleeing with him out the back of the barn. They sprinted across a plowed field and into the trees. Judging from the gunfire and shouting, it was evident that they needed to get out of the area as quickly as possible. Their only chance was to head for the weapons cache and wait for any others that might escape.

———•———

2d Company, 1st Battalion, SS *Polizei* Regiment 19, Les Berthonnets Farm, 1005, 10 October 1942—Unger's men continued to blast away at the farmhouse and the barn as they advanced across the open ground. Several bodies lay in the grass around the building, but no fire seemed to be coming from the house itself. Two Germans had been hit, proving there had been some resistance but not enough to slow the veterans down. An SS trooper reached the outside of the house and tossed a stick grenade through a window. It detonated with a deafening explosion, black smoke and flame spurting out of the shattered gap. The soldier pointed his weapon through the opening and sprayed the inside with automatic weapons fire. He stepped back, reloaded, and climbed into the room. A woman and two men lay on the floor so severely mutilated that it was difficult to tell what had killed them. Later the soldier took credit, bragging to his buddies that he was a "mean killing machine."

———•———

SS-*Sturmbannführer* Helmet Krause, 1st Battalion, SS *Polizei* Regiment 19, Oradour-sur-Glane, 1400, 10 October 1942—By early afternoon the population of the village, 180 men and 300 women and children, were assembled in the *Champ de Foire*. It was market day, so the village was crowded. With the houses emptied, the *Milice* began to systematically pillage the village of anything of value and loaded the loot onto trucks.

Krause ordered the distraught women and children marched off to the 15th-century Catholic church under the rifles of an SS detail. The procession of mothers clutching babies, grandmothers, and children shuffled down the hill to the tall church with its red Romanesque tiles and turreted spires. A woman broke away from the crowd, and before the guards could stop her, she fell at the officer's feet and begged for mercy. Krause pulled out his Luger and, without a trace of emotion, shot her in the head.

The men were divided into groups of 30 and herded into barns on the edge of town and locked in. At an officer's signal, the SS soldiers started shooting into the densely packed buildings. Screams and cries for help rent the air as bullets tore through the wooden sides. Then the shooting stopped and all was eerily silent. The Germans hauled in straw and hay, piled it on top of the bodies—some still grasping onto the last threads of life—and set the stacks on fire.

With the men finished off, Krause turned his attention to the women and children crowded in the church. A detail of soldiers lugged a heavy box into the nave and lit a fuse before rushing back outside. Thick black smoke poured out. Women and children coughed and screamed, frantically hammering on the door to get out. But their cries fell on deaf ears. "Finish them," Krause ordered. Detonation after detonation followed, as soldiers threw grenades through the windows, then raked the sacred space with machine-gun fire. To ensure total destruction, Krause ordered the village burned. By late afternoon smoke and flames reached high into the sky.

———+———

Les Berthonnets Farm, 1015, 10 October 1942—Cain crept through the knee-high undergrowth to the edge of the wood line, close enough to see the Germans searching the farm buildings. The mid-morning sun cast shadows that helped him blend in with the vegetation. He carefully parted the grass and peered out. It was a gruesome sight. The SS had already gathered the bodies of the French dead and piled them in front of the farmhouse. Soldiers were tearing boards off the sides of the house and throwing the wood on the corpses. A German officer stood off to one side directing his men. "I'd love to shoot that bastard," Cain mumbled, but with only his .45-caliber pistol and commando knife, the Kraut would live to see another day. Suddenly there was a shout as two Germans scurried across the yard carrying the team's transmitter. *Shit, now the fat's in the fire*, he thought. *They've got proof we're here.*

The discovery prompted a frenzy of activity as an SS officer began shouting orders and gesturing toward the woods. German soldiers began to spread out and start into the thicket. *Time to get the hell out of here*, Cain thought as he slowly backed away from his hiding place. But the sudden snap of twigs stopped him in his tracks. The Marine considered his options—he didn't have many. He drew the commando knife from the scabbard on his belt. If he used the pistol, the Germans would be on him in a minute. Adrenaline surged through his system and his heartrate jumped. The steps came closer and he carefully drew his legs up to spring. A German soldier appeared in front of him. *Now!* his brain screamed. Cain leaped to his feet and thrust the double-edged dagger into the unsuspecting soldier's throat. The dying man collapsed, dropping

100

his rifle and grabbing for the stiletto imbedded in his throat. Cain fell with him, landing heavily on the German's chest but keeping pressure on the blade. The dying man heaved and bucked, his legs beating a tattoo on the ground in his death throes. Cain bore down, using all his strength to slice through the enemy's neck and sever his jugular vein. Blood spurted over his hands and face. The soldier died soundlessly.

Cain stared at the German's slashed throat and almost gagged, his face inches away from the shredded flesh. The nauseating stench of fresh blood and its stickiness on his hands and face made him sick. His hand-to-hand instructors had never mentioned the gruesome reality of slitting a man's throat. *Snap out of it,* he told himself, *or you'll be dead meat too.* He rolled off the body and lay still, listening. As the sound of men picking their way through the underbrush came closer, he fought his rising panic. *Got to keep ahead of 'em.* A game trail beckoned. It was worn smooth and he was able to crawl rapidly and noiselessly several meters before he heard shouting. *Damn, they've found the body!* He could not possibly outrun them. His only chance was to hide and wait for nightfall. He crawled into a thick briar patch next to the game trail with his .45 in hand and hoped the Germans didn't have trained search dogs.

After what felt like hours, a patrol halted directly in front of Cain's hiding place. They stood there several minutes, talking and smoking cigarettes, only a few feet from Cain. *This is it,* he reasoned, as a strange sense of calm stilled his trembling body. *The Krauts have got me now.* He waited, holding his breath, and then the soldiers moved on. At one point several muffled shots rang out and he prayed that the Germans hadn't found LeGrand and the others. By early evening the shooting had stopped and the patrols seemed to have withdrawn. *The Germans don't want to be in the woods after dark,* he speculated. He decided to move and try to join the others—if they were still there. As silently as he could, he backed out of the thicket and crawled through the undergrowth, taking advantage of the evening shadows. An hour later he reached the spot where he had left his three confederates.

"LeGrand," he whispered from the concealment of a pine tree. No response, only the gentle rustle of trees. "LeGrand," he hissed louder. This time, the brush shuddered and Cain prepared to shoot or scoot.

"Hush," the police chief murmured, "you'll alert the whole neighborhood."

17

Grotte de la Draye Blanche, 3 kilometers east of Oradour-sur-Glane, 1700, 10 October 1942—Henry and Josephine hid in the underbrush near the concealed entrance to the cave, waiting for any members of the Resistance who may have escaped the massacre at Les Berthonnets farm. The cave had been designated a rally point in case of emergency. Not one fighter had shown up, and they were overwhelmed by the feeling that no one had survived the attack.

"Do you think Cain got away?" Josephine asked worriedly.

"I don't honestly know," Henry answered. "It's hard to imagine anyone getting out of the house with all that shooting." The last they had seen him was at breakfast in the farmhouse, and there had been no chance to look for him after the attack started.

The loss of the transmitter also weighed heavily on their minds. Without it, there would be no contact with London, no arms shipments, no money for the Resistance, no support of any kind—their mission would be a failure. The two were quiet for a time, lost in thought and despair. They were alone in enemy-occupied France with no way of telling who could be trusted, little knowledge of the area, no clothes other than the uniforms they had on, little ammunition, and no food. Josephine was also suffering physically. Her face and arms bore several deep scratches, and she was bruised from falling during their frantic escape through the forest. Henry was also battered and bruised. Their mud-caked uniforms were soaked with sweat and they stank to high heaven. They were a mess and hardly in any condition to wander around the forest.

With darkness fast approaching, they decided it would be better to spend the night in the cave and leave early in the morning. Even if the Germans knew about its location, it was doubtful they would attempt anything so late in the day. Just as the two started to move back into the cave, they were startled by a rustling in the underbrush. They crouched down, their carbines pointed in the direction of the movement. A shadowy figure stepped from behind the boughs of a large pine. In the darkening shadows Henry couldn't make out who it was, and his finger tightened on the trigger. Josephine reached out and squeezed his arm. "It's that crazy Marine," she whispered with relief. "I'd know his profile anywhere."

"Pierre," Henry called out, using Cain's code name. "It's us."

"Who the hell is us?" the figure called back and then broke out in a nervous laugh. "From now on that'll be our password," he joked, embracing his two teammates. Henry, Josephine, and the three exhausted Resistance leaders followed Cain into the cave entrance and collapsed.

"My God," LeGrand exclaimed, "I never thought we'd make it."

SS-*Sturmbannführer* Helmut Krause, 1st Battalion, SS *Polizei* Regiment 19, Les Berthonnets Farm, 1235, 10 October 1942— Krause was not pleased that the British agents were able to escape and took his anger out on Unger by threatening to "volunteer" him for duty on the Eastern Front. The captain was able to partially redeem himself when his men dragged an unconscious prisoner from the back of a truck and threw him on the ground in front of the commander. The prisoner had been severely beaten. His face was bloody, eyes swollen shut, and his ruined mouth gaped open, showing that most of his teeth had been knocked out.

"What information have you been able to get from him?" Krause snarled, nudging the limp body with his boot.

"So far he has refused to talk," Unger replied contritely, "but we're going to keep working on him until he does." Colonel Maude stepped forward and offered to continue the interrogation.

"Make him talk," was all Krause said as he stalked off.

The prisoner was stripped and hung from one of the barn's crossbeams, his arms bearing the full weight of his body. His feet didn't touch the ground. One of the soldiers grabbed him around the waist and pulled with all his might, forcing his shoulders out of joint. The battered man regained consciousness and screamed. Colonel Maude stepped in front of him holding a skinning knife.

Grotte de la Draye Blanche, 3 kilometers east of Oradour-sur-Glane, 0615, 11 October 1942—The fugitives spent a cold, sleepless night in the damp grotto. Temperatures had dropped into the low forties but they dared not build a fire, fearing that it might attract a German patrol. Without it, and with only the clothing on their back, all they could do was huddle together in the dark and try to stay warm. The three Frenchmen had an especially bad time of it. They had seen friends and neighbors killed by the Germans at the farm and now they were on the run, unable to seek comfort from hearth and home. What had been just a dangerous game had suddenly turned deadly.

Phillippe was deeply affected, his 16-year-old nephew among the missing. The boy had been on sentry duty directly in the path of the German assault. "It's my fault," he lamented, fearing the worst.

"I encouraged him to join the Resistance." He brooded throughout the night, vowing that he would seek revenge.

Henry set up a guard watch at the mouth of the cave. Everyone drew a straw to establish the rotation—short straw chose first. Josephine picked the first watch, which meant she could sleep most of the night—if "it wasn't so bloody cold," she lamented.

Cain ended up with the last two-hour time slot. Time dragged and he forced himself to stay awake. *Better to be tired than dead*, he mused, staring out into the pitch-black forest. The only sound was the constant drip, drip of water falling from the stalactites and the rustle of the breeze through the treetops. Finally, sunlight filtered into the cave mouth and he whispered, "Rise and shine," although it wasn't necessary; everyone was awake. Daylight seemed to have reinvigorated Phillippe to some extent, and he volunteered to switch places with Cain.

"Let's see what's in the containers," Henry said. The first container was difficult to open because the latches had jammed when it crashed into the ground.

Cain beat the latches into submission with a rock and pried open the container. "Great, just what we need," he exclaimed, examining the contents. "Socks, army boots, and uniforms. At least we'll be well dressed!"

Several other containers were more to their liking: Sten guns, ammunition, even explosives and detonators that had been wrapped in special packaging to protect them. Finally, one of the last yielded the Golden Fleece—a complete undamaged transmitter and power pack. Josephine almost broke into tears. She tested it and pronounced the set workable.

"We're in business," she said, and repacked the 32-pound Jed Set in its compartmented canvas knapsack. The final container yielded several cases of British Army 24-hour rations. "My Lord, I've gone to heaven," Josephine exclaimed, breaking the seal on one of the cardboard boxes and taking out a block of "chocolate, vitamin fortified."

Henry passed a box to each one. "I suggest you eat before the food gets cold," he said lightheartedly.

The French looked skeptically at the green tins. "What is this?" LeGrand asked.

"That's British mystery meat," Cain interjected. "It's been rejected by most civilized nations."

Josephine sniffed haughtily. "One doesn't have to eat it, one can go hungry." Her snappy retort made everyone smile, a good sign that morale was on an upswing after the previous day's disaster.

2d Company, 1st Battalion, SS *Polizei* Regiment 19, Grotte de la Draye Blanche, 0720, 11 October 1942—The 2d Company scouts easily picked up the fresh ruts that the heavily loaded wagons had made in the soft earth. The lead scout motioned for the *Unterscharführer* (sergeant) to come forward. Pointing to the furrows and a pile of horse shit that lay mounded on the side of the trail, he pushed a stick into the crusted heap and pulled it out, noting that underneath the crust it was still soft. "No more than a day old," the *Oberschütze* (private first class) gauged confidently.

The sergeant nodded and grinned roguishly. "You certainly know your shit," he whispered.

The discovery was passed back to *Hauptsturmführer* Unger, who glanced at the rough hand-drawn map in his hand and decided it was accurate. The blood-flecked diagram had been drawn by the captured terrorist after Colonel Maude "spoke to him." *A shame he didn't survive the questioning*, Unger thought. *I would have liked to have gotten more information from him.* The bloodied remains of the man had been left hanging in the barn when it was set on fire, along with the rest of the farm buildings. Unger signaled the sergeant to follow the trail that branched off toward the scarp with the exposed limestone face.

—•—

Grotte de la Draye Blanche, 0915, 11 October 1942—Phillippe sat in the shadow of the narrow fissure lost in thought, still beating himself up over the loss of his nephew. He had volunteered to take the American's place so he could be alone. *How could I have been so stupid to allow the boy to join the Resistance?* he wondered. But the youngster had pestered and pestered until he'd finally given in. *He was so naïve*, he realized, *so filled with illusions of glory and Vive la France. It was just a game to him. How will I tell his parents?* At that moment a bird took flight with a cry of alarm, startling him out of his reverie. He shrank back in the shadow of the rock. A movement next to the trunk of a larch tree caught his eye. *What is that?* he wondered, staring at a patch of green and brown foliage that seemed out of place, then quickly realized that what he was seeing was a German soldier wearing a camouflage smock. Another camouflaged figure joined the first beneath the tree ... and then more appeared, moving stealthily toward the cave opening.

No time to warn the others, Phillippe thought as he brought the Sten gun up from his lap and pulled the bolt to the rear, cocking it. The *click* of the bolt locking to the rear sounded incredibly loud, but the Germans were too far away to hear it. "Come on you *bâtards*, just a little closer," he murmured. The 9mm submachine gun was a short-range weapon—50 meters or so—and the veteran wanted to get as many of them as he could with the first burst. A rage filled him as the hated SS crept nearer. He was in a good firing position—concealed by brush, a slight downward trajectory, and a thick log gave him protection. A German stepped into the open area within range and looked right at him. Alarm registered on the swine's face. He opened his mouth to shout a warning.

Adrenaline surged through Phillippe's bloodstream. "*Vive la France!*" he shouted and pulled the trigger on the Sten. Three 9mm slugs tore into the German's chest. Mortally wounded, the soldier dropped his rifle, stood stock still for a long moment, and then collapsed like a limp doll. Phillippe swung the barrel of the submachine gun and held the trigger down. Two more Germans fell, having paid the price for bunching up. The Sten's bolt locked to the rear as the last round fired. Phillippe ducked behind the log, frantically trying to insert another 32-round magazine into the slot on the side of the weapon. He was all thumbs as a barrage of 7.9mm rounds snapped over his head and ricocheted off the limestone. A rock splinter sliced his forehead. Blood streamed into his eyes, blinding him. The closest soldier took advantage of the firing lull and left cover to throw a Model 24 *Stielhandgranate*. He grasped the pull cord, tugged it, and drew his arm back to throw the live grenade.

Automatic fire exploded from the cave entrance. Half-a-dozen 9mm bullets ripped into the grenadier's body and he collapsed. The grenade dropped from his lifeless hand and landed at his feet. Five seconds later the burning fuse reached the 6-ounce explosive charge in the sheet metal can and the grenade detonated. The force of the explosive ripped the man's body to shreds, propelled shrapnel for several yards in every direction, and wounded two others. Cain sprayed the rest of the magazine toward the Germans while Henry pulled the wounded Frenchman away from the cave entrance. Josephine wiped the blood off Phillippe's head, saw that it was merely superficial, and wrapped a battle dressing around it. LeGrand hovered over his friend. "*Ça va*—I'm OK," Phillippe said, adding, "my head is like steel." He slapped a full magazine into his Sten gun.

The explosion had momentarily halted the German advance as they tried to find the source of the fire. One of them spotted movement in the cave opening and started shooting. The others joined in with a barrage of small arms fire, causing Cain to crawl away from the opening. Bullets splattered the rock. Fragments flew everywhere.

"There's one hell'va lot of Krauts out there," he shouted over the gunfire. "We'll never be able to hold them off."

"We need time to get away," Henry said, stating the obvious.

Before they could say anything more, Phillippe gathered several hand grenades and a dozen fully loaded Sten magazines. "*Ils ne passeront pas*"—they shall not pass—he growled defiantly and took up a covered firing position close to the entranceway. Henry tried to talk him out of it but Phillippe waved him away. His mind was made up; he would make the Germans pay for his nephew.

There was nothing more to be done; someone had to slow the Germans down or they would not get away. Cain and Henry grabbed the transmitter cases, while Josephine and Alphonse filled their packs with what they considered necessary to fight their way out and survive—weapons, ammunition, maps, a medical kit, and some food. When they were ready, each of them shook Phillippe's hand. "Go now, before I lose my nerve," he insisted.

German fire picked up, signaling a renewed assault. Phillippe fired a burst to make them think twice before rushing the entrance. With a final "*Bonne chance*," Hervieux led them along the darkened passageway to an opening at the back of the cave.

Cain took one last look to see Phillippe crouched against a wall firing the Sten gun and shouting insults at the Germans. "They shall not pass," he muttered.

2d Company, 1st Battalion, SS *Polizei* **Regiment 19, Grotte de la Draye Blanche, 1015, 11 October 1942**—SS-*Hauptsturmführer* Unger shined his light on the bloodied corpse in the dirt. The terrorist had cost him five men and an hour of deadly hide-and-seek in the cavern. His men had finally cornered him in a dead-end shaft just off the main channel. Even then the *Schweinehund* had gone down fighting. He'd blown himself up with a hand grenade and took one of his men with him. A shout caught his attention.

"*Herr Hauptsturmführer*, we have found where the terrorists escaped."

Unger followed the lights and found an *Untersturmführer* (second lieutenant) pointing to the opening in the back of the cavern where the brush had been cleared away. Several sets of fresh footprints confirmed that the terrorists had gone that way. The officer directed his attention to prints in the soft mud. "Tommies," he uttered, squatting down and using his finger to point out the distinctive two rows of hobnails and traces of the heel and toe irons of a British Army boot.

"How many?" Unger asked eagerly.

"I count three people wearing military boots and two with civilian shoes, sir," the officer replied. "And sir," he added, "I believe one of them is a woman." Unger looked skeptical. "The military boot print is too small for a man, unless the Tommies are recruiting midgets." The comment brought a smile to Unger's face, not because it was funny but because it was spot on with what the captured terrorist had disclosed. He had told the interrogator that three agents had parachuted into a drop zone close to Les Berthonnets farm and one of them was a woman radio operator.

"We've got them on the run," Unger declared loudly. "Notify the battalion commander."

———◆———

SS-*Sturmbannführer* Helmut Krause, 1st Battalion, SS *Polizei* Regiment 19, Grotte de la Draye Blanche, 1100, 11 October 1942—"Well done, Unger," Krause said, patting the beaming officer on the back. The battalion commander had shown up within 15 minutes of being notified of the discovery. He was accompanied by Arnaud, a squad of his *Milice*, and several bodyguards. "I have notified the regimental commander of *our success*," he said, glossing over the fact that five soldiers had died achieving the "victory" over one poorly armed terrorist. Unger picked up the commander's emphasis on "our success" and bridled at his taking credit for the achievement. "Tell me about the ones that got away," he said. *There it is,* Unger thought, *patting me on the back for the kill and kicking me in the ass for the escape of the others.*

Unger described the footprints he'd found and the trail that led from the grotto.

"Where are the terrorists?" Krause asked pointedly.

"I sent my 1st platoon to track them," Unger replied, failing to catch the irritation in the commander's voice.

"And why did you decide to stay here?" the commander probed.

Unger was at a loss for words. He couldn't admit that the firefight in the grotto had unnerved him. Combat was not his forte; police work was more his specialty. His only previous assignment had been rounding up Jews for transport to the concentration camps.

"Well, Unger?"

"Sir, I thought it would be best to personally report to you with all the information."

Krause did not pursue the question, knowing exactly what kind of officer Unger was ... and it wasn't one who led men in action. He leveled a mocking glare at the younger officer that spoke volumes—"*I don't believe you*"—but elected to remain silent. Instead, he told Unger that he was to take the rest of his company and track down the terrorists. "I have also requested a spotter aircraft to help you locate them. It should be here within a couple of hours, which will give you plenty of time to catch up with your men, if you hurry."

Unger felt trapped. The spotter aircraft would be able to keep tabs on him. "*Ja, Herr Obersturmbannführer,* I understand perfectly."

Capitaine Bob came rushing up excitedly. "Major, one of my men used to have a farm near here and knows this area very well."

"So what," Krause snapped.

"He said there is a way around the grotto that will allow us to intercept the terrorists," he replied. Krause came alive; here was an opportunity to get rid of the terrorists once and for all … and it would look good on his record. "I can take my best men and cut them off," the *Milice* chief offered.

"Go," Krause said impatiently, "and make sure you take the parachutists alive."

Krause turned to the captured weapons and equipment that was laid out in an open area below the grotto. He picked up a Sten submachine gun and examined it.

"This is a piece of shit," he remarked to Unger. "It's all stamped metal, hardly any machined parts, not like our weapons."

"Yes sir," Unger replied, "but it was good enough to kill five of my men!"

Ignoring the insubordinate remark, Krause went on examining the captured material. He was particularly interested in the metal containers, one of which was still packed with supplies. "I believe our airborne forces would be interested in this," he said, picking up one of the 24-hour ration packs. He slit open the cardboard with his finger and fished around in the contents until he found what he was looking for. "*Schokolade,*" he said, holding up a small package. "The British can't manufacture a good submachine gun but they can make excellent chocolate."

Unger disagreed but chose not to say anything; he was in enough trouble. Anyway, he was partial to Swiss chocolate but it was so damn hard to get, particularly where he was going.

District *Milice* Chief, Forest Path, 1230, 11 October 1942—The rutted switchback trail led the *Milice* up the steep slope of the plateau. *Capitaine* Bob set a blistering pace, and within an hour and a half the *Milice* had circled completely around the grotto and intersected a well-defined trail. The local man said it led to a remote farm high up on the plateau. "I'm sure that's where they're headed," he'd said confidently. "It's one of the few places that offer shelter." They checked the trail for footprints but there were no signs of recent use in the moist soil.

"We beat them," *Capitaine* Bob declared. "We'll set up an ambush here." He positioned his men in the dense undergrowth about 15 feet off the side of the trail and issued strict instructions to wait until he gave the signal to open fire. "I want the parachutists alive," he emphasized.

———◆———

Maquis du Vercors, Forest Trail, On the Run, 1100, 11 October 1942—Henry took the lead and set a fast pace, eager to put as much distance as possible between themselves and the Germans. Phillippe could only hold them off for so long before they killed him and started after them. The trail took them upward amid stands of fir, birch, popular, and dense patches of gorse. Huge boulders often blocked the path, forcing them to detour, which cost time and energy. The three Jeds were in good shape thanks to the physical training regimen at Milford Hall, but the two Frenchmen were soon showing the strain. The steep slope played havoc with their legs. LeGrand developed painful shin splints, forcing him to slow down.

"Go on," he urged, "I'll catch up as soon as I can."

Henry spoke for all of them. "No. We'll stay together."

The Jeds divided up his load to reduce some of the weight he was carrying but the trail steepened, increasing the pain in his legs with each step. He stoically hobbled on, but he was slowing them down.

They trudged upward through the forest along a narrow ridge. It was quiet except for their footfalls on the earthen trail and the rustling of small animals in the undergrowth. No one talked, saving their energy. Their packs grew heavier; sharp edges jabbed into back muscles; pack straps pinched shoulders, cutting off circulation; and webbing rubbed raw spots on sweaty skin. An hour into the hike they heard the distant drone of an aircraft. Within minutes it was circling overhead.

"Storch," Henry said, spotting the observation aircraft through an opening in the canopy. "Looks like Jerry is trying to find us," he announced. "It'll never spot us under the trees though," he added.

"That's right," LeGrand replied, "but the forest thins out up ahead."

"Let's hope the damn Kraut gets tired of boring holes in the sky before then," Cain added.

2d Company, 1st Battalion, SS *Polizei* Regiment 19, 1130 11 October 1942—Unger was infuriated and he showed it by setting a fast pace that left men strung out on the trail. At the rate he was going, he would be lucky to have anyone left when he caught up with the 1st Platoon. His men were weighed down with 80 to 100 pounds of combat gear—helmet, ammunition, and weapons, including a heavy machine gun section. The steep trail added to their misery and it was oppressively hot. Air could not circulate through the dense forest. Thirty minutes into the speed march, the men were sweating like pigs. Many had already emptied their canteens, and there were very few wells or springs on the plateau where they could fill them. The plateau's porous limestone allowed the rain to pass through the rock and drain into underground streams that flowed downhill toward the lowlands.

Unger's fury was fueled by the way the battalion commander had treated him. *That Hurensohn had all but accused me of being a coward*, he fumed. *I'll show him!* In his anger, Unger failed to see that his men felt the same way about him as he did about the battalion commander. He had never won any popularity contests; in fact, many of the men swore that in the next firefight their esteemed company commander would be the victim of a bullet in the back. An NCO heard the traitorous grousing but did not do anything to stop it; he agreed with them. Maintaining the morale of the 2d Company was not Unger's strong suit. He was a brutal commander who instilled fear in his subordinates, and they reacted by being cruel and ruthless to the French people, as if they needed any incentive. Most of them were former concentration camp guards, for whom wanton brutality was a way of life.

Two hours into the march a scout reported that the 1st Platoon was only a half-mile up the trail and was waiting for the exhausted company to catch up. Over a third of the unit was strung out along the trail. A veteran NCO risked Unger's wrath by reminding him that the plateau was terrorist country, and, with the company spread out, they were risking an ambush. Unger brushed him off. This was a chance to catch the terrorists and finish them once and for all.

18

Maquis du Vercors, Forest Trail, On the Run, 1125, 11 October 1942—Henry held up his hand and stopped. Something didn't seem right; the forest was too quiet. Suddenly a pair of grouse exploded out of the undergrowth. They instinctively reacted, bringing their weapons up and crouching down, ready to shoot. LeGrand stepped in front of them and shouted, "*Je suis Français*, don't shoot."

A voice shouted back from the side of the trail, "*Deposez les armes.*"

"Do as he says and put down your weapons," LeGrand said, recognizing the voice. "He's a friend." The Jeds lowered their Stens. A figure rose out of the undergrowth and cautiously made his way toward them. The man carried an old hunting rifle loosely pointed in their direction.

"François," he called out contritely, using LeGrand's first name. "I'm sorry. I thought they were *Boche* and were using you as a hostage." He made a motion with his hand and dozens of men suddenly appeared. "Les Maquis du Vercors," he announced.

The newcomer embraced LeGrand happily. "I thought you were dead," he said. "I was told everyone in the village had been killed."

"What do you mean?" LeGrand demanded with a puzzled expression on his face.

"Then you don't know?" the man replied sadly.

The policeman shook his head. "No, I've been in a cave hiding from the Germans."

The man looked stricken. "Oh François," he muttered sadly, "the SS *Polizei* killed almost everyone in the village. There were only a few survivors."

The blood drained from LeGrand's face. "Everyone?" he repeated, unwilling to believe such a heartless act.

"I'm afraid so," the man replied miserably, reaching out and grasping LeGrand's shoulder. "The villagers were rounded up and murdered, except for a few who managed to escape."

"My wife, my children!" the chief uttered.

His friend merely nodded. "I'm so sorry, François."

LeGrand stumbled to the side of the trail and slumped to the ground, holding his face in his hands. His shoulders shook with emotion.

"My God," Henry muttered, unable to understand how anyone could be so inhuman. "They're butchers." He turned to the others and whispered, "Let's leave him alone in his grief."

"Those bastards," Josephine swore. "I hope they rot in hell!"

"We intend to send the Germans and *Milice* on that journey," François's friend declared in heavily accented English. "Every man in the Maquis du Vercors has sworn vengeance."

Cain simply nodded, feeling better knowing that the German he killed at the farm was one of them. *The son-of-a-bitch was part of that gang of butchers*, he declared to himself.

The newcomer introduced himself. "I am known as 'Jacques'," he said, shaking hands with each of the Jeds. "I am François's deputy." Within minutes they were surrounded by dozens of Maquisards, a repeat of the previous night's welcome. Henry didn't like it one bit and reminded Jacques that the Germans might be on their trail. "Not to worry, my friend," he replied confidently. "One of my men

is scouting your back trail. If he sees anything, he'll let us know."
He had barely uttered the words when a wild-eyed young man
sprinted up the trail.

"*Les Boche,*" he said, trying to catch his breath. "They're coming
this way!" he gasped.

The boy's report swept through the ranks of the Maquis. Suddenly
everyone was talking at once. "Quiet," Jacques demanded, "the *Boche*
will hear you." He turned to the youngster who was bent over with
his hands on his knees trying to recover. "How many Germans are
there?" he asked.

The boy straightened up. "I counted over a hundred and they're
about a mile behind me."

"This is what we've been waiting for," Jacques said excitedly.
"They'll be at our mercy—no heavy weapons and on our ground—
ripe for an ambush."

LeGrand pushed his way into the circle. His face registered
anguish but his eyes burned with vengeance. "*Ils ne passeront pas!*"
he said passionately and raised his rifle in the air.

"*Ils ne passeront pas!*" the men repeated enthusiastically. Everything
rested on his shoulders. The Maquis were full of enthusiasm but
were lightly armed and lacked the discipline necessary to stand up
against the well-trained Germans.

LeGrand took charge and issued orders to set up an "L"-shaped
ambush. He picked a straight section of the trail that ran for over
a hundred yards through undergrowth. The site provided excellent
concealment, yet good fields of fire. The Jeds were impressed. It was
obvious that the Maquisards knew what they were doing. They found
out that many of the men were former soldiers and had trained their
compatriots on ambush techniques. The instruction had paid off.
Within minutes they were spread out in the undergrowth along one
side of the trail. They had a French FM 1924/29 light machine gun
which LeGrand placed at the far end of the ambush at a 90-degree

angle so it could fire along the long axis of the trail. Limiting stakes had been driven into the ground to keep the gun from firing too far to the left and hitting his own men.

LeGrand positioned himself with the automatic weapon. When the Germans were in the killing zone, he would tell the gunner to shoot—the signal to trigger the ambush. He stressed to everyone not to open fire until they heard the machine gun. "I will shoot any man who fires before the signal," he emphasized sternly. "Wait until the *Boche* are all in the killing zone. Our lives will depend on killing as many of them as fast as we can. We don't have enough ammunition for a long fight."

Jacques positioned himself on the far end of the line, so he could see the enemy enter the kill zone. LeGrand asked the Jeds if they would participate. "We would be honored," Henry responded, and joined the Maquis chief close to the machine gun. Josephine was sent with a four-man security detachment to the Maquis base camp further up the plateau, in a stand of hardwood that made it difficult to see, even from the air. Josephine pitched a fit. She didn't want to miss all the fun. After listening to her complain for a moment, Henry impatiently explained that he outranked her and she was to do as he ordered. "I don't have a lot of time to explain," he said forcefully. "You're an essential element in our success or failure. Everything depends on your communication skills, not on how many rounds you can put down range. End of discussion, now get going!"

<hr />

Maquis du Vercors, Forest Trail, Ambush Position, 1235, 11 October 1942—Jacques pressed his face into the rich forest loam, heavy with the odor of decaying vegetation. He lay absolutely still, hardly daring to breathe as the Germans tramped by, barely 5 feet from his hiding place. He was so damned scared that his heart throbbed wildly. In his hyperactive mind he imagined that the *Boche* could feel the vibrations. Nervous sweat ran down his face in rivulets, stinging his eyes and soaking his heavy wool shirt. The incessant whine of mosquitoes reminded him that the pests were sucking his blood and there was nothing he could do to stop them. A slap was out of the question; any movement might attract the attention of the Germans. To top it off, he needed to pee and he had an insane urge to sneeze. He concentrated on the sneeze first—noise would get him killed; a urine stain would only get him teased. With a mighty effort, he stifled both impulses. The Germans trudged by him completely unaware they were walking into an ambush.

The lead elements of the German platoon approached the Jeds' concealed position. From their vantage point, they watched the enemy soldiers walk openly on the trail with complete disregard for basic security precautions—weapons slung, helmets off, tunics unbuttoned—skylarking. *These guys aren't just careless,* Cain thought, *they're dumb shits. They're going to pay for it, as long as the Maquis don't screw up the ambush.* He risked a glance at Henry hunkered down beside him. The colonel's face positively radiated with energy. *My God,* he thought, *the man loves this shit! He's like a racehorse at the starting line, can't wait for the gate to open.* Henry stared back at Cain with his good eye and winked.

The hundred or so Maquis du Vercors, many of them teenage boys in their first combat, waited nervously for the signal to open fire. With the *Boche* only feet from their rifle barrels, they suddenly realized the seriousness of what they had gotten themselves into. It was one thing to practice target shooting but an entirely different matter to actually kill another human being. Still, not one of the Maquis opted out. They pointed their hodgepodge of ancient shotguns and single-shot rifles and waited for the signal to start the killing.

2d Company, 1st Battalion, SS *Polizei* Regiment 19, 1235, 11 October 1942—SS-*Untersturmführer* Hans Schmidt was worried. The company commander was pushing him to go faster. Because of the press for speed, his platoon was forced to stay on the trail. There was no flank security. "Don't worry about it," Unger told him angrily. "Speed is essential. The terrorists are trying to escape and I want to catch them before they get away. Now push it out and stop bitching!"

The plateau is dangerous, Schmidt wanted to scream. There were rumors that armed terrorists were gathering in large numbers. Several patrols had already been ambushed and had taken casualties. *I shouldn't be here, particularly under a shithead like Unger*, he thought. *The man is incompetent.*

Schmidt's lead scout stopped briefly in the middle of a long open stretch of trail. It just didn't look right, but before he could check it out, his *Obergefreiter* (squad leader) told him to get the lead out of his ass and keep moving. The scout shrugged his shoulders as if to say, "Screw it" and stepped out. No one else in the column noticed anything unusual, and within a few minutes the stretch of trail was filled with men from the 1st Platoon. Most of the men in Schmidt's 25-man platoon were not combat infantrymen. They were a mixture of foreigners and ethnic Germans drafted under threat of punishment. For the most part they were an unruly and undisciplined lot who were difficult to control, even if the newly assigned officer wanted to. He was more interested in shacking up with his French mistress in Grenoble than tromping around the boonies with a bunch of losers. In fact, as he tilted his canteen up to suck the last few drops of water, the thought struck him that less than 24 hours ago he was enjoying a drink in the officers' club.

Maquis du Vercors, 1238—LeGrand watched an enemy soldier stop in the middle of the trail about 50 yards away. He wore a camouflage smock gathered at the waist by a leather belt that held an ammunition pouch and two stick grenades. A Schmeisser submachine gun hung by a strap from his shoulder. The German scanned the underbrush. *What does he see?* the Maquis chief wondered anxiously. Just as he was about to give the signal to the machine gunner to open fire, he risked a quick glance at Henry. The veteran soldier shook his head—not yet. The German hesitated for a long moment and then started walking forward again. LeGrand breathed a sigh of relief. But as the minutes ticked by, he worried that one of his men might say to hell with the order and shoot the first German that appeared in his sights, spoiling the ambush and putting them all in deadly peril. *Come on, you bastards, hurry up,* he mouthed silently. The tension increased. The lead German was so close Cain could clearly see the "whites of his eyes." Suddenly he remembered the Revolutionary War slogan, "Don't fire until you see the whites of their eyes." *Damn,* he breathed anxiously, *they're close enough—shoot the bastards!*

LeGrand lay next to the machine gunner, the gun fully charged, bolt to the rear, and the 25-round curved box magazine fully seated on top of the receiver. The gunner nervously grasped the pistol grip of his weapon, finger on the trigger, waiting for the chief's signal. With the lead German only a few feet away, LeGrand quivered with excitement. "Fire!" he cried out. The gun roared. A lethal spray of nickel-jacketed 7.5mm bullets tore into the unsuspecting German, shredding flesh and muscle. He collapsed in a heap, dead before he hit the ground. LeGrand's mind registered the moment of the soldier's death—the puffs of dust from the German's uniform where the bullets struck, the grimace on the man's face from the shock and pain—and it gave him a little satisfaction. Nothing could bring back his wife and children, but killing the *Boche* might ease the pain.

For a split second there was just the loud chatter of the automatic weapon—and then a torrent of fire erupted from the underbrush. Germans collapsed in agony; others fell soundlessly. The air was filled with the buzz of bullets smacking into flesh and the shrieks of wounded and dying men. The German column dissolved in panic. Terrified survivors scrambled for protection from the terrible onslaught that cut into their ranks.

✦

2d Company, 1st Battalion, SS *Polizei* Regiment 19, 1238—Schmidt was thinking of his *Fräulein* when the Maquis opened fire and a stream of 7.5mm bullets tore through his chest. It was the last thought that he would ever have. He collapsed, his face frozen in a smile, with the empty canteen still in his lifeless hand. Bullets scythed through the 2d Company, leveling men like a field of wheat. Those who didn't die instantly thrashed about on the ground until they bled out or died from another wound. The handful of survivors in the kill zone hugged the forest floor, pinned down and struck dumb with terror. The men who had escaped the initial burst of fire were content to remain under cover, waiting for the company commander to tell them what to do. Only a few Germans used their weapons, not enough to gain fire superiority over the Resistance fighters.

No orders were issued, the company commander paralyzed with fear. Nothing in Unger's career had prepared him to deal with the calamity that had overtaken his company. He lay behind a fallen log staring into the sightless eyes of the dead SS-*Oberscharführer*—company sergeant. Only minutes before the two men had been talking … and then the deadly barrage of machine-gun fire. The sergeant cried out, and a gush of blood spewed out of his mouth into Unger's face. The officer stood immobilized in the middle of the trail, transfixed by the ghastly spectacle. His brain finally registered the deadly peril. He leaped behind a fallen log, instinctively curling into a tight ball, his legs drawn into his chest and arms covering his head. As bullets cracked overhead, he squeezed his eyes shut. The screams and piteous calls for help from the wounded barely registered in his terrified brain.

With no one to lead them, what discipline there was quickly broke down. First one soldier, and then another, edged backward away from the ambush. No one stopped them; the officers were dead, and the surviving non-commissioned officers were frozen with fear. Bullets continued to find targets. Suddenly a wounded NCO jumped to his feet, shouting, "Pull back!" He was immediately cut down, but his death spurred the survivors into action, and they fled from the ambush, every man for himself.

———◆———

Maquis du Vercors, 1240—In their excitement, the machine gunner blew through four magazines—100 rounds—before he realized he was down to the last 25 rounds. "François," the gunner yelled, "I'm almost out of ammunition!" He wasn't the only one; firing was dying down all along the line. The Resistance fighters only had a limited supply of ammunition. LeGrand knew it was time to give the withdrawal signal. Just as he was about to blow the whistle, his men started cheering.

"The *Boche* are fleeing!" they shouted. The news brought the fighters out of their ambush positions. Several of them started to chase the fleeing Germans but Jacques called them back.

"Let them go, we've done enough today," he said, looking at the bodies that lay scattered on the trail.

The Maquis were jubilant—shouting joyously, pounding each other on the back, bragging, with no thought of security. Henry brought them back to reality, instructing LeGrand to send Jacques and a small party of men to follow the retreating Germans to make sure they didn't return. He then advised the Maquis chief to begin an organized search of the killing zone to collect all the weapons, ammunition, and anything else they could use. The two Jeds joined in searching the grisly remains. An overpowering smell of fresh blood and shredded tissue hung in the air, sickening several of the younger men. It was one thing to talk about killing but it was quite another for them to observe the gory results at first hand.

"Here's an officer," one of the search party exclaimed, holding up a Walther P-38 pistol as evidence.

Henry examined the body. The officer had been shot in the chest, leaving three small holes in the man's uniform jacket. Surprisingly, there was little blood. What was remarkable about the cadaver was the smile on its face. "Must have died a happy man," he quipped heartlessly, pawing through the corpse's assault bag. A young fighter heard the remark and looked askance at the hard-edged expression on the Jedburgh's face. "The bastard tortured and murdered innocent men, women, and children," Henry declared. "He deserved to die." With that he dumped the contents of the German's bag on the ground. It contained an antique silver cross that he knew had belonged to Madam Berthonnet.

"Here's a live one," a fighter shouted, catching Henry's attention as he hauled a *Schutzstaffel* officer to his feet. The man had been hiding behind a log. The captive struggled, crying out, "*Nicht schießen!* Don't shoot!" Several fighters gathered around the terrified man, spitting, shoving, and punching the captive, threatening to kill him. LeGrand pushed his way roughly through the circle and grabbed the German, forcing him to his knees. He pointed his pistol at his head. The two Jeds stepped forward.

"Don't kill him," Henry demanded. The Maquis chief lowered his gun and turned hate-filled eyes on the officer.

"He deserves to die for what he has done," he spat. "He is a butcher!" His men agreed, shouting for his death. No one felt compassion. It was becoming a tense standoff.

Henry did not have a comeback. It was not his friends and family that had been taken hostage, then brutally tortured and killed by the *Schutzstaffel* for nothing more than being at the wrong place at the wrong time. He stepped back, deciding that he didn't want to fight his friends to save an enemy. The German began to cry and beg for mercy. He clutched at a fighter's jacket.

"Bastard," LeGrand shouted and brought the 9mm pistol up, pointing it at the side of the officer's head. He pulled the trigger. Blood sprayed from the wound, splattering the circle of men. The body collapsed and lay quivering on the ground. "Rot in hell," LeGrand cried, and spat on the corpse. The men turned away from the scene and searched for other wounded. Shots rang out as other *Schutzstaffel* were discovered. There would be no prisoners.

"Rough justice," Henry remarked to himself.

The Maquis stripped the dead and stacked the booty in a pile. The haul included 36 Mauser rifles, half a dozen Schmeisser submachine guns, hand grenades, a goodly supply of ammunition, uniforms, helmets, and useable equipment ... enough to equip an entire Maquis company. A godsend for the Resistance, which was long on volunteers but chronically short of weapons and ammunition. The Germans had levied a labor quota on Vichy France, known as the *Service du travail obligatoire* (Compulsory Work Service). Thousands of young men and women had been rounded up and shipped to Germany to work in the war industry. The quota had caused a widespread revolt among the young people, and they had flocked to the Resistance safe havens in the mountains. It was these resisters that the Jedburghs were organizing and equipping to fight the Nazis.

Cain looked at the pile of enemy uniforms and equipment. He could understand why the Maquis wanted the equipment, but there didn't seem an obvious use for the uniforms.

"Why the uniforms?" he asked.

LeGrand replied that his men had used them to infiltrate a German facility. "They might come in handy again," he related confidently.

Before leaving the ambush site a heated debate broke out on whether to bury the corpses or leave them to decompose where they had fallen. One of the fighters, a priest, argued for burial because it was the Christian thing to do, but LeGrand was vehemently opposed: "Let the bastards rot in the open after what they did to our people!" The deciding factor boiled down to the fact that they had neither the tools nor the time to dig graves. As a "final solution," the priest gave them a hasty benediction, which LeGrand was quick to point out was more than they'd given their victims when they stood them against a wall or burned them alive.

19

Milice Ambush, Forest Path, 1240, 11 October 1942—*Capitaine* Bob positioned himself so that he had a clear view of the trail and then settled down to wait. It was hotter than hell. The pine trees formed a tight screen, blocking air flow and trapping the heat on the forest floor. Rivulets of sweat made his uniform stick to his body. He felt drowsy. It would be easy to fall asleep. The only sounds to keep him awake were the chatter of birds and drone of insects. He wondered how many of his men had succumbed to the impulse to nap, but there was no way to check without making noise. He'd have to depend on them to remain alert. They were his best men but that wasn't saying much. Most of them were petty criminals that had been given a choice—prison or *Milice française*. It was not an easy choice. The *Milice* was universally hated by the ordinary French citizen for collaborating with the Germans, and mistrusted by the Germans simply because they were French. The Germans issued them secondhand weapons and barely gave them enough ammunition to protect themselves. The Maquis had begun an assassination campaign, and the *Milice* were screaming for heavier weapons to protect themselves. Two of *Capitaine* Bob's men had been killed in the past month.

"I can hear someone coming up the trail," one of the men whispered, interrupting the *Capitaine*'s thoughts. Seconds later, five armed men hiked into view; four of them carried rifles and were dressed in rugged civilian clothes, while the fifth wore a British Army uniform and had a submachine gun slung over his shoulder. *Terrorists*, the *Milice* chief thought, tightening his finger on the trigger of his rifle. As they came closer, he saw that the one with the automatic weapon was the British woman that Major Krause was after. *He will pay a handsome reward if we can bring her in alive.*

Capitaine Bob's pulse raced wildly as he sighted in on the leading terrorist's chest, his hands shaking nervously. He jerked the trigger. The bullet hit the terrorist in the shoulder and knocked him down. There was a moment of shocked silence, then the terrorists whirled toward the sound of the gunshot and grabbed for their weapons. A hail of bullets from the hidden *Milice* ripped into them. Two of the terrorists collapsed so quickly that it seemed as if the earth had been jerked out from under their feet. Another took three rounds in the chest. He stood stock-still for an instant, a look of intense surprise on his face, and then fell face first into the dirt. Bullets ripped into the fourth man, sending him crashing headlong into the woman. Both dropped to the ground. "*Merde!*" *Capitaine* Bob swore in frustration, seeing the woman's crumpled form lying on the trail. *Major Krause is not going to be happy.*

His men broke cover and rushed to check the bodies on the trail. Two were still alive ... the man *Capitaine* Bob had shot and, much to his relief, the woman, who had only been knocked out when the terrorist slammed into her. He dragged the corpse off the woman and turned her over. She groaned in pain but he could not see any wounds, except for a sizeable lump on the side of her head.

"Hold the bitch up," he ordered. Two of his men pulled the semi-conscious woman upright and held her as another stripped off her battle jacket, leaving just her wool flannel shirt. The man ran his hands roughly over her body, much to the delight of the men who had gathered to watch.

"Strip her!" they urged hungrily. "Maybe she's concealing something." The tormentor ogled her chest and savagely ripped her shirt down the front, exposing her brassiere. He reached out to rip it off when *Capitaine* Bob interceded. He wanted information, not sport.

"Where are the others?" he screamed at her in French. "What are you doing here?"

She didn't answer. He slapped her face, hard, bringing tears to her eyes—but she remained silent. He shouted the questions over and over. Each time the punishment for not answering was more severe. The abuse left her face swollen, eyes blackened, and several loose teeth. Enraged and frustrated that she wouldn't talk, he punched her in the stomach. The vicious blow doubled her over. She vomited and collapsed on the ground, gasping for breath. The *Milice* chief saw that it would take more persuasive measures to get the British agent to talk.

"Get her up and tie her hands behind her back," he ordered. "We're going to take her to headquarters."

One of his thugs made a big show of tying a loop in a 10-foot-long rope. He stared heartlessly at the woman, a cruel smile on his face, as his hands fashioned the knot. When he finished, he dropped it over her head and pulled it tight, forming a noose. He yanked it, tightening the noose and choking her. She fell to her knees, about to black out, when her tormentor loosened the rope.

"We don't want you dead," *Capitaine* Bob said callously, "at least until you've given us what we want to know. Get up," he ordered, kicking her in the side. She struggled to her feet, but the effort made her dizzy and she went down on one knee. *Capitaine* Bob grabbed her by the arm and yanked her to her feet. "Now start walking," he shouted, shoving her roughly.

Maquis du Vercors, Forest Trail, 1420, 11 October 1942—"Chief, chief," an agitated voice shouted from the head of the column, "come quickly!" LeGrand hurried forward past the line of heavily laden men. By the time he reached the front of the column, several men were standing in the middle of the path talking excitedly with the young scout that had been sent to reconnoiter the trail. They were plainly upset about something.

"What is it?" LeGrand demanded. "What's happened?"

"The security team—they're all dead!" the frenzied scout exclaimed. The news was stunning and caught LeGrand completely by surprise.

"How ... where?" he stammered, trying to make sense of the startling news.

"Ambushed," the man cried out, prompting another round of excited chatter. Everyone had a question they wanted answered.

"Quiet," LeGrand thundered. "Let him talk."

The distraught scout's entire body shook as he related how he had discovered the four mutilated bodies of the security team—literally stumbling over their bloody remains. One corpse was partially hidden in the underbrush just off the side of the trail. "I thought it was a log," he said, "and then I saw ..." He broke into tears, unable to continue.

Hervieux gave him a moment to gather himself together. "Where did you find the bodies?" he asked.

"On the main trail where it joined a footpath that led off the plateau."

LeGrand knew exactly where the site was located. He had used the path many times in the past few months. By now, the two Jeds had worked their way to the front of the column. Henry broke into the conversation.

"You said four bodies. Was one of them a woman?"

The scout thought for a moment and shook his head. "No, monsieur, but she may have been lying in the undergrowth," he replied.

132

"Or she may have been able to escape," Henry said hopefully. He turned to LeGrand. "Cain and I will hurry on ahead. Bring the rest of the column as fast as you can."

Maquis du Vercors, Forest Trail, 1420, Ambush Site—Henry crawled behind a fallen tree while Cain inched through the underbrush to a spot where he could see the four bodies lying on the trail. The forest seemed abnormally quiet, as though the horrific violence had frightened the animals into hiding and driven the birds away. There was a cloying stench of death in the air. The two Jeds watched and listened for several minutes just to make sure the ambushers were gone and then approached the bodies from two different directions. "Can never be too careful," Henry cautioned. The bodies had been stripped and mutilated; insects were attacking their exposed skin. Cain bent down to examine a corpse more closely. Its face had been bashed in and the genitals had been cut off and stuffed in the maw that had been its mouth.

"Fucking animals," he exclaimed hotly. "What kind of man does something like this?"

"A band of murderous thugs that want to instill terror," Henry answered vehemently. "They want to terrify the population so they won't support the Resistance, but it's not going to work with LeGrand's band. It'll have the opposite effect. You saw how he handled the Germans at the ambush … it's a blood feud, tit for tat." They searched the ambush site and noted there weren't any empty cartridges near the bodies. "Never got a shot off," Henry remarked. "Probably never knew what hit them."

They found Josephine's battle jacket in the undergrowth next to the trail but no signs of her body. "No bullet holes or blood," Cain said, scrutinizing the blouse closely. "Now where the hell is she?"

"Look at these," Henry said, pointing to dozens of overlapping footprints in the hard-packed dirt trail. He knelt down. "See this?" He indicated the faint trace of a British ammunition boot. "The bastards have got her." They followed the footprints to where they branched off on a path that led off the plateau before turning back to the ambush site. "We've got to find out where they're taking her," Henry declared.

SS-*Sturmbannführer* Helmet Krause, 1st Battalion, SS *Polizei* Regiment 19, Grotte de la Draye Blanche, 1230, 11 October 1942—Major Krause was still at Grotte de la Draye Blanche loading the captured supplies when the traumatized survivors of the 2d Company debouched from the forest. They were completely unnerved, and it took him some time before he was able to make sense of what had happened to them. He was so incensed over the poor performance of the company that he took the two most senior NCOs—two corporals—and had them shot. The other members of the company were immediately arrested, placed under guard, stripped of their weapons, and forced to load the trucks.

The actions did little to calm the irate officer. Seething, he took out his anger on the first village they came across on their return to Grenoble. Krause ordered his soldiers to round up 30 men, put them against a wall, and shoot them as an example of what happens to those who support the terrorists. The fact that none of those he shot had anything to do with the ambush meant nothing to him.

Ambush Site, 1820, 11 October 1942—The Maquis column reached the ambush site late in the day after a four-hour climb up the steep terrain. Upon their arrival, the Jeds briefed LeGrand on what they had found and showed him the rough graves they had scraped out on the forest floor in a natural clearing. The site was in the heart of a grove of old pine trees, which added an element of tranquility, despite the violence that had been inflicted on the men that lay beneath the forest canopy. "*Merci Monsieurs*," LeGrand uttered, his voice choked with emotion. "They died for France."

When he found out the bodies had been disfigured, LeGrand went into a rage, swearing revenge against the men who had killed them. Henry waited until the Maquis chief calmed down before telling him that Josephine had been captured. "We have to find out where they have taken her and try to rescue her," he insisted. LeGrand quickly agreed and sent two of his most trusted men to follow the trail of the ambushers.

Unlike the Germans they'd killed in the ambush, LeGrand insisted on holding a memorial service for his four dead soldiers. The Maquis formed two ranks in front of the earthen mounds. The priest stepped forward and in a low voice said a solemn prayer over each of the graves. His invocation offered solace to the young men in formation whose comrades lay beneath French soil. When the priest concluded his prayer, LeGrand gave an order for the Maquis to fire a rifle salute. The ragged volley was deafening in the close confines of the clearing.

"Jesus," Henry muttered, "that's loud enough to wake the dead."

Cain heard the callous remark. *Jesus Christ*, he thought to himself, *Henry is one tough son-of-a-bitch.*

Milice Headquarters, 28 Cours Berriat, Grenoble, 1830, 11 October 1942—*Capitaine* Bob watched his men drag the British terrorist along the basement corridor and throw her bodily into the jail cell. The narrow concrete underground lockup was about the size of a large closet. It was windowless, pitch black, with no furniture, just a bare concrete floor. The rough treatment was all part of the softening up process he used to cower the prisoners and get them in the right frame of mind for interrogation. "Pain and fear are wonderful tools to break even the strongest captive," he lectured his men. He would enjoy breaking this British terrorist.

The day had gone well and Bob felt good—four terrorists killed and a British agent captured.

"The Germans will be most appreciative," he declared to Colonel Maude standing at his side.

"I agree," she replied. "This calls for a special celebration."

The *Milice* chief smiled with anticipation; Maude's celebrations usually left him spent and hung over. *The woman is an Amazon*, he reflected, staring hungrily at her uniform blouse which barely contained her large breasts. Maude caught him eyeing her chest and deliberately arched her back, straining the buttons even further. Excited by Maude's exhibition, Bob made a quick decision. "I will interrogate the terrorist in the morning," he decided.

"I was hoping to question her now," Maude countered.

"*Patience, ma chérie*," he replied, taking her hand and leading her toward the basement stairway.

The guards shook their heads knowingly as they watched the two disappear up the stairs.

"I'd like to be in his shoes," one muttered.

"Ha," his partner snorted, "you couldn't handle her. She'd turn you inside out."

"*Ja*, but what a way to go," he replied. The two were careful to keep their comments quiet, well aware of the duo's cruel and sadistic temperaments. Anyone that got on their bad side lived to regret it … if they survived the couple's special attention.

20

La Ferme d'Ambel, Maquis du Vercors Base Camp, 0630, 12 October 1942—The Maquis band finally reached the isolated farm early the next morning after an exhausting all-night march along a faint alpine path that ran through the heavily forested uplands. The stone farmhouse and three sturdy wooden outbuildings, one of which was a sawmill, were located in a desolate valley in the northeastern corner of the plateau. It was an ideal location, tucked under a high ridge, in a thick stand of trees that made it almost impossible to be seen from the air. A rough track across a stone bridge over the river used to power the sawmill provided the main access to the farm. LeGrand estimated that the farmhouse and outbuildings could accommodate over 100 men.

The farm was an important timber concession that bordered the Ambel Forest, producing charcoal-based gasoline that powered French Gazogene automobiles and trucks in the Grenoble area. Having confiscated all supplies of regular gasoline for their own use, the Germans had left the locals to fend for themselves, so they wheezed around the streets of Grenoble and struggled up the steep grades of the plateau in clouds of wood smoke. The farm offered good cover for the large number of able-bodied young men in the vicinity, whom the Resistance supplied with false identity cards showing them to be loggers working for the concession. It was also closely linked to the owners of the local transport company, who supplied trucks to haul the lumber and also provided support for the Resistance.

Immediately after reaching the farm, Cain broke out the B2 Jed Set, while Henry prepared an enciphered status report for SOE headquarters. Using the one-time pad, he carefully encoded an account of Josephine's capture, noting that the Maquis was trying to find out where she had been taken. After checking his work, Henry attempted to raise the intercept station, using his coded name and call sign. His first attempts went unanswered, and he grew concerned that the transmitter had been damaged during the hike. Finally, he heard a "Send your traffic" signal through the earphones. Heaving a sigh of relief, he started lightly tapping the telegraph key—not as fast as Josephine—but he got the job done, as far as he was concerned. After completing the message, he signed off and shut down the transmitter to save the batteries. He'd turn it on at the next scheduled broadcast time.

———————

Station 53a (Intercept Radio Station), Grendon Hall, Grendon Underwood, England, SOE Signals Center, 0645, 12 October 1942—The FANY operator on duty heard the faint transmission but did not recognize the fist and hesitated to answer it in case it was a German deception attempt. She called to a supervisor, who listened in and decided to respond. The yeoman copied the message word for word, and when the transmission ended, she passed it to the decoder in the next room. Unfortunately, the message was delayed in being deciphered because the woman had already begun working on another message. After an hour of attempting to make heads or tails of the message, she gave up and placed it in the "indecipherable" box, where a special team would "attack" it, in an attempt to make it readable. By contrast, Henry's message was easily deciphered, and within ten minutes the decoder passed it to her supervisor, who read through it, recognized its importance, and stamped it "Operational Immediate." The message was sealed in an envelope and handed to a motorcycle courier for delivery to headquarters.

Milice **Headquarters, 28 Cours Berriat, Grenoble, 0530, 12 October 1942**—The strike of the jailer's hobnailed boots on the concrete floor sent shivers up Josephine's spine. Fearing they were coming for her, she shrank back from the door as far as the tiny cell allowed. She knew it was only a matter of time before she was hauled out to be questioned. The goons had been dragging prisoners from their cells all night long and interrogating them somewhere in the prison's upper floors, the victims' tortured screams piercing the air. Much as she tried to steel herself for the interrogation, Josephine was deathly afraid that she wouldn't be able to resist their brutality. The classroom instruction she had received on how to resist interrogation was a far cry from the shocking conditions she found herself in—bedbugs, lice, fleas, isolation, and, above all, fear. In England she had been among friends, and unhurt. Here the reality was grim—her face was badly bruised, with one eye completely sealed shut, nose broken, and her lips split and swollen. Agony gripped her every time she moved, and she thought several of her ribs might be broken or cracked. The pain weakened her resolve, but she was determined to hold out as long as possible without giving anything away.

The footsteps stopped in front of the cell door, as keys grated sharply in the heavy metal lock. The door burst open. Before she knew what had hit her, two *Milice* jailers charged into the cell and grabbed her violently by the arms, sending a wave of pain coursing through her body. She screamed but her cries fell on deaf ears. They dragged her roughly into the brightly lit corridor where a powerfully built woman wearing a *Milice* officer's uniform stood under the glaring lights. A holstered pistol hung on a belt around her ample waist, and she wielded a riding crop in her hand, which she tapped against her thigh impatiently. Josephine knew instantly that this was the infamous Colonel Maude.

"Take her to my special room," the woman ordered harshly.

F Section, Special Operations Executive, Norgeby House, Room 52 (Signals Section), 83 Baker Street, London, 0845, 12 October 1942—Loreena looked up just in time to see the uniformed motorcycle courier come through the door and head toward her desk. As Head of Signals, she and her assistant were the only ones authorized to sign for the decoded messages he brought from Grendon Hall. The courier saluted and handed her a sealed envelope. She quickly checked to make sure it had not been tampered with. *Can't be too careful*, she thought, then signed the receipt he handed her, acknowledging that the messages had been delivered. "Thank you, sergeant," Loreena said as the man came to attention, saluted, and marched purposefully out of the room.

As was her habit, Loreena broke open the envelope and skimmed the messages to determine which staff member to send them to for action. The first message caught her eye; it was highlighted in red and stamped "Operational Immediate." She looked at the header to see who originated it. *Team Alexander!* Her heart skipped a beat and she paled. "Oh my God," she whispered, fighting the sinking feeling in the pit of her stomach that something had happened to James. She read further and heaved a sigh of relief; he was OK, but the team radio operator had been captured by the Germans and was being held at the Gestapo headquarters in Grenoble. She felt guilty for thinking only of her man. Setting aside her thoughts, Loreena locked the rest of the messages in her desk drawer and hurried to her superior's office.

A trim woman in a tweed suit was seated at a table concentrating on a document when Loreena entered the office. Vera Atkins had been informally assigned as "F Int" for F Section Intelligence, which she amusingly called "interference" on the personnel chart, but she was really Colonel Buckmaster's formidable assistant and Loreena's boss. As Buckmaster himself had noted in her personnel file, "She has a fantastically good memory and quick grasp." She also had a strong personality and did not suffer fools gladly, which several bootlickers learned to their discomfort.

Atkins was also tasked with overseeing agents that were dropped into France. This responsibility largely meant sifting through all intelligence about life on the ground in France. She tracked the latest information on what papers an agent would need to move about; on whether ration cards were issued monthly or weekly; on the hours of curfew; or on the latest trend in hats in rue Royale. Gleaning the facts from magazines, intelligence sources, and returning agents, she circulated highlights in little leaflets for the staff called "Titbits" or "Comic Cuts" after popular magazines.

Atkins looked up and smiled. "Sit down, Loreena," she said, and gestured to the hard-backed chair in front of the table.

"Miss Atkins," Loreena began—no one ever called the woman Vera, always Miss Atkins or Madam—"I have an 'Operational Immediate' message that I thought you might like to see," she said, and handed it across the table. As her superior read through the brief message, her facial expression hardened.

"I know this woman. Josephine is one of my girls," she remarked passionately and leaned back in her chair. She thought back to the chat she'd had with the three Jeds before their mission. Slowly she plucked a Dunhill cigarette from an ornate silver box, lit it with a gold lighter, inhaled deeply, and held it for a long moment before exhaling. "We're going to do our best to get her back," she declared resolutely, fixing Loreena with her icy blue-gray eyes.

———◄——————

La Ferme d'Ambel, Maquis du Vercors Base Camp, 1645, 12 October 1942—The Jeds crowded around a rough plank table with the surviving leaders of the Maquis du Vercors—LeGrand and Commandants Alphonse and Jean—in the kitchen farmhouse to hear the report of the two scouts that had been sent to locate Josephine. The scouts had made contact with a member of the Resistance in Grenoble. He had seen the blue uniformed Vichy police drag a woman in a torn uniform into the *Milice* headquarters. With that, the room grew somber. Everyone knew that meant torture and execution. Dozens of captured Resistance fighters had already met that fate at the hands of the *Milice*—death by firing squad or the hangman's noose after a brutal interrogation. Even now over 50 accused Resistance fighters were awaiting their fate in the basement cells of the *Milice* headquarters.

The thought of Josephine undergoing torture and death brought a demand from the Jeds.

"We have to try and rescue her," Henry stated.

"Impossible," Commandant Alphonse interjected hotly. "There is a German battalion billeted in the city, and the *Milice* headquarters is built like a fortress and heavily guarded by *Milice* and *Feldgendarmerie*. It would be suicide to attempt a rescue. I will not sacrifice my men needlessly." The other *chef de bataillon* nodded in agreement.

"No one is asking you to sacrifice your men," Henry replied calmly. "All I'm asking you to do is consider the possibility of mounting a rescue."

LeGrand had remained silent up to this point. "I have been in the building several times on official business," he announced, "and like Commandant Alphonse pointed out, a rescue attempt would be suicidal. If we fail, what happens to the other prisoners? The *Milice* will kill them in revenge." His statement seemed to settle the issue. Without the Maquis du Vercors, there was nothing the Jeds could do.

Henry was not about to give up and prodded the Maquis for information. "Describe the building," he asked LeGrand.

The Maquis chief shrugged his shoulders, as if to say, *Sure, but it won't change anything.*

"The five-story headquarters building is located on a dead-end street in the center of the city. It's surrounded by high masonry walls and has only one entranceway, and that is heavily guarded 24 hours a day."

"What's the inside of the building look like?" Henry probed.

"The building has been extensively remodeled," LeGrand explained. "The upper floors have been turned into office spaces for the Gestapo. The *Milice* have offices on the second floor. The basement and first floor have been made into holding cells and torture rooms."

Henry nodded. "Are there any troops billeted in the building?"

"No," LeGrand replied, "they are billeted in a barracks next to the headquarters building. The *Milice* commander, *Capitaine* Bob, and his mistress have a suite in the Hotel Moderne, two blocks away. It's the best hotel in the city and caters only to German officers and their French whores," LeGrand declared angrily. "It has luxuries that are simply unavailable anywhere else in the city."

"Who the hell is this *Capitaine* Bob?" Cain demanded.

"He is a murderous bastard," LeGrand growled, unable to keep his temper. "He collaborates with the Gestapo and is responsible for the torture and death of dozens of our people who have fallen into his hands. He is nothing more than a Nazi butcher. We have tried to kill him several times, but his network of informers and collaborators alerted him each time and he escaped."

"What about his mistress?" Henry interjected. "Any chance of working through her to get him?"

"Colonel Maude is worse than he is," LeGrand replied. "She enjoys inflicting pain and often takes the lead in the interrogation and torture sessions."

Following the conversation, the Jeds sent an encrypted message to Grendon Hall reporting the information they had received from the Maquis, emphasizing their conviction that Josephine and the Maquis prisoners "had" to be rescued. Headquarters acknowledged the message and immediately transmitted a response: "Standby for instructions." Cain began copying the coded message. The FANY operator at Grendon knew that the team's regular operator was unavailable and deliberately slowed the transmission of the message. As it was, Cain sweated bullets taking it down—reading code was not his strong suit. The decoded message was startling in its directness: "This headquarters supports rescue. Initiate reconnaissance of target and commence operational planning. Report support requirements upon completion. Good luck."

Milice Headquarters, 28 Cours Berriat, Grenoble, 0535, 12 October 1942—Josephine was dragged up the stairs to a room on the first floor. She inwardly recoiled with fear at what she saw—a torture chamber. Meat hooks were suspended from the walls; chains and handcuffs were haphazardly scattered around the room; and a variety of clubs and truncheons were lined up on a table. An atmosphere of brutality and barbarism permeated the very air. Before she could move, the jailers seized her arms and twisted them behind her back, tying her wrists so tightly that it lacerated her skin. Maude appeared and told her that she should talk or "it will be very hard for you." Despite the pain, Josephine told her that she had nothing to say. "It's no good trying to hide the truth from me. We are very well informed," Maude bragged. "Not everyone in the Maquis is as loyal as you."

The woman nodded to one of the jailers, who looped a rope around her bound wrists and passed it over a wooden beam in the ceiling. "Your last chance," the woman stated. When she didn't respond, the jailers pulled the rope until she was hanging from her arms, her weight forcing her shoulders out of their sockets. She screamed and passed out from the intense pain.

She regained consciousness to find the woman slapping her face. "Talk," was all her tormentor shouted over and over. She hardly noticed the blows because the pain from her damaged shoulders was overpowering. Blood streamed from her mouth. "Talk!" the woman screamed. Josephine prayed for relief—*God, I can't stand this!*—and blessedly passed out for the second time. She woke to find herself back in the cell with her hands untied. There was a tingling sensation in them but no feeling in her arms. They hung limply at her side.

21

La Ferme d'Ambel, Maquis du Vercors Base Camp, Massif du Vercors, 0830, 13 October 1942—Despite his opposition to a rescue attempt, LeGrand had sent four of his best men into Grenoble to gather information. They returned the next day with startling news: the Gestapo was going to execute all the prisoners that were being held by the *Milice* in retaliation for the Maquis ambush. Shocked and angered, the Maquis leadership resolved that "we have to do something." They could not simply stand by and let the Nazis execute their friends and neighbors without lifting a finger to save them. LeGrand was the first to reverse his earlier position.

"I believe there is a chance to rescue them, if we receive the proper support." All eyes turned to the Jeds. "What can you do for us?" LeGrand asked.

This was the opening Henry had been waiting for. "SOE backs the rescue," he responded. "They have requested an operational plan and support requirements before finalizing approval for the support."

"Very well," LeGrand interjected, "let's get to work."

They gathered around the kitchen table where one of the scouts laid out a rough, hand-drawn sketch of the streets surrounding the *Milice* headquarters. The penciled drawing showed the building sitting at the end of a dead-end street at 28 Cours Berriat. "There's

146

a roadblock here," the scout said, pointing to where Cours Berriat intersected the main cross street. "It's a wooden barrier gate manned by four Germans." Henry drew the military symbol for a roadblock on the sketch and labeled it in French, intending to use the sketch to brief the rescue force. The scout pointed to the front of the compound. "The entrance is here, guarded by two men."

"There is a courtyard inside that you have to cross before reaching the entrance to the main building," LeGrand added. "Two more guards check identification cards here. There are at least ten guards on duty at any one time inside."

The scout pointed to a structure adjacent at the north end of the headquarters building. "This is the guard barracks and mess hall," he said. "All the guards, except those on duty, eat lunch here at the same time every day. That will be the best time to attack."

Finally, the scout pointed out an open area two blocks from the barracks. "This is where their vehicles are staged. We counted three trucks and a half-track inside a barbed wire fence," he explained. "A single guard checks the vehicles in and out."

Henry turned to LeGrand. "We'll need those vehicles."

LeGrand nodded. "I have several men who know how to drive." He turned to his second in command. "Andre, you will lead the carjackers." The comment brought a knowing laugh from the men. Andre had a pre-war reputation for appropriating vehicles without their owners' consent.

The men turned their attention to a set of architectural drawings one of the scouts had laid on top of the sketch map, which showed the interior of the three-story building. Henry was amazed. "Where did you get these?"

The scout smiled. "The stupid *Milice* used local architects to draw up the remodeling plans, and it just so happened that one of them is a Maquisard." The men closely examined the building's first-floor plan, particularly the layout of offices, hallways, and the location of the basement stairway.

147

LeGrand pointed to a large room near the basement stairway. "This is the torture room," he said with revulsion. "The prisoners are brought up the stairs from the basement cells and interrogated here. According to our sources, *Capitaine* Bob and his whore often participate in the interrogation. Their specialty is electric shock. They attach wires to their hands, feet, genitals, chest, neck, and breasts and crank up the voltage until they talk."

Henry turned his attention to the basement floor plan, which showed small cells spaced along each side of a narrow corridor. "What do you know about them?" he asked.

"The prisoners are jammed together," Commandant Alphonse replied knowingly. He had experienced the 'hospitality' of the *Milice* firsthand. "They have to sit on the floor; often there are so many that they can't stretch out. There's no toilet facilities, just a bucket. They're fed once a day. The guards bring their food in a large pail. It's almost impossible to adequately describe the appalling conditions. I was lucky. I only spent three days in a cell before they let me go." He pointed to four cells at the far end of the corridor. "This is where the high-value prisoners are kept; the ones that *Capitaine* Bob and his mistress reserve for their 'special' treatment. Conditions here are even worse than they are for the other prisoners. I expect that's where Josephine is being kept." Cain thought about his teammate being held in those atrocious conditions and swore vengeance on the bastards.

The discussion turned to planning the rescue. Initially LeGrand wanted to use his entire force of over a hundred men, but as the plan unfolded, it became obvious that a large number of men would not be feasible. There was no place big enough to stage them prior to the assault, and it would be almost impossible to conceal their presence from collaborators, who would be only too happy to curry favor with the Nazis by informing on them. After reviewing their options, they decided that 32 men would be sufficient—16 to attack the *Milice* headquarters, ten to kill or capture the *Milice* chief in the hotel, and a six-man carjack team. They decided to use the four Gazogene lumber trucks for transportation, but it would mean leaving before dawn and breaking the curfew. LeGrand was not that concerned. His drivers had special German permits that authorized them to pass through the roadblocks.

After going over the plan several times, LeGrand dropped a bombshell. "We have a man inside the building with access to the prisoners."

"Can he get a message to them?" Henry asked excitedly.

"Maybe," the chief replied. "He is a handyman and is often called upon to do repair work inside the building. He has a pass that allows him to go anywhere without supervision."

"If the rescue is a go," Henry said, "we'll need to have him get the information to everyone so they can be ready."

Milice **Headquarters, 28 Cours Berriat, Grenoble, 2000, 14 October 1942**—Josephine was in agony, her body a throbbing mass of pain. The past two days had been one torture session after another. She was barely holding out. The sessions were getting worse because she wouldn't tell the interrogators what they wanted. The woman interrogator was the worst, a veritable Amazon—tall, big-bodied, muscular arms and legs. A savage, cruel, and sadistic bitch who delighted in inflicting pain, routinely beating and punching Josephine. When that wasn't enough, she resorted to using a rubber club to pound across her bare feet. The pain was excruciating. After one such session, the woman promised to continue the interrogations until Josephine told her everything she knew. "The only way you're going to leave here," she screamed, "is in a coffin."

That night Josephine had been huddled against the wall of her cell when she heard a man whisper her name. At first she thought she was hallucinating but the voice continued insistently. Josephine crawled closer to the door. "I'm here," she murmured thickly, hardly able to form the words because of her mangled mouth. Her lips were split and swollen and she had unconsciously bitten her tongue during the beatings.

"Do not despair, we are working to free you," the man uttered quietly. "Be ready tomorrow."

Josephine heard his footsteps fade and she was alone again—but this time with a measure of hope.

F Section, Special Operations Executive, Norgeby House, Room 52 (Signals Section), 83 Baker Street, London, 1000, 14 October 1942—Loreena was caught completely by surprise when Vera Atkins marched purposefully into her office. The boss had never ventured there before. Normally the staff were summoned to her office for briefings. "It's on," Atkins announced without preamble. "RAF command has been tasked with the mission." Loreena felt like cheering. The past several days had been filled with anxiety, ever since F Section had requested RAF support for the raid on the *Milice* headquarters in Grenoble. Colonel Buckmaster had convinced the head of SOE that the raid was essential. His support carried the day. "We must send the 'execute' message immediately," Atkins stated. "The raid is scheduled for lunchtime tomorrow."

No. 141 Wing, 28 Squadron RAF, RAF Hunsdon, Harlow, Essex, England, 0700, 15 October 1942—The eight aircrews came to attention as Group Captain Nigel Fox-Perry entered the dispersal hut's briefing room. "It's on, lads!" he thundered to the accompaniment of cheers from the pilots and navigators/bombardiers. They had been practicing cross-country low-level precision bombing for the past few days and were raring to get on with the mission—any mission, as long as it got them back in the war. Fox-Perry stepped up to the large chalkboard and pulled the covering away, exposing a large 4- by 5-foot aerial photograph of the target. "The building in the center is the *Milice* headquarters in Grenoble, the target you've been practicing so hard for." He paused to let them get a good look before continuing. "It's not only a headquarters but it's also a prison. Intelligence reports indicate that the French Resistance fighters that are being held there are scheduled for execution." He paused again to let the information to sink in. "There is another important reason for the mission. One of our Special Operations agents is being held there. She has valuable information that can't be allowed to fall into enemy hands." The mention that a British woman was in the jail got the pilots' undivided attention.

"Lads," Fox-Perry continued, "our low-level strike is part of a rescue attempt by the French Resistance. They will launch a ground attack immediately after our aerial assault." He tapped the photograph with his swagger stick. "This is our primary target, the main building. It is a three-story stone and brick structure. The prison cells are located in the basement. Each aircraft will carry four general-purpose 500-pound MK IV bombs instantaneously fused, giving us just enough time to get away from the blast. They are designed to penetrate and destroy the top floor but not the basement—so I'm told, although I'd hate to be in the building when our bombs detonate over their heads." Fox-Perry then pointed to a wooden structure on the east side of the main building. "This is the guard barracks, which has to be destroyed before the Resistance fighters attack.

"Gentlemen, it's time to get down to how we're going to pull off this little stunt," Fox-Perry announced. "Jimmy," he said, addressing Flight Lieutenant James Bruce. "I want your two-plane section to blast a hole in the outer wall at the southern entranceway. First aircraft in use the entrance road as the guide. Second aircraft break right at 10 miles from the target and stay at sufficient height to observe the first strike. After explosions, follow the same route to launch your attack."

Fox-Perry turned to Flight Officer Clyde Dickens. "Clyde, your section is to attack the south side of the main building three minutes after Jimmy's attack. Use the same route to the target as the first section. Attack in column with enough separation to avoid lead's bomb fragments." Fox-Perry paused to answer any questions. There were none. The third section was under the command of Flight Lieutenant Paddy Grenier. "Paddy, your two-plane section is to attack the guard barracks two minutes after Clyde's section pulls off the target." He pointed to it with his swagger stick. "Paddy, attack in column with enough separation to avoid bomb blasts."

After covering the mission profile, Fox-Perry pointed to the coordinating instructions on the blackboard:

Operation *Jail Break*

Zero hour: 1200
All aircraft will attack at rooftop height
Close escort will be provided by Typhoons from No. 257 Squadron
Rendezvous point after attack east of target

"That's it, lads," Fox-Perry announced. "We've only got one chance to do this right, so let's make it a good show. Remember, in fast and get the hell out fast."

The flight crews shuffled out of the hut headed for the flight line, lugging their parachutes, leather flying helmets, Mae Wests, maps, briefing bags packed with lists of frequencies and call signs, beacon identification, and code letters of the day. The armed and fueled Mosquitos stood ready on the hardstand, lined up in their take-off order. The crew did a detailed walk-around inspection, paying particular attention to the four dark green 500lb bombs with their distinctive red and green bands on the nose, safely tucked away in the bomb bay. A poorly secured bomb could ruin a crew's day if it came loose on takeoff. The two men climbed up the telescoping ladder and squeezed into the cockpit, sitting side by side.

"How does a big bloke like you manage to get into this plane?" Fox-Perry's navigator groused.

"I don't get into it, I put it on," the captain laughed.

Fox-Perry pressed the starter button and booster coil buttons, starting the engines. The ground crew pulled the chocks away and gave a thumb's up to the pilot.

"All set?" Fox-Perry queried.

"Set," the navigator replied.

Fox-Perry slowly opened the throttles and released the brakes. The aircraft raced over the grass surface of the runway, gathering speed from its two Rolls-Royce engines. Two hundred yards from the end of the runway, Fox-Perry pulled back on the control column and the Mosquito lifted off, quickly followed by the others, one after another. The take-off sequence was to make sure there was sufficient distance between them so one aircraft didn't start moving off until the aircraft in front of it was just leaving the ground.

22

La Ferme d'Ambel, Maquis du Vercors, 0450, 15 October 1942—
Well before dawn the men selected for the rescue mission were up
and preparing the four Gazogene trucks for the three-hour drive to
Grenoble. They stacked lumber in the truck beds, leaving a space in
the center large enough for seven men and their equipment. It would
be a tight squeeze, but it was the only way to conceal the men from
the German sentries manning the checkpoints and roadblocks.

With a last *"Bonne chance"* from their comrades staying behind,
the men climbed aboard the trucks. Planks were then laid on top
of the space so that they were completely concealed from prying
eyes. The trucks coughed into life, and amidst a gnashing of gears
the convoy slowly made its way along the moonlit stretch of rutted
logging track off the plateau. A large cloud of suffocating grayish
wood smoke and dust marked their passage.

Two and a half hours later, just as dawn was breaking, the convoy
reached the outskirts of Grenoble. A German roadblock appeared
out of the gloom. The driver of the lead vehicle slowed down and
cautiously inched it forward toward the armed soldier standing
in the middle of the road with his rifle casually pointed in their
direction. The driver spotted a machine-gun team and several
heavily armed members of the roadblock casually watching their

progress. LeGrand loosened the pistol tucked in the waistband of his pants.

"I'll handle this," the driver cautioned. "I know him." The men in the truck bed readied their weapons and prepared for action.

"Don't do anything unless I give the signal," LeGrand whispered just loud enough for them to hear.

The German sentry climbed onto the running board and shined a flashlight inside.

"Pierre," he said in heavily accented French, "what are you doing here so early in the morning?"

"*Bonjour mon ami,*" the driver responded resignedly. "The boss forced me out of my warm bed and the arms of my *jeune fille* to deliver this accursed lumber to your supply depot."

The soldier laughed. "They're all alike," he sympathized, "still in bed while we're freezing our balls off." He took a breath. "Did you bring anything?"

"I didn't forget you, my friend," the driver replied and handed him a paper envelope containing 200 francs, the standard bribe for letting vehicles through the roadblock.

"Have a good day," the soldier offered, tucking the envelope inside his uniform blouse. "I'll see you next time." He jumped down and signaled to the members of the roadblock that everything was OK and waved the convoy on.

Three of the trucks made their way along the deserted streets toward the *Milice* headquarters in the center of town, while the fourth truck headed for the hotel. A block from the headquarters, the trucks pulled into a narrow alley and stopped behind a two-story garage that concealed them from the main street. The men piled off. Andre led his carjack group along the alley toward the parking area, while the other group rushed through the back door of the building. Inside the garage, half-a-dozen mechanics were quickly rounded up, bound hand and foot, and locked in a room off the shop floor. Two of the mechanics were members of the local Resistance cell and had provided information to the raiders on the guard schedule of the garrison. Tying them up provided a legitimate alibi when the Germans launched the inevitable after-raid roundup of suspects.

As the raiders gathered near the double doors of the garage and peered nervously at the headquarters building, they all wondered, *Will the British aircraft come?* Cain caught LeGrand nervously glancing at his watch. "They'll be here," he whispered to the Resistance chief, although he said it with more confidence than he felt.

———◆———

Maquis du Vercors, Hotel Moderne, 0745, 15 October 1942—Two *Milice* guards were sitting at a table beside the entrance to the hotel casually reading a newspaper when they heard the unmistakable rumble of a Gazogene truck approaching. It turned the corner, a telltale plume of grayish charcoal smoke following along in its wake. "Lumber truck," one muttered, looking up from the newspaper he was sharing with his partner. "Probably on its way to the supply dump." Neither man gave it a second look. Clearly, they were guards in name only. They were doping off because it was common knowledge that the non-commissioned officer who was supposed to check on them never showed up until late in the morning. Besides, nothing ever happened, and they were bored. What could possibly happen here?

The truck pulled brazenly to a stop directly in front of the entrance. The guards looked up from their papers. "You can't park here," one shouted angrily, motioning the driver with his hand to move along. Henry, dressed in the uniform of a German non-commissioned officer and carrying a Schmeisser submachine gun, jumped out of the cab. Before the guards realized that something was wrong, Henry raised his weapon and unleashed a deadly barrage of 9mm bullets. The burst raked the guards and left them slumped over across the table, blood soaking into the newspapers. Any chance the guards had of resistance had been lost due to their apathy. Their rifles stood propped up against the door frame, mute testimony to their carelessness.

Before the sound of gunfire died away, the seven Maquisards concealed by the stacked lumber in the truck bed threw off the planks and followed Henry at a run toward the hotel's entranceway. Speed was essential. They had to capture *Capitaine* Bob before he realized what was happening. In less than a minute they burst through the ornate front door into the lobby, where three German officers were in the process of checking out. The gunfire and the sudden appearance of the soldiers in German uniforms momentarily stunned them into inaction. One recovered quickly and made the mistake of reaching for his sidearm. He paid the price for his speedy reaction and was instantly gunned down. The other two were mercilessly clubbed to the floor and put out of action. The stunned desk clerk put his hands up and was pushed roughly against the wall. Two of Henry's men took positions to cover the stairway to the upper floors, while the others rushed into the dining room. The entire action took less than a minute and a half.

The small dining room was filled with a dozen German and *Milice* officers and their French doxies eating a leisurely breakfast until gunfire erupted in the lobby and the Resistance fighters burst into the room. The diners sat openmouthed as the raiders quickly spread across the front of the room and pointed their weapons at them. "What's the meaning of this?" an officious German staff officer demanded. Several officers instinctively pushed away from the tables, intending to confront the intruders. Henry nipped the insipid challenge in the bud by firing a shot into the ceiling in a shower of plaster dust. As it suddenly dawned on the diners that the intruders were not German soldiers, the room erupted with panicked cries of alarm.

"Sit down and shut up," Henry bellowed menacingly. They quickly obeyed, although several women continued to weep. Henry's plan was designed to cower the officers and make them easier to control, with the understanding that terrified prisoners were not prone to be heroes. It worked perfectly. The officers remained stiffly in their seats, hoping for rescue.

"*Terroristen*," *Sturmbannführer* Krause whispered alarmingly to the *Milice* chief and his mistress sitting beside him at the table.

"Oh my God. They'll kill us once they know we're here," *Capitaine* Bob muttered, loud enough to be overheard.

"Shut up, you fool," Colonel Maude hissed menacingly. "Maybe they won't be able to identify us."

Krause was alarmed. If the *Terroristen* discovered that he was the architect of the Oradour-sur-Glane massacre, they would show him no mercy. Very slowly and carefully, he reached up and withdrew his identification card from the pocket of his field uniform, slipped it under the tablecloth, and tried to cover it with his plate. In his nervousness, he knocked over a water glass which he tried to grab but it slipped out of his grasp and fell onto the floor, smashing into pieces. The commotion attracted attention.

"You there," Henry shouted, "stand up!"

Krause didn't move, pretending that the demand was meant for someone else. A muscular Maquisard standing a few feet behind the German officer shoved his way through the closely packed tables, grabbed the man by the neck with one hand, and forced him to his feet. "*Schweinehund!*" an infuriated Krause shouted and grabbed for his holstered pistol. Before he could draw his weapon, the Resistance fighter bashed him viciously on the side of the head with the butt of his rifle. Krause collapsed on the table, overturning it and landing in the half-eaten remains of breakfast and broken crockery.

"Get up," the fighter demanded, kicking the German.

As Krause got shakily to his feet, the raider took the officer's pistol and patted him down. In the process, the Maquisard glanced down and spotted an ID card lying in the litter on the floor. He thumbed the card open to the first page, where a wallet-sized photograph was glued. A name was typed below it—*SS-Sturmbannführer Max Krause.* It suddenly dawned on him that this man was the same bastard that was responsible for the massacre of his friends and neighbors in the village.

"Murderer!" he bellowed, and in a fit of rage slammed his rifle into Krause's back, knocking him to the floor. The fighter raised his rifle to finish him off. Before he could pull the trigger, Henry knocked the rifle aside.

"*Arretez,*" he said commandingly. "We'll take him to LeGrand for a decision on what to do with him."

"Line everyone up against the wall and search them," Henry continued. The fighters spread out among the tables and used their rifles to unceremoniously push and prod the laggards into line. "Which one of you is *Capitaine* Bob?" Henry demanded in French. No one responded. "I'm not going to ask again," he repeated, pointing his submachine gun menacingly at the line of men and women.

"Don't hurt us," a distraught woman sobbed and pointed to an overweight, pasty-faced *Milice* officer, who was trying his best to be inconspicuous. "It's him," she cried. *Capitaine* Bob was pulled roughly out of line and forced to his knees.

"Don't shoot me," he squealed piteously. Henry was taken back. Was this coward the butcher everyone feared?

"Tie him up," Henry ordered brusquely. The *Milice* chief's hands were roughly bound behind his back and he was shoved into a corner.

"What about her?" the same distraught woman cried, pointing to a fleshy, mean-faced woman wearing a *Milice* officer's uniform. "She's Colonel Maude, his whore!" Before anyone could react, Maude shrieked and threw herself on the snitch. They collapsed on the floor in a tangle of arms and legs. Maude, cursing wildly, got her hands around the woman's neck and started squeezing.

"Enough," Henry shouted and motioned two of his men to separate the women. They grabbed Maude's arms, but she broke free and turned on them, kicking and scratching violently.

Maude's claw-like fingernails raked a fighter across his cheek, breaking the skin and leaving a strip of torn flesh. Enraged, he hauled her off and punched her in the face, knocking her to the floor. Blood gushed from her smashed nose and mouth, leaving her moaning in pain.

"Tie her up," Henry ordered. A fighter stepped forward and callously twisted her hands behind her back and tied a knot. Other fighters moved along the line of German officers and female collaborators, tying their hands behind their backs.

23

German Vehicle Park, Maquis Carjack Team, 0745, 15 October 1942—Andre stepped out of the alley and walked toward the German soldier guarding the vehicle park. In his right hand he gripped a knife, concealed by his coat sleeve. His heart thumped wildly in his chest as adrenaline surged through his bloodstream. The young-looking sentry stepped into his path. *A teenager,* Andre thought and called out, *"Bonjour,"* in an effort to appear nonchalant, despite the butterflies in the pit of his stomach. The sentry ignored the greeting and motioned him away. Andre kept walking toward him.

"Halt!" the soldier shouted threateningly, starting to unsling his rifle. Andre sprang forward and plunged his knife into the sentry's throat with a vicious slash, severing his windpipe before the German could react. Eyes wide with shock, the sentry dropped his rifle and instinctively grabbed the gaping wound and tried to staunch the flow of blood that poured over his hands and down his uniform. He gagged and fell to his knees.

The Maquis fighter was transfixed by what he had done. The gory sight of the dying German writhing in agony turned his stomach. He had never killed with a knife before ... shooting a man with a rifle was one thing, but using a knife to take someone's life was totally different. "*Mon Dieu*," he mouthed, "what have I done?" Just then blood gushed from the sentry's throat, and he fell forward and lay still. Andre stared at the corpse and then looked at his hand, which still held the bloody knife. He grimaced and loosened his grip to let it fall to the pavement.

A teammate rushed up. "Come on Andre, snap out of it. Help me get this body out of the road," he shouted, spurring the shaken leader into action. The two men dragged the corpse into the parking area and dumped it in the sentry hut. A trail of blood on the pavement led to the hiding place but there was no time to clean it up; speed was of the essence. The airstrike was due any minute, and the carjack team had to pick up the freed prisoners before the Germans recovered from the bombing.

Andre climbed into the cab of the half-track and fired it up. Before he could put it in gear, a truck driver signaled that there was a problem. The trucks needed fuel in order to make it to the Resistance base camp. "Shit," Andre exclaimed, nervously glancing at his watch. "We're running out of time." The 3-ton trucks were essential; there was no other choice. Without them there wasn't enough transportation to haul the freed prisoners back to camp. He jumped out of the cab and motioned the drivers to pull over to a large stack of 20-liter jerrycans partially covered by a tarpaulin.

———◆———

No. 28 Squadron RAF, Operation *Jail Break*, **1125, 15 October 1942**—The eight camouflaged B MK IV De Havilland Mosquito fighter-bombers—nicknamed "the Wooden Wonder" because of their plywood construction—flew just a few feet over the Channel's wave tops to avoid detection by the German coastal radar installations. They were in a tight four-section formation—almost wingtip to wingtip. Their week-long, low-level formation flying was being put to the test. With their wingtips a few feet apart, they had to keep their attention riveted outside the cockpit. All the aircraft controls—pitch, flaps, trim, etc.—had to be done instinctively. A moment of inattention could mean disaster.

The formation climbed slightly as it flashed over the French coast, going flat out at well over 300 miles an hour, and headed west, staying just above the treetops. The weather was near perfect—clear skies and bright sunshine, which gave the pilots unrestricted visibility. Flight Officer Dickens said he had never seen better flying conditions in his life. Fox-Perry chose a route that took the flight away from the major population centers, particularly those that had large German garrisons protected by antiaircraft batteries. An hour into the flight, the formation intersected the Isère River north of Grenoble and turned south, following the waterway toward the target.

At 1156 the city appeared on the horizon. The squadron broke into sections to commence their attack. Fox-Perry pulled away from the formation so he could observe. Flight Officer Bruce waggled the wings of his aircraft, a signal to his wingman to pull off and wait until he finished his attack. Flight Lieutenant John Cary, Bruce's bomb-aimer, unhooked his seatbelt and scrambled forward to the Mark XIV Computing Bomb Sight in the nose.

"Bomb doors open," he announced. "Target coming up, Jimmy." He gripped the bomb release while staring intently through the sight's optics.

"There it is—straight ahead," Bruce replied, as he concentrated on maintaining the Mosquito on course.

At 1202, Bruce was just 2 miles from the target.

"Open bomb doors," he ordered.

"Bomb doors open," the navigator replied.

Bruce picked up the entrance road and adjusted his heading slightly. Seconds later, he spotted a German formation outside the entranceway to the outer wall and gave them a short burst from his machine guns, knocking several down. Almost instantly, Cary announced, "Steady—hold it—bombs gone." All four bombs were released. Bruce pulled the aircraft up sharply, helped by the loss of weight, and cleared the rooftop by only a few feet. The southern wall of the headquarters building was located just inside the outer wall. Fox-Perry observed the detonations. One bomb bounced off the inner face of the wall and exploded with an angry red-orange flash, leaving a boiling cloud of grayish-black smoke and sending an enormous spray of shattered bricks into the air. The second bomb bounced along the ground, coming to rest against the southern end of the main building. It exploded, caving in one wall. The other two bombs missed the compound altogether and detonated in a field outside the wall without causing any damage.

Bruce's wingman began his run just after the bombs exploded, the billowing pall of smoke from the first attack concealing the wall. "I can't see the target," the bomb-aimer exclaimed, taking his thumb off the bomb release button. The aircraft flashed over the headquarters building at breakneck speed and followed his section leader to the rendezvous point.

Exactly three minutes later, Flight Officer Dickens' second section roared into the attack. The smoke from the previous explosions had partially dissipated, giving Dickens' bomb-aimer a clear view of the target. An image from the camera in his aircraft showed debris flying into the air as his four bombs tore through the slate roof. The bombs were armed with instantaneous fuses that detonated on the slate roof, destroying the upper floor of the building. Fox-Perry observed flame and rubble shooting out of the building's windows. Dickens' wingman made his run. He was not as accurate; his first bomb landed in the courtyard, the second and third tore through an outside wall of the target, and the remaining bomb missed the building entirely and exploded outside the compound.

Paddy Grenier's third section roared in from the east, just 70 feet above the ground, dropping their bombs right on target, totally destroying the guards' barracks. The section pulled round into a tight right-hand turn and headed for the rendezvous point.

Fox-Perry remained behind to assess the damage, circling the target. There was a strong east wind blowing thick clouds of smoke across the western end of the target. He observed a partially collapsed wall in the south face of the headquarters building, whose upper floor seemed to be engulfed in flame. A large section of the outer wall had collapsed, leaving a 20-foot gap. He saw a number of men running toward the breach in the outer wall as he pulled away from the target.

Maquis du Vercors, *Milice* Headquarters, 1203, 15 October 1942—A roar filled the garage as an aircraft flashed over the Maquis' hiding place. No one saw the bombs drop, but their detonations violently shook the building, and for a moment it appeared the structure would collapse. A wave of concussion shattered windows, hurling glass shards into the interior of the building, barely missing the raiders. Even though they knew the raid was coming, the sudden overwhelming noise and violence caught them by surprise.

As the last bombs exploded, LeGrand, Cain, and a dozen fighters dashed across the street toward the shattered breach in the outer wall of the compound. A 10-foot pile of collapsed bricks and debris filled the gap, forcing them to scramble over the unstable mound, slowing their assault. LeGrand was the first man over the top. Dazed members of the *Milice Franc-Garde*—the armed wing of the *Milice*—staggered across the courtyard, fleeing the smoke and flame of the badly damaged headquarters building. Without missing a beat, LeGrand pointed his submachine gun at them and fired a burst into the unarmed crowd. Four of the hated paramilitary police crumpled to the ground. The rest skidded to a halt and raised their hands. "*Ayez pitié*, don't shoot!" they cried, but it was too late for them.

LeGrand ordered two of his men to remain at the breach to cover their withdrawal, while the rest darted for the gaping headquarters entranceway. Sprawled on the steps lay the grotesquely mangled bodies of the two guards. Heavy black smoke billowed out of the opening where the doors had once stood. The assault force paused long enough to put on the German gas masks they had captured in the ambush. It had been Cain's suggestion to bring them along.

Cain took the lead, LeGrand and the rest of the team following closely behind. Slowly they worked their way into the heavily damaged building, relying on their flashlights to cut through the smoke. Even then visibility was limited to a few feet. The gas masks proved their worth. Without them they would never have been able to proceed. Even so, the lenses started fogging up, further reducing their vision. For the untrained fighters, the damn things were suffocating, causing one of them to panic and throw off his mask. He sucked in a lungful of smoke and collapsed, choking and writhing on the floor. Following LeGrand's order to take him outside, two men quickly hauled him into the open air, leaving only eight fighters to search the basement where the prisoner cells were located.

The further they advanced into the darkened building, the more difficult it was to navigate through the debris that littered the corridor from the bomb-damaged floor above. "Dark as a drill instructor's heart," Cain muttered as his team of fighters cautiously picked their way past hastily abandoned *Milice* offices. They reached the stairs to the basement and warily made their way down step by step. At the bottom, Cain and LeGrand shined their flashlights along a narrow corridor, revealing rows of cells extending along each side. Dozens of emaciated faces stared back at them through small barred openings in the cell doors. The air was clear and they took off their masks. Recognizing the Maquis fighters, the prisoners begged, "Let us out!", hardly daring to believe that rescue was at hand. LeGrand's men immediately attacked the locks on the cell doors. They had to hurry before German reinforcements arrived.

"Josephine, where are you?" Cain hollered over the clamor.

"Here," a muffled voice cried out. He shined his flashlight toward the sound of her voice.

"Over there," he declared, seeing a bare arm sticking out through the bars of a cell's porthole window. Cain rushed over and grasped Josephine's hand.

"Thank God you've come," she cried, overcome with emotion.

"We'll get you out of here," he said. "Move away from the door, I'm going to shoot the lock." He fired his pistol. The gunshot was deafening in the enclosed space. The heavy .45-caliber bullet shattered the iron lock and the door flew open.

Josephine lay sprawled in a corner, softly crying. Cain took her in his arms, shocked by her appearance. Her face was grotesquely swollen, her lips split and blood-encrusted, her eyes nothing but bruised slits surrounded by deep purple and crusty red tissue. Her nose was broken, and it looked like her cheekbone was fractured.

"You're safe now," he soothed. "We're taking you out of here." He tried to lift her up but she groaned in pain.

"I think my ribs are broken," she gasped. Cain turned to LeGrand.

"We need something to carry her on."

LeGrand rushed from the cell and returned a few minutes later carrying several blankets. Two of his fighters carried a door they had torn off its hinges for a stretcher. "This is all we could find," he said.

LeGrand folded the blankets and placed them on the door for padding. Cain knelt by the injured woman. "We're going to have to lift you up," he cautioned. Josephine nodded and steeled herself as the men gently placed her on the makeshift stretcher. Her face grimaced with pain but she did not cry out. Each man took a corner of the door and carefully maneuvered it out of the cell into the corridor.

<hr/>

Maquis Carjack Team—With a gnashing of gears the trucks lined up beside the stack of jerry cans. The Maquisard drivers jumped out of the cabs and, in a frenzy of activity, started filling the gas tanks. They were behind schedule, the British bombers due at any moment. There was no time to lose. The trucks had to be in position to pick up the prisoners or the whole operation would fail.

At 1203, just as they finished topping off, the first Mosquito bomber flashed overhead, so low that its two 1,280 horsepower Rolls-Royce engines filled the street with a deafening heavy-throated roar. Seconds later ear-splitting explosions rent the air, followed by a blast wave that struck the surrounding buildings, shattering windows and hurling broken glass and debris in all directions. The powerful concussion briefly stunned the carjack team, even though they were two blocks from the target. They had never seen an airstrike, much less been this close to one.

Andre took the lead in the Sd.Kfz. 251 half-track and headed for the billowing smoke cloud marking the *Milice* headquarters building. The small convoy, joined by the three Maquis vehicles, arrived just as the first prisoners climbed through the gap in the perimeter wall. As they staggered into the open, gulping in the fresh air, the rescue vehicles pulled alongside them. Initially, the fleeing men were horrified by the sight of the German vehicles, but Andre and his men calmed them down. "*Nous sommes français*—we are French!" Andre and the other drivers shouted, waving a French flag bearing the Cross of Lorraine, the symbol of the Free French.

24

Norgeby House, Room 52, Special Operations Executive Signals Room, 83 Baker Street, London, 1210, 15 October 1942—Vera Atkins was studying one of the many classified documents that crossed her desk when a FANY signals clerk knocked on her door.

"What is it?" she asked.

"Miss Atkins, a priority message has just been received by the signals room that the raid has started."

Atkins quickly scooped up the documents, locked them in her desk, and started walking toward the signals room through the cordoned-off security area. As per protocol, an armed guard requested to see her identification, despite the fact that she passed his post several times a day. Atkins herself had chewed him out when he'd allowed her entry without checking her ID.

She passed through a steel blast door and entered the signals room, where a large blackboard listed the call signs for all teams that were being monitored by one of the FANY radio operators. Team Alexander was highlighted in red, indicating that Atkins was to be notified immediately upon receipt of any communication from or about it. The duty petty officer caught her eye and held up a message form.

"Ma'am, we just received this from No. 28 Squadron, but we don't know what it means— 'Tally Ho. Humpty Dumpty has no place to sit. His walls came tumbling down.'"

Atkins broke out with a big smile. "That's all right, petty officer, you know how peculiar those pilots are."

———●———

Maquis du Vercors, *Milice* Headquarters, 1212, 15 October 1942—The stretcher party carrying Josephine came out the shattered entranceway of the headquarters building just as Andre and the vehicles pulled up outside the shattered wall. "Over there," Cain said, pointing to the prisoners climbing over the debris obstructing the gap. The men were exhausted from carrying the makeshift stretcher through the building but made one last effort and clamored over the rubble to reach the line of lorries. Andre spotted them and beckoned them to bring Josephine to the half-track.

The area around the vehicles was crowded with escaped prisoners intent on celebrating their freedom despite the pleas of their rescuers to get aboard the vehicles. After several frustrating minutes, LeGrand had had enough and fired his Sten gun into the air to get their attention. At the same time, Andre gunned the half-track's engine, making it appear that the convoy was going to leave. The combination of the two was enough to get the prisoners' attention, and they quickly climbed onto the crowded lorries.

Cain took a last look around for any remaining prisoners, climbed aboard the half-track, and motioned for the convoy to follow him to the Hotel Moderne.

———●———

Hotel Moderne, 0805, 15 October 1942—Half a dozen German officers and their French girlfriends—"horizontal collaborators," as the Maquis called them—stumbled through the hotel's entranceway, prodded by Schmeisser-carrying Resistance fighters. *Capitaine* Bob was stiff with fear every time Henry casually pointed his Schmeisser in his direction. Maude, however, was unrepentant, despite the pain of her broken nose and badly bruised face. Eyes burning with pure hatred, she glared at her captors but reserved a special contemptuous look for her partner. "Weakling!" she hissed. Krause, the last man out, walked haltingly, under no illusions about his fate; it was just a matter of whether the end would be quick or drawn out. The French women cried and asked for mercy from the hard-eyed fighters, but their pleas fell on deaf ears.

The group was herded over to the Gazogene lorry where two muscular fighters grabbed each prisoner by the arms and lifted them onto its flatbed. With their hands tied behind their backs, the prisoners would not have been able to climb up by themselves. Another armed fighter took a position on the cab of the vehicle, ready to fire down on anyone foolish enough to try to escape.

Within minutes the vehicles from the prison drove up. LeGrand jumped off the half-track and was immediately surrounded by half a dozen agitated Maquisards, all talking at once and pointing to the German officers on the truck.

"Be quiet," he declared, trying to make sense of what they were saying. That got their attention.

One spoke up. "We've captured the murderer who killed our women and children."

LeGrand's face turned red with anger. "Get him off the truck!" he roared.

In an attempt to shield himself, Krause pushed into the middle of the prisoners. They wanted nothing to do with him and forced him to the rear of the vehicle, where a brawny Maquisard grabbed him around the waist and pulled him down. Krause lay cringing on the pavement as LeGrand stood over him, his pistol raised.

"Get up," he demanded, "or I'll shoot you where you lay!" The terrified man slowly rose to his feet. "This is for the people in Oradour-sur-Glane," LeGrand said venomously, and shot him in the stomach, again and again, being careful to avoid killing him outright. Kraus screamed and collapsed. "Let him suffer and die, slowly," LeGrand declared.

The two Jeds witnessed the retribution and did not feel one ounce of pity for the Nazi bastard. They knew he would die in agony, but in their minds it was still not enough for what he had done. Hopefully he would rot in hell!

Cain ordered the convoy to take off, hoping to escape the city before the Germans mounted an effective response to the prison break. Krause was left crying for help on the side of the road.

The convoy reached the city's outskirts without challenge, but there was still the roadblock to deal with. In an attempt to deceive the soldiers, Cain mounted a machine gun over the cab of the captured half-track and manned it with a fighter dressed in a German uniform. It was not to be; the Germans had been warned by *Funkgerät*—radio device—and were ready.

The convoy were speeding along the tree-lined roadway, when suddenly bullets ricocheted off the armor plate of the half-track, making a sharp crack as they passed. Sparks marked their impact on the metal. Henry, the veteran, marked the location of the automatic weapon by its sound.

"It's in the tree line by the bend in the road," he shouted. The fighter on the cab opened fire, spraying the wood line.

"Drive through the ambush," Cain bellowed to Andre. "Don't stop!"

Stepping on the gas, Andre headed straight for the German position, bullets ricocheting off the sloping frontal armor. One struck the half-track gunner, flinging him off the cab into the troop compartment. It was now a contest between the German machine-gun crew and the armored vehicle. There could only be one outcome, and it happened quickly. The 8-ton vehicle crashed through the sparse foliage and crushed the three-man crew before they could escape.

"Gutsy play," Henry remarked, looking at their remains. The half-track pulled back on the road, and the convoy continued its road march to the Maquis base camp.

La Ferme d'Ambel, Maquis du Vercors Base Camp, Massif du Vercors, 1530, 15 October 1942—Immediately after reaching the base camp, LeGrand sent for a doctor in Grenoble, who had a pass which allowed him to travel freely. The man arrived a few hours later and brought word about the reaction to the prison break. The furious Germans had set up dozens of roadblocks and were scouring the countryside for the escaped prisoners. They promised retribution if the perpetrators were not turned in and had taken influential hostages, including several local mayors.

After passing on the information, the doctor examined Josephine. Afterwards, he privately told Cain and Henry that she needed far more medical treatment than he could provide, and because of the increased security, it would be impossible to treat her in any local facility. The Jeds decided that she had to be evacuated. Cain set up the Jed Set and sent a message requesting a supply drop and an emergency medical evacuation, as well as a replacement radio operator. He also gave the location of the drop zone which they used as a secure landing area. The message was acknowledged and Cain was told to stand by.

Special Operations Executive, Norgeby House, Room 52 (Signals Section), 83 Baker Street, London, 1539, 15 October 1942—As soon as Vera Atkins reviewed Cain's message she rang up the Special Duties Squadron. The duty officer assured her that an evacuation flight would be scheduled immediately, and he would call her back with the flight schedule.

Twenty minutes later Vera received the schedule and relayed it to F Section for transmission. The pickup was scheduled for the following evening—one of the last full moon periods of the month.

———✦———

Special Duties Squadron, A Flight No. 161 (Special Duties) Squadron, RAF Tangmere, 1600 16 October 1942—Flying Officer Hugh Totenberg sat at a table in the operations room of "The Cottage"—a small two-story house located just inside the main gate of Tangmere RAF station in West Sussex—absorbed in working out a flight plan for the evening's mission to evacuate an injured Jedburgh and insertion of a relief agent onto a high mountain pasture known as the Darbonouse. He was working from up-to-date information supplied by agents on the ground in France and incorporated in the Air Transport Form he had just received. The ATF contained a detailed description of the landing field, including the location of any obstacles that might hinder the operation; dimensions of the field; time of pickup; the Morse code recognition signals; and the topographic references that would help him locate the site.

A high-resolution photograph of the landing field lay open on the table in front of him, showing a large, rolling pastoral stretch of countryside. It lay a few hundred yards to the north at the end of a semi-sunken track with dense woods to the west and a bocage of thick bushes and low scrub to the east. It was about 900 yards long and half as wide and seemed free of any obstacles that could pose a problem.

The field was tight, but the photo interpreters had noted that it sloped from north to south. Totenberg planned to land in the southern end of the field, using the slight upward grade to slow the plane enough to keep him out of the sprawling patchwork of rambling woods and brakes to the north of the landing field. The downward angle would also aid him in taking off. All in all, it seemed to be a satisfactory landing site, if the weather would cooperate. Several recent flights had been cancelled because of heavy fog.

After familiarizing himself with the details, he started working on the flight plan. He marked out the flight route on his 1:500,000 map and then carefully cut it into strips so that his flight path was in the middle of the strip with about 50 miles showing on either side. He folded the finished product so he could hold it in one hand and study two strips while flying. The last two strips were twice the scale (1:250,000) to provide more detail as he approached the objective.

Satisfied with the preliminary planning, Totenberg sat back in his chair and carefully reviewed each facet of the mission, as was his habit. He was a careful man, his squadron mates describing him as "meticulous to a fault." But he was still flying while others were not. The flights called for a high degree of skill, courage, and initiative. He had to map-read his way by the light of the moon and make a landing on a field he had never seen before, while being guided by hand-torches manipulated by partisans. And that was the reason he had been assigned this difficult mission.

The flight to evacuate the agent was deep in France, at the extreme range of his Lysander, which would mean a lengthy exposure to German night fighters and antiaircraft batteries. His only defense was his expertise and the plane's maneuverability. Having considered the risk, the squadron commander had picked Totenberg because of his experience with similar undertakings. He knew Totenberg would need all his flying skills to carry out this assignment.

Finished with the planning, Totenberg went across the hall to the dining room where his passenger was just finishing dinner. The young man rose and stuck out his hand.

"Sir, I'm Robert," he offered calmly.

An American, Totenberg thought to himself. *And a big one at that; well over 6 feet tall, broad shoulders and chest, and large hands and thick wrists. I certainly wouldn't want to get on his bad side.*

The two men briefly chatted until a flight sergeant stuck his head in the room. "Time, gentlemen," he said cheerfully. They picked up their carry-ons and went outside. A weapons carrier took them to the remote dispersal site, where a high-winged Westland Lysander monoplane, affectionately called a "Lizzie," was waiting. Totenberg performed a "walk-around" of the matte black-painted aircraft, looking for any obvious signs that the plane was not ready for flight. He carefully inspected the 150-gallon external fuel tank that was suspended under the fuselage. It extended the aircraft's range to about 600 miles in each direction, or eight- or nine-hours' flight time. Satisfied that everything looked in order, he signed off on the acceptance form, signifying he was now responsible for the Lysander. Meanwhile, a ground crewman fitted Robert's parachute harness and showed him how to clip the reserve chute onto his chest.

Robert used a permanently attached port-side steel ladder to climb into the rear cockpit. He stowed his carry-on under the wooden seat and strapped himself in. The ground crewman plugged his helmet into the intercom system and showed him how to switch his microphone on and off.

Totenberg placed his escape kit containing a wad of French money, a map of France printed on silk, a compass, fishing hook and line, and some concentrated food tablets into the starter handle locker. He then slipped his feet into a series of toeholds on the port side of the fuselage and climbed up to the cockpit. He settled into his seat, slid the canopy shut, and performed all his pre-flight checks. Finding everything in "green," he primed the engine and started it up. He waved the chocks away, taxied onto the grass runway, opened the throttle, and took off, heading over the English Channel toward the rendezvous.

The Darbonouse, High Mountain Pasture, Massif du Vercors, 2200, 16 October—Two hours before the scheduled arrival of the Lysander, the reception committee made its way to the landing site on foot by the light of the full moon. Josephine was carried on a stretcher, sedated, and wrapped in blankets. A six-man security detachment, armed with Tommy guns and hand grenades, surrounded the site in case the Germans tried to interfere with the evacuation. Nothing was left to chance.

Cain gave three men handheld red-lensed electric torches and had them stake out a flarepath 150 yards long in the shape of an inverted "L," which the pilot would use for landing. He instructed them that when he spotted the Lysander approaching the landing site, he would flash the agreed-upon letter in Morse code. The pilot would acknowledge the signal with his own light, then Cain would have the three men on the ground switch on their lights, forming the flarepath.

With everyone briefed and deployed, all the reception committee had to do was wait, which was often the hardest part. To help pass the time, they stood around talking and smoking vile-tasting French Gauloises cigarettes, with one thought weighing on everyone's mind: *Will the aircraft show up?*

Westland Lysander, 0015, 17 October 1942—Totenberg held the 1:250,000 strip map in his hand and compared it with the ground he was flying over. He estimated that the landing site should be coming up very soon, if his dead reckoning was accurate. Trying to find a spot on the ground using just a map, compass, and the light of the moon, while flying at low altitude, was devilishly difficult.

Suddenly, he spotted a flicker of light off the nose of the Lysander. It was a letter in Morse code. "That's it," he mumbled to himself, "the signal!" Relief washed over him as he flashed the recognition signal using his downward-pointing Morse code lamp. After a few seconds, three lights came on, indicating the flarepath.

Totenberg reduced speed and altitude and flew along the base of the "L" to check for obstacles. Satisfied that the landing site was clear, he lined up on the south end of the field and started a gentle descent. He reduced speed to 70mph with slats out, deployed the flaps, and floated to the ground close to the third light. He put on the brakes, made a U-turn, and taxied back to the first light where the reception committee waited. He didn't shut down and made ready to take off, aiming to spend as little time as possible on the ground.

Almost before the aircraft had stopped moving, the stretcher-bearers carried Josephine to the aircraft, hurriedly removing the blankets as they struggled to hoist her up to the rear canopy. Robert finally leaned down and took her under the arms. Through brute strength, and a push from Henry, he managed to lift her into the rear cockpit. Even though she was sedated, the rough handling brought out cries of pain. Robert strapped her in, which played havoc with her broken ribs. There was no thought of putting her in a parachute harness.

Robert climbed out of the cockpit, closed the canopy, and gave Totenberg a thumbs up. The aircraft started rolling forward, and in less than 150 yards it took to the air. Total elapsed time on the ground—seven minutes.

25

La Ferme d'Ambel, Maquis du Vercors Base Camp, Massif du Vercors, 0630, 18 October 1942—Early the next morning the leadership of the Vercors Maquis—LeGrand, Alphonse, and Jean—met with Cain, Henry, and Robert in the kitchen of the farmhouse to plan attacks on the Germans. The highly successful prison break had brought dozens of new men into the fold, and LeGrand was anxious to launch attacks by capitalizing on the excitement and patriotic fervor it had created.

"The lack of weapons and ammunition remains a major stumbling block to effective action," he emphasized.

Commandant Alphonse echoed his comment. "The Maquisards in my sector are anxious to take action, but we need weapons," he stressed.

Cain listened intently; this thirst for action was just what he was looking for. He could now confidently report that it was time to arm the Vercors Maquis. He composed a message requesting a drop of arms and ammunition, including 1,000 pounds of C-2 plastic explosives, and told Robert to send it to London.

Cain was in the farmhouse the next morning talking with Henry when Robert burst into the room, calling out excitedly, "It's on, It's on!"

"What's on?" Cain asked, taken aback by Robert's excitement. "The arms drop is scheduled for tomorrow night!"

———✦———

857th Bombardment Squadron/801st Bombardment Group (Provisional), Massif du Vercors, Operation *Carpetbagger*, 1400, 19 October 1942—The ground crew finished the last-minute maintenance on one of the squadron's specially modified B24D heavy bombers, nicknamed "Supply Store," when the loads started coming in by truck from Area H, the OSS logistics base at Holmewood, England. The trucks were loaded with 30 containers and packages crammed with weapons, ammunition, explosives, rations, and anything else the Jed teams wanted or needed. There were two types of containers, "C" and "H." The standard load for an "H" container was five Sten guns with 15 magazines, 1,500 rounds of 9mm ammunition, five pistols with 250 rounds of ammunition, 52 grenades, and 18 pounds of explosives. The weight of this container was 281 pounds. In one standard load, a "C" could hold two British Bren light machine guns complete with 16 magazines and 2,000 rounds of .303 ammunition, weighing 300 pounds.

Supply Store's crew supervised the loading, and once they were finished they waited until well after dark. Then the "Liberator" four-engine aircraft took off on its mission, crossing the English Channel at 2,000 feet to avoid German coastal radar, then up to 4,000 feet over the French coast to stay clear of the coastal defense machine guns. After safely passing over the coast, Supply Store immediately dropped down to between four and five hundred feet to make navigation easier. It also kept the German night fighters from attacking from below, forcing them to attack from above where the B24D could bring its two top turret guns to bear. At one point, Supply Store experienced light flak on the way to the target, but it was ineffective.

At 40 miles from the drop zone, the B24D's "Rebecca" transceiver and antenna system picked up a signal from the Jedburghs' ground-based transponder, nicknamed Eureka. The signal indicated the aircraft was slightly off-course. The navigator gave a correction to the pilot who initiated the course change to home in on the signal. At 2 miles, the pilot visually sighted the drop zone.

<hr />

The Darbonouse, High Mountain Pasture, Massif du Vercors, 0100, 20 October 1942—In the distance, LeGrand heard the unmistakable sound of aircraft engines. "They're here. Get ready!" he shouted, and ordered his men to display the glide path. He aimed his light toward the sound and flashed the code letter. An answering light flashed back the same code. The engine noises grew louder.

The pilot spotted the lights of the reception committee and approached upwind of the drop zone for a straight-in run on the target. He reduced the throttle, lowered the landing gear, and extended the wings to half flaps, to slow the aircraft to between 120 and 130 miles per hour. The slower speed was near the stall speed of the B24D, but it reduced the opening shock of the parachutes and lessened the chance of damage to the containers' contents.

As soon as the pilot lined up on the target lights, he lost sight of them under the nose of the aircraft, and the bombardier riding in the glassed-in nose had to guide him into the release position. The plane leveled off at 600 feet, and when it reached the container release point, they were salvoed all in one pass over the target. With the drop completed, the pilot raised the landing gear, moved the throttles to maximum power, and started a gentle climbing turn to the right and headed for home. His tail gunner reported that all the parachutes had opened.

To protect themselves from the rain of bundles descending on the drop zone, the reception committee took cover in the tree line. The moon's luminosity revealed the blossoming parachutes, making them look like giant mushrooms sprouting from the B24D. A cheer went up from the overjoyed Maquisards. It was all they could do to keep from running onto the drop zone. Fortunately, they didn't; several bundles separated from their parachutes and plunged downward at speed, leaving a deep hole in the ground—the impact certainly could have killed a man.

As the last bundle hit the ground, the Maquisards swarmed onto the drop zone and started collecting the containers and loading them on the Gazogene logging trucks. In a bit of irony, the stolen German trucks were used to whisk the British weaponry to a barn where it was hidden under mounds of hay and guarded by a squad of Maquis. Within days the weapons and ammunition would be distributed.

Cain found it hard to keep the Maquis from immediately attacking any German they saw. He cautioned patience and development of a plan to hit the Nazi transportation and communications network. At the mention of transportation, Commandant Jean provided information that he had received from one of his sources: the Germans were using the Valence–Moirans railroad, a major transportation hub between Valence and Grenoble, to transport a large number of troops within the next two days.

———————+———————

Valence–Moirans Railroad, 0445, 21 October 1942—The Maquis leaders discussed and approved an operation to derail the train. LeGrand thought a successful attack would raise morale and bring in new recruits. It was decided that their first foray would be led by

Cain and LeGrand. Commandant Jean volunteered to be the guide, as he was intimately familiar with the area.

Just before dawn, a ten-man raiding party climbed aboard the captured German half-track and set out on their mission. They believed the half-track would enable them to get by any roadblocks they encountered, particularly since the entire party wore German uniforms and several of them could speak German like a native.

They traveled on secondary roads to avoid traffic and made good time, until they reached the crossroads leading to Vassieux-en-Vercors. A German motorcycle with a machine-gun-mounted sidecar came barreling around the corner, barely missing the half-track but careening into a ditch on the side of the road. The driver flew over the handlebars and the machine gunner ended up tangled in the banged-up wreckage. Both men were knocked unconscious and lay concealed in the waist-high grass.

It all happened quickly, before the raiders could react … and then, vehicle headlights appeared in the distance.

"Back! Back!" Cain shouted. The frantic driver tried to shift into reverse, but in his haste and unfamiliarity with the vehicle, all he did was grind the gears. Finally, he jammed the vehicle into reverse and backed it into the secondary growth that lined the road—just in time. Four trucks loaded with German troops sped past at high speed, oblivious to the men in the ditch.

"I'll take care of them," one of the Maquisards threatened and started to jump off the half-track.

Cain grabbed his shoulder. "Leave them," he said. "If you kill them, their buddies will start looking for us."

The raiders kept a wary eye out for other vehicles, but the road remained clear. An hour later they spotted the railroad line in the dim light and followed it to the stationmaster's outbuilding. Brazenly, the driver pulled up in front of the darkened building. Cain and

LeGrand slipped through the unlocked door, while the other raiders cut the telephone line and provided security.

The stationmaster must have been a late sleeper, for within a couple of minutes, an old man wearing a night shirt stumbled down the stairs.

"What are you doing here?" he demanded nervously, staring wide-eyed at the two heavily armed strangers.

"We're patriots," LeGrand answered, "and we're here to derail the troop train. Will you help us?"

The old man paled, opened and closed his mouth a time or two, and finally blurted out, "*Vive la France!*" He stepped forward and grabbed LeGrand's hands, repeating "*Vive la France!*" several times, as tears rolled happily down his cheeks.

Cain took in the scene. "I guess we've got a helper," he mumbled to himself.

LeGrand reminded the stationmaster that if he stayed, the Germans would undoubtedly kill him and invited him to join the Maquis.

"I'll get my things," the old man volunteered.

The stationmaster confirmed that a troop train was scheduled to come through within a couple of hours. "That gives us time," Cain said. "But just in case, we'd better get to it." He gathered the demolition crew and their explosives and hiked along the tracks until he came to a sharp curve on a downward grade. "This is the best spot," Cain remarked. "We'll place the explosive on the outboard side of the tracks."

The men unpacked the explosive charges that perfectly fit the indentation in the steel rail. The charges had been developed by scientists at Station IX, the Special Operations Executive factory that made special weapons and equipment. The Composition C-2, a soft, moldable explosive, was easy for them to work with. They duct taped the charges in two places, 3 yards apart, on the outside of the railroad curve. After inserting the blasting caps in the charges, they strung the detonating cord from the charges to a pressure switch placed just up the track. When the train's front wheels ran over the switch, it would detonate the explosives and dislodge the rail. With the rail gone, the engine would continue forward, pulling the rest of the train down a steep slope to the bottom of a draw.

After double checking the demolitions to ensure they were laid properly, Cain signaled his men and they retraced their steps to the stationmaster's outbuilding. LeGrand met him outside. "We wrecked all the equipment inside," he said. "It'll never be used again."

Twenty minutes later, the raiders were on a hill overlooking the railroad when the seven-car troop train approached the demolition site. At first there was the faint sound of an explosion, then the locomotive failed to make the curve and plunged into the draw. Car after car followed, smashing into each other until there was a huge pile of twisted wreckage clogging the depression. The sound was overwhelming.

Cain was aghast; he never expected there would be so much destruction. The wooden cars completely disintegrated. Their steel chassis knifed through the kindling, adding to the death and devastation. Nothing moved, except the settling of the debris.

After observing for several minutes, the raiders piled into the half-track and sped away from the scene before rescuers arrived.

***

La Ferme d'Ambel, Maquis du Vercors, Massif du Vercors, 22 October 1942—Word of the Maquis involvement in the train derailment spread far and wide, and dozens of eager volunteers rushed to join the Maquis du Vercors, swelling the Resistance to over a thousand.

The word also reached the *Milice française*, who had infiltrated several of the Maquis bands and passed the information on to the Gestapo. Within days the Germans launched a series of deadly raids against known or suspected members of the Maquis. Dozens were arrested or killed based only on the statements of the *Milice*.

"The bastards," LeGrand swore. "Something has to be done to stop them." He talked it over with Cain and the two of them came up with a plan to terrorize the local thugs. They would raid the militia post of the *Franc-Garde* that was stationed near Vassieux-en-Vercors, at the base of the massif. Commandant Alphonse's former headquarters had been located in the village before the *Franc-Garde* established their militia post, and he was intimately familiar with the layout of the village.

Alphonse established contact with a villager whose sympathies lay with the Maquis and asked him to gather information about the militia. The man quickly responded that the garrison was composed of about 30 poorly armed volunteers housed in a building in the middle of town. He described them as bullies who strutted around town terrorizing the locals. It was well known that many of them were former convicts who had only volunteered for the *Garde* to get out of jail. On most nights their officer and NCOs were in the local bar, drunk, or often *enchaîné* (shacked up) with the local collaboration *horizontale*. There was a nightly patrol but in name only; the men were more interested in being comfortable than walking around in the dark.

Alphonse sketched a diagram of the *Franc-Garde* headquarters, the bar, and the surrounding streets to use for planning the strike. The objective was a hit-and-run raid and prisoner snatch to terrify and bring a halt to the *Garde's* traitorous activities. The leaders of the raid, Cain and LeGrand, decided to keep the number of raiders to a minimum—only 16 of the most experienced and reliable men, which they split into two sections: a prisoner snatch section (LeGrand) and an attack by fire section (Cain).

The Maquis parked their captured German truck on the outskirts of Vassieux-en-Vercors just after 0130. The drive down the mountain had taken two hours, which put them in position just at the time when the members of the *Garde* would be at their most vulnerable—sound asleep.

The two sections split up. Cain led his men along the darkened streets toward the *Garde* billet, while Hervieux's section surrounded the bar, where the sympathetic owner let the drunken *Garde* officer sleep it off. The two NCOs had rooms on the second floor where they "entertained" various available women.

Prisoner Snatch, 0200, 23 October 1942—At LeGrand's signal, his men broke through the front and back doors. They found the *Garde* officer passed out, slumped over a table strewn with empty bottles and puddles of spilled beer. While the officer was being tied up, LeGrand and three men rushed up the stairs and found themselves in a long hallway lined with closed doors. They kicked one in. LeGrand was about to bust in the second door when it suddenly flung open. A half-dressed *Garde* threw himself on the Maquis chief. The unexpected attack caught LeGrand off-balance, and he crashed to the floor underneath his assailant. The goon pinned LeGrand's arms with his knees and got him in a choke hold, but only for a brief moment before a Maquisard bashed him over the head with the muzzle of his Sten gun.

"Thank you, Marcel," Hervieux declared, as he got shakily to his feet. "I'm afraid *le bâtard* got the best of me."

At that moment, a semi-dressed woman ran screaming out of the room, heading toward the stairs. Marcel knocked her to the floor. "*Pouffiasse!*" he snarled. "Get up, floozie!" The woman swore and kicked, but her efforts were futile. Marcel hauled her up, twisted her arms behind her back, and tied them, none too gently.

The second *Garde* NCO was frog-marched roughly out of a room, his face blood-smeared. "I caught him trying to escape through a window," his captor declared, "and he didn't want to come peacefully." The *Garde*'s "girlfriend" was hauled out of the same room, her hands tied behind her back.

After making sure all the other rooms were vacant, the Maquisards herded the captives to the main floor, where the men's hands were tied securely behind their backs.

"Take them to the rendezvous," LeGrand ordered, and then turned to the women. "You have collaborated with the enemy," he declared. "Patriotic Frenchmen have been imprisoned and killed, and for that there is no forgiveness."

The distraught women were forced to sit down. A Maquisard produced a pair of scissors and proceeded to cut off their hair as a symbol of their shame. "Let everyone know that those who help the Nazis will suffer the same fate ... or worse," LeGrand thundered. "This punishment is not just for sleeping with the *Milice* but for adultery to your country!" In the process of trying to cut their hair as close to the scalp as possible, the "barber" nicked it. Thin rivulets of blood ran down the sides of their crudely shaved heads. Within minutes, piles of hair littered the floor. The men turned away from the women's grisly humiliation, leaving them alone in their misery.

The sudden rattle of automatic weapons fire caught LeGrand's attention.

"Cain's men are attacking the *Garde*," he exclaimed.

Attack by Fire, 0220, 23 October 1942—Cain split his section. Four men went around to the back of the *Franc-Garde*'s headquarters to cover the rear entrance. They were given 20 minutes to get in position. The other section broke into the empty building across the street and took up firing positions on the second floor facing the headquarters, providing an excellent vantage point to observe the headquarters and a good field of fire. They watched the lone *Milice* stand guard outside the front entrance. It was easy to see that he was a guard in name only. He carried an obsolete Berthier 8mm bolt-action carbine carelessly slung over his shoulder. At times he leaned against the door frame smoking a cigarette, seemingly oblivious to what was going on around him.

Cain checked his watch; the men in the rear should be in position. "Stand by," he warned his men. "Fire!" The initial burst of fire cut down the guard and tore up the front of the station, shattering windows and flinging wood fragments into the air. A hurricane of 9mm bullets tore through the interior rooms. Those unfortunates who leaped out of bed were killed or wounded. Most of the men were simply too shocked and traumatized to do anything but hug the floor, pinned down by the storm of bullets.

After emptying two magazines, the Maquisards broke off the attack and headed for the rendezvous. As they left the building, LeGrand left behind written warnings that if the *Garde* continued to collaborate with the Germans, they could expect similar attacks.

Within ten minutes everyone had been accounted for, and the truck, with its load of 16 Maquis, Cain and LeGrand, and three prisoners, headed for the massif. There was no pursuit.

26

La Ferme d'Ambel, Maquis du Vercors, Massif du Vercors, Retribution, 1200, 25 October 1942—Two days after his return to the farm, LeGrand convened a kangaroo court to try the three *Franc-Garde Milice* for "crimes against the French people." The men were tried in a large field before five hardened members of the Maquis chosen to act as judges. A large crowd of Maquisards watched silently as the three battered men were dragged before the court. Some rough justice had already been meted out ... but more was yet to come. Several witnesses were called upon to testify. Their description of what the three men had done elicited enraged howls from the armed crowd. LeGrand was able to restore some measure of order, but it was obvious that revenge was high in everybody's mind. These men had not only collaborated with the Nazis—but worse, had acted in cooperation with the Gestapo by denouncing and killing other Frenchmen. The verdict came quickly—they were to be shot by firing squad.

Cain and Henry watched from a distance. They had been ordered not to interfere in local affairs and could not intercede even if they wanted to. LeGrand told them in no uncertain terms that the trial was strictly a Maquis affair. But still, the fast court martial and firing squad gave them pause.

The three were marched to the edge of the field and tied to sturdy poles that had been erected earlier that morning. The Jeds could not help but note that the "court's" sentence had been preordained. The two *Garde* NCOs faced the six members of the firing squad with stoicism and refused to be blindfolded, but the officer cried out for mercy. His cries went unheeded, and the rifles barked. LeGrand walked behind each body and delivered the coup de grace with his pistol. Afterward the remains were taken deep into the woods and buried in unmarked graves.

That night, LeGrand sent three Maquis teams against the major rail lines again. They reported back the next morning. One team was able to place their explosives without interference and dislodge over 50 yards of rail. The other two teams couldn't even get close to the track because of increased German foot patrols. It was obvious that the Germans were on high alert and were willing to commit a large number of men to protect their major rail line. In addition, scouts reported that their engineers were getting better at repairing damaged tracks quickly. They needed a different tactic.

Cain turned to the latest volunteer, the stationmaster, for help. "Tell me about the railroad bridge between your station and Vassieux-en-Vercors; it's our next target."

Recognition registered in the older man's eyes. "Perfect," he exclaimed and added that the bridge was a chokepoint. It had never been widened to accommodate the addition of new rail lines. The line was suffering the effects of German neglect.

A complicated routing schedule had been devised to ensure that trains did not all arrive at the same time and create a backlog as they waited for their turn to cross. The bridge was continually used by German supply trains. If it was damaged or destroyed, it would paralyze the entire line and cause the Germans an immense amount of disruption.

The stationmaster volunteered to accompany the raiders. Cain thanked him but said he was too valuable in the

Résistance-Fer—Railway Resistance—the organization composed of railroad workers and *cheminots*—engineers. The stationmaster had been instrumental in encouraging the organization to cooperate closely with the Maquis in sabotaging the *Société nationale des chemins de fer française*, France's national state-owned railway.

The *cheminots* succeeded in blowing up several trains, including baggage and transport cars carrying German soldiers, inflicting heavy losses. Over the coming days and weeks, they regularly dynamited dozens of tracks in several important military sectors, unbolted strips of track, and caused derailments by throwing the wrong switch. One, a reserve crew train officer known as "Georges," successfully disabled five engines before being caught and shot by the vengeful Gestapo. Their activities became so pervasive that the Germans were forced to send in a large contingent of their own railroad workers to keep an eye on the French.

The Railroad Bridge, 0130, 26 October 1942—Cain and six hand-picked Maquis volunteers silently picked their way through the undergrowth on the south side of the railroad bridge. Ahead of them stood a 200-yard-long iron girder bridge spanning a deep ravine. The local Maquis reported that a foot patrol crossed from one end of the bridge to the other during the hours of darkness. However, the waning moon's weak light cast shadows on the superstructure, making it difficult to spot movement on the walkway.

Cain signaled a halt. His men sank down in the undergrowth, watching and waiting. They were keyed up and jumpy; it was easy for the untrained Resistance fighters to imagine Nazi supermen hiding in the shadows. The night sounds seemed magnified as they strained to hear something out of the ordinary—a whisper, a footstep, the snap of a twig.

Cain motioned them forward. The ominous shape of a bunker loomed out of the darkness. They could hear muffled voices. Without warning a door opened, illuminating the entranceway and silhouetting two Germans emerging from inside. The Maquisards sank deeper into the shadows and held their breath while the Germans talked and shared a cigarette in front of the open door. Cain carefully pulled the pin from a Mills bomb and lobbed it toward the entranceway. His throw was perfect. The 22-ounce serrated cast-iron hand grenade sailed into the bunker and bounced on the floor with a loud metallic clunk. "*Was ist das?*" someone inside shouted. The grenade's 70 grams of TNT exploded, sending lethal shards of iron scything through the interior of the bunker and killing the four men inside.

The two Germans outside spotted Cain's movement and started to unsling their rifles, but it was too late. A Maquisard loosed an entire magazine of 9mm bullets from his Sten gun, killing them instantly.

Cain jumped to his feet and directed the Maquisards to follow him onto the bridge deck. Time was of the essence. They had to place the explosives and blow the bridge before German reinforcements arrived. He had his men lay out the 2-pound blocks of C-2 high explosives and start molding it into long strips, 3 inches wide and 2 inches thick. He planned to place the strips on the outboard plate girder, which supported the weight of the bridge on that side. Looking at the 40-pound mound of plastic explosives, Cain thought it would be more than enough to bring down the bridge or at least put it out of commission for some time.

Cain tied a rope around his chest and had the Maquisards lower him over the side of the bridge, leaving him dangling 30 feet over the ravine's rushing water. His hands were free to attach the C-2. He braced his feet against the lower flange and leaned back, calling to mind the rappelling class at the commando training center.

The Maquisard passed him strip after strip of C-2 until he had a string of explosive that ran the entire width of the girder. He inserted a blasting cap into the explosive, checked to see if everything was ready, and had his men haul him up.

The team wasted little time in finding shelter, where Cain attached the wires from the blasting cap to the "Hell Box," or blasting machine. As soon as everyone was under cover, Cain gave a twist to the handle, sending an electric charge through the wire to the blasting cap. The cap exploded, setting off the 40 pounds of C-2. The terrific explosion blew a large piece of the girder hurtling high into the air and falling within feet of the huddled team. When the dust and smoke cleared, Cain could see that the bridge was still standing, but there was a large section of the plate girder completely missing, as well as much of the deck. The bridge superstructure itself was perilously close to toppling into the ravine. In Cain's estimation, it would be impossible to repair unless the structure was first torn down and a new bridge built. The Maquisards were exhilarated, jumping up and down in celebration, until Cain brought them back to earth and reminded them they were in great danger and had to leave immediately.

———

La Ferme d'Ambel, Maquis du Vercors, Massif du Vercors, 0900, 26 October 1942—There was great excitement at the farm upon the team's return. Against the advice of the Jeds, LeGrand insisted on a celebration. "We don't want to attract too much attention," they urged. However, he was dead set on trumpeting their successes: a train derailment, an important bridge heavily damaged, railroad tracks cut, and the communication system disrupted throughout the area. He sent messengers throughout the Vercors informing the various Maquis groups, "We are fighting back against the Nazis."

Cain wrote a message on his one-time pad spelling out the Maquis Vercors' success and directed Robert to send it to head-quarters. Robert waited until his scheduled report time and quickly established contact with Grendon Hall. He was concerned with the message length, because it required him to be on the air longer than usual. Nevertheless, he set up the Jed Set, and right on time he started sending the message. Robert was known to the girls at the intercept station as a "ham fisted" operator because he always seemed to be beating the telegraph key rather than lightly tapping it. Nevertheless, his messages were, for the most part, readable and free of mistakes.

Grendon Hall acknowledged receipt of Robert's message and told him to stand by for traffic. Seconds later he picked up their signal and copied the short message, which he decoded and passed to Cain. The message notified the Jeds of a parachute drop the following night.

Unknown to Robert at the time, a German long-range D/F counterintelligence radio intercept station picked up his signals and plotted them for follow up by local Gonio radio-detector vehicles (*voitures de radiogonio*). The plots, which did not pinpoint the exact location, were good enough to provide an approximate position. The information was forwarded to a radio intercept company attached to the 157th Reserve Division.

---

609 *Feldgendarmerie* **Quimperlé, 1000, 26 October 1942**—When the report of the destruction of the railroad bridge reached the commanding general of the 157th Reserve Division, he went through the roof and demanded an immediate operation to locate and destroy those responsible for the attack. The commander of the 609th *Feldgendarmerie* Quimperlé, *Oberleutnant* Hans Snell, was ordered to hunt down and kill the saboteurs without mercy.

The 27 non-commissioned officers and men of the 609th specialized in combating Allied special forces and Maquis groups. The unit had a brutal reputation for showing no mercy with those it captured. The *Feldgendarmerie* was backed up by the national police, a composite force of the *Groupes mobiles de reserve* (GMR, mobile reserve groups), and the *Gestapo française*, a unit comprised of convicted criminals.

Snell immediately began a campaign of intimidation and reprisal by rounding up 40 men from the local villages surrounding the bridge site and machine gunning them in a field facing the bridge. He sent patrols into one of the villages where the *Gestapo française* broke into houses and shot down a dozen men in front of their families. Others were hung from lampposts. Their actions terrorized the locals but they also enraged the Maquis du Vercors, who increased their attacks on the communications and transportation infrastructure and opened assaults on individual German soldiers and collaborators. In the countryside, German patrols and couriers were attacked, supply convoys ambushed, buildings blown up, informants and collaborators assassinated.

In one case, a German posing as a deserter was brought to a Resistance group by a local man who was well known to them. After interrogation, the German admitted he had been sent to infiltrate the group and report on their location and morale. He had used the collaborator to help with his mission. After a summary trial, both men were shot.

Snell developed an army of civilian informers, who were paid for results. A French couple in Grenoble provided information on the local Resistance to the Gestapo who, assisted by the *Milice*, gutted the organization. A surviving member of the Resistance was able to catch the couple walking home after dark and shot them. He pinned a note on the man's shirt: "Death to all collaborators."

The Germans also offered large rewards for information, but it was not enough because of the Maquis threat. They tried another tack by taking hostages and offering to return them unharmed if they provided the names of Maquisards and locations of their hideouts.

The Maquis became bolder, even as the German onslaught continued. A force of two dozen Maquisards attacked a Group Mobile Reserve command post and managed to capture it, along with several prisoners, including the commander. In the process of disarming them, the GMR commander drew a concealed pistol and killed the Maquis leader. He was immediately cut down along with several of the prisoners. The rest were taken back to La Ferme d'Ambel.

27

Free Republic of the Vercors, 20 November 1942—Thousands of young, military-aged men flooded into the massif to escape the Vichy government's increase in the *Service du travail obligatoire* (Compulsory Work Service) quotas. The men, called *réfractaires*—those refusing to be drafted for compulsory labor—would rather take their chances on the mountain than be deported to Germany and be forced to work as slave labor. They were placed in nine camps. "I believe Vichy is doing a better job of recruiting for the Maquis than we could," Cain remarked to LeGrand. The Massif du Vercors plateau had become the center of resistance in southeast France.

Cain learned that LeGrand was being pressured by the area's professional military commanders to make the Vercors into a "Resistance redoubt"—a geographic fortress behind the German lines from which to launch attacks on their transportation and communication infrastructure. LeGrand favored a continuation of hit-and-run guerrilla tactics and resisted the pressure. However, it became too great when the British and Americans promised parachute reinforcements if and when there was a German attack. The illusion that untrained men, with little help, could take on battle-hardened German troops took hold with the leaders of the Maquis, and they decided to declare the entire plateau the Free Republic of the Vercors.

A ceremony was conducted in the village of Saint-Martin. Armed Maquisards standing in ragged ranks lined the tiny square. In the center stood the Commissioner of the Republic, De Gaulle's representative. Fascinated onlookers watched as the flag of the new Republic—a French tricolor emblazoned with the Croix of Lorraine with a letter V, signifying Vercors, at its base—was raised. The Maquisards were ordered to present arms and the "Marseillaise" was played. Afterward, the Commissioner stepped forward, and with great dignity, read the proclamation declaring the founding of the Free Republic of Vercors—the first independent territory in France since the beginning of the German occupation in 1940. After the ceremony, special printed notices were posted in public places throughout the plateau: "Starting from this day, the decrees of Vichy are abolished and all the laws of the republic have been restored … Long live the French Republic. Long live France." Several villages on the plateau flew the new flag.

The Jeds tried to talk LeGrand out of the declaration. "Your Maquisards are getting very good at hit and run, and sabotage," Cain pointed out, "but standing and fighting the Nazis in a pitched battle is an entirely different story."

"For one thing," Henry added, "you don't have heavy weapons. The Germans will hit you with artillery, mortars, and heavy machine guns."

LeGrand nodded in agreement. "I know," he replied, "but the Maquisards are bored with training and planning. They are demanding action." Cain could see that LeGrand had made up his mind and it was senseless to argue with him.

Operation *Bettina*, 1 December 1942—It didn't take long before the proclamation notices fell into the hands of the Germans. Not surprisingly, they were furious and refused to tolerate a French republic in their backyard. The Nazi commander for the south of France issued a directive: "The 157th Reserve Division will immediately take all steps to eliminate the concentration of powerful enemy forces in the Vercors area." *Generalleutnant* Karl Pflaum of the 157th, one of the most experienced anti-partisan officers in France, was assigned the mission. He commanded over 10,000 men, including his own division, a specialized airborne unit, an armored battalion, police and security units, and a force of Red Army soldiers from the Soviet republics of the Caucasus or Central Asia taken prisoner by the Germans and formed into units known as the "Mongols." They were used to sow terror by indiscriminate killing, looting, and raping.

Pflaum's tactical plan, designated Operation *Bettina*—the largest operation conducted against the Resistance in Western Europe—included two components: encircle and cordon off the plateau in a simultaneous ground attack from four separate directions to keep the defenders from concentrating a force against one point, and an airborne assault into the heart of the plateau using glider-borne *Fallschirmjäger* (paratroopers). Their first task was to track down and annihilate resistance groups and destroy their camps; second, all captured weapons and ammunition were to be gathered in and taken away; third, all men aged 17 to 30 were to be arrested and assembled into labor squads; fourth, all buildings used by the Resistance were to be burned down; and finally, livestock was to be taken away.

Within days, the Germans started mobilizing and deploying their force, which was quickly reported to the Maquis Vercors. The Germans commenced Operation *Bettina* by encircling the plateau with infantry. At the same time, the *Geschwader Bongart*, a dedicated anti-partisan aviation unit, conducted the first airstrikes of the operation. Fourteen Italian Reggiane Re 2002 fighter-bombers dropped 500-pound bombs on four of the surrounding villages—La Chapelle, Malleval, Cognin, and Vassieux. The planes also indiscriminately strafed everything that moved, in a preview of worse atrocities to come.

The Maquis *Comité de Combat* (Fighting Committee) responded with an order for all men on the plateau between the ages of 20 and 24 to report for duty. The order was not universally popular, and some men "forgot" to report. LeGrand helped them remember by rounding up the laggards.

La Ferme d'Ambel, Maquis du Vercors, Massif du Vercors, 1 December 1942—With the Jeds' help, LeGrand set up a conventional command post at the farm. Cain suggested a traditional staff section organization—personnel, intelligence, operations and logistics/communications setup—overseen by a chief of staff. LeGrand accepted their recommendation and quickly named Cain as his operations officer. Henry was named chief of staff, because of his "warm personality," Cain declared, tongue in cheek. Former French military officers and NCOs filled the personnel, intelligence, and logistics sections. Other former military served as their assistants. Robert was designated as communications officer, as he had the Jed Set, their only link to the outside world. There were no radios for internal communications; LeGrand had to depend on runners to maintain contact with his scattered forces.

In the first hour of the German attack, LeGrand's crowded command post was a scene of frantic activity—until Henry stepped in. Standing on top of a table, he thundered, "*Tais toi*—shut up!" in his best parade ground voice. His angry shout reverberated through the room and caught everyone's attention. There was instant silence. "I will not tolerate this commotion!" he declared. Before he could say more, the outside door flew open and a teenage Maquisard burst into the room.

"The Germans are coming!" he shouted.

For an instant everyone stood frozen with shock; then it was pandemonium as everyone grabbed for weapons and started for the door. Again, Henry's bellowed command, "*Arrêtez!*" brought them up short.

"What do you mean?" he calmly asked the distraught runner. Henry's unruffled question after his outburst had a settling effect on the boy, and he remembered why he was here.

"Pierre sent me to report that hundreds of Germans are advancing on the road from Saint-Nizier."

———————

Kampfgruppe Luger, Reserve *Gebirgsjäger* Battalion 100, 1000, 1 December 1942—Major Heinz Luger's orders were to advance from the northeast along the well-maintained road from the town of Saint-Nizier and penetrate into the heart of the plateau. He didn't expect to have too much difficulty; after all, they were just terrorists. They could never stand up to his superbly trained and blooded 800-man battalion. He was looking forward to coming to grips with them after losing several men to their hit-and-run attacks. Revenge was on his mind.

Pillars of smoke marked the progress of his battalion from Grenoble. His men had taken vengeance by shooting all the men they encountered and burning every building in the vicinity of the road. Luger had done nothing to discourage them and, in fact, encouraged the destruction. *Nothing like a little cruelty to bring the swine to heel*, he believed.

Through his binoculars Luger studied the wooded ridge in front of his lead company. He didn't see any movement in the jumbled growth and ordered his men to "move out faster." His radio operator passed the order over the *Feldfunk-Sprecher*. Luger was anxious to be the first combat group into the plateau. It would look good on his record—and if truth be told, that's all he cared about, for he was a careerist and would do anything to further it.

The commanding officer of the 3rd Company, *Hauptmann* Walter Jürgen, was not in a good mood when his radio operator gave him the message. Since assuming the lead for the battalion, Luger had been on his back and it was grating on him. In his opinion, the battalion commander was a jerk; all he was interested in was himself. On several occasions, Luger had sacrificed men in order to look good. However, Jürgen knew that if he didn't follow his orders to the letter, he would be the next to be sacrificed.

The only way the 3rd Company could move faster was to disregard flank security, so Jürgen called them in. In violation of sound tactical doctrine when close to the enemy, the company reformed on the road. Luger overlooked the violation. All he was interested in was in being the first on the plateau.

Maquis Defense, Overlooking the Saint-Nizier Road, 1000, 1 December 1942—The two 150-man Maquis companies were concealed in trenches along the military crest of the ridge overlooking the Saint-Nizier Road—the Brisac Company on the right, and the Goderville Company on the left. Both company commanders were former French Army officers and experienced combat leaders. They had chosen the ground well—good fields of fire for the four Bren light machine guns and Maquis riflemen. They could sweep the road and fields on either side with lethal fire.

Although the commanders may have been experienced combat veterans, their men were hardly more than boys. Many were still in their teens and this was their first time under fire. They were quick to cover this lack of experience with bluster and boasting; however, despite the bravado, they were clearly worried about the forthcoming battle.

***

3rd Company, Battalion 100, 1000, 1 December 1942—The men of the 3rd Company were in a lighthearted mood, full of themselves after torching the terrorist homes—once they'd looted them, of course. They were old hands at pillaging, having plundered their way across France, their packs filled with stolen trinkets. Anyone who had a twinge of conscience about stealing rationalized it away: *What difference does it make? The houses are going to be burned anyway.*

It was a warm day, unusual for this time of year, the winter sun beating down. Not a cloud in the sky. Much of what they had stolen now littered the roadway behind them. *What the hell do I need this for?* several decided, growing more fatigued as the road led upward toward the plateau's high ground.

The lead platoon commander had given up trying to keep his men spread out, reasoning that it was just too damn hot and not worth the effort. He had not seen a single military-aged male in days. *The terrorists are cowards and won't stand against us,* he defended to himself. In the absence of guidance, his men started bunching up on the road. As they marched up the steep incline, the platoon commander failed to notice the line of dirt spoil running along the ridge under the trees.

Suddenly, a storm of gunfire swept the platoon. The surprise was complete; in an instant half a dozen men collapsed, wounded or dead, before instinct kicked in and they took cover. There was no one to tell the stunned survivors what to do; their negligent officer lay in the middle of the road with a bullet in his head.

Maquis Defense Position, 1000, 1 December 1942—The two Maquis company commanders couldn't believe their luck. The Germans were walking in clusters on the road. They waited until the formation was a hundred yards from their positions before giving the word to open fire. Even their untrained men could not miss. The Maquisards continued to fire long after the Germans went to ground, the temptation to shoot at live targets too strong to resist. This was their chance to hit back at the men who'd invaded their country and killed friends and neighbors. It was payback time!

Suddenly the snap of bullets caught their attention. A Maquisard abruptly pitched backward in a spray of blood and brains. The boys on either side stared in horror at the sight, traumatized by their friend's sudden death. Realization that death was at hand quickly sank in.

3rd Company, Battalion 100, 1005, 1 December 1942—Despite the initial shock of the deadly fire, the well-trained Wehrmacht infantry executed their anti-ambush drill. *Hauptmann* Jürgen ordered the 1st Platoon to lay down fire from covered positions, while he led the 2nd Platoon around the Maquis flank. "Follow me!" he shouted. Whatever deficiencies Jürgen may have had, lack of courage was not one of them. He sprang from cover and ran toward a stand of pine trees on the lower slope of the ridge, the 2nd Platoon hard at his heels. Three men fell to the fire from the ridge, but the rest made it to the shelter of the trees.

Jürgen let the men catch their breath while he looked for a way around the Maquis positions. He could not see the trenches because of the trees, but the sound of firing gave him an idea where he needed to go. "On your feet," he called out, motioning with his hand, and started moving laterally across the slope. Within a dozen meters he intersected a game trail that led upward.

———————◄|———————

La Ferme d'Ambel, Maquis du Vercors, Massif du Vercors, 1015, 1 December 1942—Henry continued to question the runner but didn't get much additional information other than there were "hundreds of Germans." Finally, exasperated by the lack of information, Cain turned to LeGrand. "I'll go see for myself," he said. "If it's as bad as the runner makes it out to be, they'll need help. I'll take the Alpine Platoon to reinforce them."

Cain set a fast pace and finally reached a point where he could plainly hear the sound of firing. *At least they haven't been overrun*, he thought to himself. "Faster," he urged his men. The rattle of gunfire grew louder. He could hear shouting, and then he spotted several Maquisard wounded clustered in an open space.

"Pierre?" he called. "Here I am!" the heavily bandaged man responded. "Thank God you're here. The Germans are trying to flank us on the left." Hearing that, Cain rushed his men forward and put them in position, tying in with the Goderville Company on the right, and extending the Maquis lines.

They had no sooner taken cover when a German officer appeared, followed by what looked like a line of soldiers. Cain quickly realized that the dense forest had forced the attackers to advance in a single file. Only the lead man could shoot, while Cain's men were spread out and everyone could blast away. "Fire!" he yelled. A deluge of bullets tore through the file of Germans, felling them before they even knew what had hit them. The officer leading them was blown away, tossed aside like a rag doll. Cain could plainly hear the thud of bullets striking flesh as one German after another fell like ten pins until there were no more in sight. "Cease fire!" Cain yelled. Suddenly the forest was deathly quiet. A thin acrid bite of burnt gunpowder hung in the air as Cain collected half a dozen Maquisards to check the bodies to ensure there were no "sleepers" waiting for a chance to shoot a careless Maquisard.

Cain warily approached the game trail, finger poised on the trigger of the Thompson submachine gun. He crouched down. The body of the German officer lay a few feet away in the underbrush. He could see the man had taken several rounds to the upper body, which left the remains pretty well chewed up. Directly behind him lay another body, and another, and several more lying on the trail or in the underbrush. He counted at least 15 corpses. He turned to the men behind him. "Search the bodies and take any documents you find, as well as any weapons or equipment that we can use."

The youngsters reluctantly moved among the dead, gingerly searching them. One boy spewed the contents of his stomach in the grass after turning a body over and discovering it had no face. No one laughed because they were all pretty queasy. Most of them had been to funerals where the deceased was carefully posed in a coffin, but this was different; the bodies were bloody, torn apart, brutally ravaged by high velocity bullets and lying in the careless positions where death had found them. Most had been cut down individually, but here and there two or three bodies fell in a pile, as if they had died trying to protect one another. The secluded forest game trail had become a charnel house.

Cain searched the officer's body, patting down the man's uniform to see if there was anything in his pockets before examining his leather map case. He found his name and photograph on an ID card that was in his left breast pocket—"Hauptmann Walter Jürgen" was

207

handwritten under a photo showing a severe-looking officer with close cropped hair and the ubiquitous dueling scar on his cheek. "You won't be dueling anymore," Cain said to himself, "you Nazi bastard!" and roughly stuffed the card back in the dead man's pocket.

The map case turned out to be a treasure trove. *Looks like this guy never threw anything away,* Cain thought. The case was stuffed with documents, but the biggest prize of all was a detailed 1:25,000 map of the plateau showing strongpoints, camps, supply dumps, roadblocks, and command posts, including LeGrand's. He also noted penciled arrows with unit symbols indicating obvious attack routes and the units involved. "Christ," he exclaimed, "the collaborators have been busy spying on us."

He stuffed the map in his pocket and went after an even bigger personal prize—the dead man's pistol, a Walther P38. He tugged the pistol belt loose from around the corpse's waist and took the weapon out of the holster. He quickly examined it. "Beautiful," he murmured, ejecting a cartridge from the chamber and trying the action. *Smooth, and not a speck of rust anywhere.* He buckled the pistol belt around his waist.

Shouts jolted him back to attention. His novice men were celebrating their victory by making a pile of weapons and equipment, ignoring the fact that a large force of Germans was only a few hundred yards away.

Kampfgruppe **Luger, 1130, 1 December 1942**—After his lead company was chewed to pieces by the small arms fire, Major Luger realized he had made a major tactical error in failing to acknowledge that the terrorists would stand and fight. Now his dead and wounded littered the landscape, and the enemy still controlled the entrance onto the plateau. He should have used his mortar platoon and supporting artillery battery to batter the terrorists before sending his men against them.

Resolved not to make the same mistake again, he summoned his mortar platoon commander and ordered him to set up his weapons in a dry stream bed and be prepared to fire on his order. Next, he had his *Vorgeschobene Beobachter* (artillery forward observer) plot the coordinates of the trench line and radio them to the 7.5cm *Gebirgsgeschütz* 36 mountain artillery four-gun battery. The battery was in direct support of Luger's *Kampfgruppe*.

As Luger's first wave of assault troops got into position, he had the mortar and artillery fire blanket the ridge with high explosive. The first round was short, so the artillery observer told the battery to add 500 yards. His estimate was right on, and he radioed the battery to "fire for effect." The rain of steel blanketed the terrorist positions. The observer saw several terrorists running from the trenches toward the safety of the forest. He adjusted the fire: "Add 500, fire for effect." The 12.7-pound high-explosive rounds landed right on top of the fleeing terrorists.

———◆———

Maquis Defense Positions, 1145, 1 December 1942—The first ranging shot hit at the base of the ridge, startling the Maquisards who had never been exposed to high-explosive artillery and mortar fire. The scream of the incoming round, followed by the deafening explosion, was completely unnerving. By contrast, the mortar fire was virtually silent. The shells made a whispering sound, which could not be heard. As the Germans adjusted their fire, the rounds kept coming closer and closer until they enveloped the trenches. Even disciplined troops lost heart under incoming fire … and the Maquisards were not in that category. At first, a couple boys jumped out of the trench and ran for safety. Then more followed, until the trickle became a flood, with many being cut down by shrapnel in their panic to escape the deadly fire. Soon the trenches were empty except for a few crumpled bodies.

Cain tried to stop the Maquisards, but blind panic had completely taken hold of them. There was nothing more he could do. He had little choice but to join the retreat. However, unlike the Maquisards, he chose to pull out when there was a cessation in the shelling. After scrambling out of the shoulder-deep trench, he sprinted 50 yards before the scream of incoming rounds sent him to the ground. Shrapnel slapped through the undergrowth. He narrowly missed being crushed by a severed tree limb. Each round felt like it was going to hit him in the back. *Got to get out of the kill zone*, he told himself. Before another volley came in, Cain jumped to his feet and dashed another 50 yards. This time the shells landed well behind him. He kept running until he felt safe.

Kampfgruppe **Luger, 1150, 1 December 1942**—Luger ordered his men forward after the artillery and mortars ceased shelling the Maquis positions. His infantry advanced to the bottom of the ridge without taking fire. They gained confidence that the terrorists had retreated and quickly scrambled up to the abandoned positions, where they found several bodies and a few abandoned weapons scattered in and around the shell-blasted trenches. In a fit of revenge, they mutilated the corpses.

Luger notified headquarters that his battalion had seized the northern entrance to the plateau. "Continue to advance and join *Kampfgruppe* Schmidt on the plateau," he was told. Meanwhile, a search team discovered the gruesome remains of the 2nd Platoon. They had been stripped of weapons and equipment, but they had not been mutilated, as was the habit of some German troops. Luger was beside himself. *How could a platoon of my soldiers be annihilated by untrained terrorists?* he wondered. *They must have had help*, he concluded. It was his way of rationalizing the loss of so many men. The abandoned British weapons lent credence to his belief. At least it helped take the sting out of the thrashing.

After burning all the deserted buildings in the vicinity, *Kampfgruppe* Luger pressed on, intending to join *Kampfgruppe* Schmidt as soon as possible.

Maquis Command Post, 1400, 1 December 1942—The command post was in turmoil when Cain arrived. Clearly something was very wrong. He caught Henry's eye and, with a nod, motioned him outside where there was less commotion. LeGrand joined them.

Before Cain could say anything, LeGrand blurted out, "The Germans are attacking the three entrances onto the plateau. They've got us outnumbered and we can't hold them."

Cain agreed, relating his experience on the Saint-Nizier Road. "We desperately need reinforcements," he added. "What does London say?"

Henry shook his head. "Robert has been trying to reach them all morning, but the Germans are blocking our signal. The last we heard from London was, 'we'll try.'"

"That's not good enough," LeGrand emphasized strongly. "We have hundreds of men to think about. I don't want to see them all killed."

Just then a runner approached, shouting, "Gliders! Gliders! The Americans are coming!"

28

Fallschirm-Kampfgruppe Schäfer, 0630, 1 December 1942—
Oberleutnant Friedrich Schäfer, veteran commander of the airborne
Kampfgruppe, watched as his heavily laden *Fallschirmspringers*
boarded the DFS 230 transport carrying gliders (*Lastensegelflugzeug*)
lined up on the runway at Lyon. Their mission was to land right in
the heart of the Vercors plateau, capture the town of Vassieux, and
push inland to block the Saint-Nizier Road. Schäfer planned to bring
in his force in two waves. The first wave of DFS gliders would bring
in 200 infantrymen with light weapons and equipment. It was a gutsy
call, because the initial wave would be on their own in the midst
of hundreds of terrorists until the second wave arrived, bringing
an additional 200 men as well as heavier weapons, ammunition,
and equipment.

Schäfer had a severe, cruel-looking face, with the obligatory
dueling scar, and a "high and tight" haircut. He looked the part of
a Nazi superman—slender, fastidious, his uniform festooned with
decorations and medals that he received for carrying out Hitler's
"New Order," with a ferocity that earned him his superior's praise.
A veteran of the glider-borne attack on Eben-Emael—the Belgian
defensive fort—at the beginning of the war, he presented himself
as a tough, demanding leader. In actual fact, Schäfer was a brutal,

merciless killer, who believed that taking prisoners was a waste of time and manpower.

Schäfer took his seat on the narrow bench in the middle of the cramped fuselage. He sat behind the pilot, who was also designated to man the single machine gun mounted on the canopy. He settled in for the butt-numbing three-hour flight to the landing zone. At a little after 0730, the Heinkel He 111s revved up their two Daimler-Benz engines and slowly took up the slack in the 40-meter tow ropes. The experienced Luftwaffe pilots knew exactly how to nudge the gliders into the air without breaking the tow ropes. As they became airborne, the gliders dropped their landing gear, depending on a skid under the fuselage for landing.

The noise inside the flimsy "flying coffins," as they were known affectionally by the *Luftlandetruppe* (glider men), prevented anyone from talking. Instead, the veterans fell asleep, which they claimed they could do anywhere, anytime. One of the men got airsick, earning the ire of the rest of the eight-man stick. The stench was nauseating, affecting even the strongest stomach. At that point in the flight, the men were willing to do anything to get out of the glider.

Twenty-one twin-engine bombers, towing gliders, emerged from the clouds and flew over LeGrand's command post. Maquisards poured out, shouting and cheering in celebration: "The Americans are here!"

With tears running down his face, LeGrand walked over and shook Cain's hand. "Thank God help has arrived," he cried, overcome with emotion.

Henry slapped his fellow Jed on the back. "You Yanks certainly know how to stage a demonstration."

They watched the aircraft circle a large open space and then cut the gliders loose. As the gliders came in for landing, their sides became visible to the men on the ground. Instead of American stars or British rondels, black German swastikas were painted on the fuselages. The men stood in stunned silence.

At 3,000 feet, the glider pilots cut the tow ropes and started the gut-wrenching 60-degree dive angle. Schäfer thought the steep angle would give them an edge by putting them on the ground before the terrorists could react. At 1,800 feet, the gliders were slowed down by small parachutes which blossomed from the rear. As they touched down, two small retro rockets fired, bringing them quickly to a stop.

Cain was the first man to shake off the shock of the airborne attack. "Germans!" he bellowed, pointing at the gliders. Henry ran to a nearby Bren gunner and told the young Maquisard to "SHOOT!" Frozen in place, the boy didn't grasp the significance of the gliders. The one-eyed Jed wrestled the weapon from his grasp, braced the 19-pound light machine gun against his hip, and blazed away at the nearest glider. He was able to place ten of the magazine's twenty .303 bullets into its nose and canopy. The pilot slumped over the controls, pushing them forward, causing the glider to smash into the ground. The metal fuselage crumpled and ended up in a pile of jumbled wreckage and broken bodies. Another glider fell victim to Maquisard fire, but the remainder landed safely.

The *Fallschirmspringer* disgorged from the surviving aircraft, formed into assault squads, and stormed the village of Vassieux, the pilots providing covering fire from the onboard machine guns. Schäfer was in the forefront, indiscriminately shooting anyone he came across. Without hesitation he gunned down a woman and child, and his men followed his example. They found only women and children in the village; the men were all in the forest with the Maquis. The women hoped the Germans would spare them. They were wrong. Schäfer's men went on a killing spree, slaughtering every living thing in Vassieux: old men, women, children, even animals, in a blood lust encouraged and condoned by their commanding officer. Schäfer himself murdered several inhabitants in cold blood, after which he celebrated the *Kampfgruppe's* "great victory."

The Maquisards quickly recovered and rushed in to attack the *Fallschirmspringer*. However, their uncoordinated and piecemeal attack was easily repulsed, and they were forced to pull back. The Jeds gathered them together and organized them into squads with strict instructions to surround the village and keep the Germans under fire but not to directly attack them. An intense firefight broke out with losses on both sides. However, the Germans could ill afford the loss. The destruction of two gliders and the casualties they suffered during the initial assault had cost them two pilots and 25 parachutists.

Fallschirm-Kampfgruppe Schäfer, 1400, 1 December 1942—After the abortive Maquisard attack, the *Kampfgruppe* established a defensive perimeter using several houses in the middle of town as strongpoints. Schäfer himself staked out a command post in one of the farmhouses—a poor choice. Small arms fire penetrated the wooden walls and wounded two of his men before he fled to the basement. As the day went on, Schäfer became more and more worried about his situation. His men were outnumbered, and they were running out of ammunition. The terrorists were much stronger than he had anticipated, and he expected them to launch an attack at any time. *If the reinforcements don't get here soon, it may be too late,* he mused.

But help was already on the way in the form of a second wave of 20 DFS and three Gotha GO-242 gliders carrying over 200 infantrymen and heavy weapons. As before, the Heinkel He 111s circled the landing zone and then the gliders were cut loose. This time, however, the Maquisards were alert and ready to welcome them. The gliders started taking fire long before they reached the ground. The embarked troops were helpless inside the fragile aircraft. Several men were killed and wounded by bullets passing through the fabric-covered fuselage before the gliders slid to a stop.

The embarked soldiers scrambled to get out of the death traps, helped by covering fire from Schäfer's men in the village, and a section of Focke-Wulf Fw 190 fighter-bombers that swept down to strafe the exposed Maquisards. This suppression fire enabled the bulk of the reinforcements to reach safety and brought German strength to over 350 combat-hardened *Fallschirmspringer* and a 20mm Flak 38 antiaircraft gun which was recovered from one of the GO-242 gliders. Schäfer used the gun to target the enemy positions and to cover the reorganizing of his force as they prepared to assault the Maquis.

Maquis Command Post, 1500, 1 December 1942—LeGrand gathered his commanders together. "Gentlemen," he began, "I believe it's time to face the situation. In my opinion we have only one course of action: to disperse. We can break up into small groups, infiltrate through the German lines, and continue the fight in the forest and mountains of the massif. I believe it's our only choice." His comment was met initially with stunned silence, so he summarized their situation, making it painfully obvious there was no hope. "The Nazis have broken through our defenses on the north, east, and south, and now we have a considerable force right in front of us." With that he sat down, waiting for his commanders to speak. One spoke emotionally about a last stand.

"At least we'll die with honor," he stressed. Another offered his opinion that an organized breakout as a fighting force was the answer. LeGrand countered, saying that it was impractical when most of the Maquisards were still in contact with the Germans and there was no way to communicate a plan to them. It became obvious to everyone that the only viable option was to follow LeGrand's proposal. They finally agreed to disperse in small groups starting that evening.

The Jeds were in agreement with LeGrand and offered to accompany him. In the meantime, they tasked Robert to contact London and let them know the plan. LeGrand asked them to allow him to send a last message, which they agreed to. In it he criticized De Gaulle and the Allies for not supporting the Vercors Maquis: "We have fought the Nazis without your promised support and suffered a great number of casualties. Now we must take to the forests and mountains to save our lives. For this we hold you responsible. You are criminals and cowards. Let me be clear, we consider you criminals and cowards." Robert sent the message as written.

An hour later, as Robert was about to shut down the Jed Set, he received a message from London for his two bosses. The message read: "Jedburgh Team Alexander be prepared for extraction in three days from Rayon Drop Zone." Short and sweet, no mention of why.

Cain exploded after reading it. "What the hell is this all about?" he thundered.

The normally calm Henry was equally upset. "We can't leave our friends!"

Cain ordered Robert to request clarification. In perhaps the speediest response they had ever received, the reply simply stated, "Comply with orders."

LeGrand took a different view; he supported the orders. "I believe you should go back and tell them what happened here. Tell them we were depending on them to help us ... and they didn't. Their promises were worthless."

The small party, including the three Jeds, LeGrand, and a local man to serve as a guide, left the command post late that afternoon. They wanted to infiltrate the German encirclement after dark. The group used little-known trails to work their way off the mountain, secure in the knowledge that the Germans seldom ventured into the forest for fear of ambush. By late evening they had passed through the porous enemy lines and reached their waystation for the night, a farm that belonged to a member of the local Maquis.

The farmer furnished them with food and cider. He seemed quite nervous, but they attributed it to the proximity of a German garrison. Nevertheless, Cain suggested they keep a sharp eye on the man just in case.

The exhausted men bedded down in the barn but rotated one man on watch throughout the night. Sometime before dawn, during Henry's rotation, he noted the farmer slipping out of his house and riding down the lane on his bicycle. *What the hell?* Henry thought. *Is the guy going to turn us in?* Almost immediately the farmer returned, furiously peddling his bike. He threw it down in the courtyard and ran into the barn, shouting, "Germans!" The fugitives sprang out of their straw beds, grabbing for weapons.

The farmer quickly explained that a patrol was at the end of the lane and would be at the farm in a matter of minutes. The fugitives snatched up their rucksacks and weapons and fled out the back of the barn just as the German patrol appeared. The sight of four armed men fleeing across an open field caught the patrol by surprise, giving the fugitives time to reach a tree line. Several shots rang out but no one was hit.

"Now we're in for it," Henry groused, as they plunged further into the trees. "The Jerries will be on us like white on rice!"

"Great analogy," Cain panted, trying to catch his breath. "Now they know we're in the area, they'll increase their patrols." The fugitives stopped to check on any pursuit. Their luck held; the Germans were not anxious to pursue them into the forest.

The German patrol's discovery of the fugitives dramatically increased the possibility of their capture or death and caused them to be even more careful as they made their way to the pick-up zone. The thought was in the Jeds' minds, *Will we be on time?*

29

A Flight No. 161 (Special Duties) Squadron, RAF Tangmere, 0639, 4 December 1942—Flying Officer Hugh Totenberg happened to be sitting in the kitchen of "the cottage" when the mission was posted. He was on the roster for the next extraction, so he was given the Air Transport Form to study. He noted that the landing field had been used in the past as a drop zone for the insertion of agents. The attached high resolution aerial photograph showed a clear meadow free of obstacles but surrounded by thick forest. The field was large enough for his Lizzie, so he didn't anticipate any problems with landing and taking off. However, he was a little concerned that the Germans may have discovered it had been used to infiltrate agents, although there was no indication they had it staked out. He copied the Morse Code identification signals on his knee pad and then worked up his flight route and prepared his map so that it would be easy to handle while flying.

Finished with the planning, he was tempted to have a mug of tea but then decided against it. The flight was long and he didn't want to have to pee during the flight; using the "necessary" while flying was a real pain in the buns. He caught a ride to the dispersal site and did the usual walk-around inspection of the Lizzie. A ground crewman accompanied him, ready to make any minor corrections.

Everything seemed to be OK, so he signed the acceptance form he was handed and put on his Mae West and parachute. He climbed into the cockpit and settled into his seat. After performing the pre-flight check, he primed the engine and started it up. The ground crewman pulled the chocks. The tower gave him clearance, and he released the brakes and taxied out. He took a last look at the cockpit gauges. Found them all in the green and took off. His fifth mission of the month.

Rayon Drop Zone, 2000, 4 December 1942—Cain lay in the tree line scoping out the meadow. "I can't see anything," he said to Henry and Robert lying next to him. "Maybe we lost them."

"We should be so lucky," Henry replied. They were referring to a German patrol that had spotted them that afternoon as they crossed a road. The patrol had come on hard, and they had been forced to run for their lives. Thick vegetation had helped them lose the pursuit, but they didn't know if there were other patrols in the area.

The moon had risen and was casting its light on the meadow, making it easier to see, but the forest surrounding it could hide an entire army. There was just no way to scout the area before the pickup. LeGrand and his men were in the meadow ready to flash the signal as soon as they heard the aircraft. The Jeds were on edge. The last few days had worn on them mentally and physically. They felt like they were abandoning friends, or as Henry said, "running out."

Cain thought he heard the faint sound of an aircraft engine. "Here comes our ride," he muttered.

"Have you got our tickets?" Henry responded, releasing some of the tension he was feeling. The sound grew louder.

Flying Officer Hugh Totenberg, 2000, 4 December 1942—Totenberg peered out the side window of the Lysander and spotted what he thought was the pick-up field. "Now all I need is the light code," he mumbled to himself. A tiny pinpoint of light flickered in the darkness. "There it is!" He felt a familiar thrill of excitement. The rush of adrenaline revved him up, making his senses come alive. He thought it made him a better pilot.

Totenberg expertly brought the aircraft lower and lower until the flarepath was clearly visible, making a perfect landing—"right on the money," as the Yanks would say. He taxied over the rough ground to where the "pick-ups" were standing, wheeled the Lysander around, and prepared to take off. "Come on chaps," he muttered, "haven't got all night."

The three men sprinted for the Lysander, Cain in the lead. He stopped at the ladder to let Robert be the first to climb into the aft cockpit. "Hustle!" he shouted, urging the young NCO to get his ass in gear. Henry was next. Just as he reached the cockpit, gunfire exploded from the left-side tree line. Bullets tore through the aircraft's aluminum fuselage. Henry fell head first into the cockpit. Cain jumped onto the ladder, shouting, "Go! Go!" and started climbing as Totenberg "poured the coal" to the engine. Cain struggled to climb as the Lysander gained speed.

More bullets struck the fuselage. One entered Totenberg's forward cockpit and struck him in the left side of the neck. He flinched and grabbed the wound with his left hand but continued to maintain control of the "stick" with his right. Blood streamed down his flight suit, and for a moment he felt lightheaded … but his superb airmanship and self-discipline took over. The Lysander reached take-off speed and he lifted it into the air, just as Cain fell into the cockpit.

The three passengers struggled to sort themselves out in the cramped cockpit as the aircraft gained altitude. The Lysander was built to accommodate two passengers, three in a pinch, for which the current situation qualified.

As blood loss and shock began to take its toll, Totenberg struggled to keep from passing out. There was nothing the passengers could do for him, except pray. At one point the Lysander dipped dangerously low over the English Channel and it looked like they were going for a swim. Somehow Totenberg regained control. Finally, after three tension-filled hours, Tangmere's grass runway appeared in the windscreen.

The crew manning the tower observed the Lysander's erratic flight and asked for confirmation if the pilot needed assistance. Totenberg's muffled response confirmed their suspicion. The base crash crew and medical staff were alerted. The duty ambulance sped out to the runway.

In a last desperate effort to maintain consciousness, Totenberg brought the Lizzie in for landing. He bounced at least three times before finally bringing it down, proving the sturdiness of the landing gear. Gingerly, the crash crew lifted the wounded pilot out of the aircraft. A medical officer put a large battle dressing on his neck to stop the bleeding and placed him in the "meat wagon," as the ambulance was called, and it sped away.

The three Jeds slowly uncoiled themselves from the cockpit and shakily climbed down the ladder. Robert dropped to his knees and kissed the ground. The two old salts took their return in stride. "All in a day's work," Cain voiced. The ground crew wasn't so sure. They had to patch over 20 holes in the Lizzie's fuselage.

Victory Services Club, 1000, 5 December 1942—Cain and Loreena walked hand in hand up to the reservations clerk and asked for their room key.

As he handed it over he asked, "Weren't you here the night of the big air raid?"

"Yes, but we spent the night in the Tube," Loreena replied.

"I remember now," he said. "I loaned you blankets." Cain reached for his wallet. "There won't be any charge," the clerk continued. "You didn't make use of the room, so this night's free."

Cain couldn't tell whether the clerk's comment had a double meaning, but, he figured, *what the hell, take what you can get.* Loreena was under no such illusion and her face turned red. The two walked away, leaving the clerk smiling with understanding.

"There's a war on, you know," he said to himself.

30

Special Operations Headquarters, 64 Baker Street, London, 0900, 7 December 1942—The two Jeds sat in the outer office of SO 3, Operations. They had been scheduled to meet with its elusive director for the past two days, but something always came up to preclude it from happening. Today was the final day before their leave was up and they had to report for duty. After an hour, a Wren ushed them into the "Great" man's office. He started the conversation. "I read your report and it seemed quite complete. I shared it with the boss." Before either one could comment, a male clerk entered and handed them folders. "Gentlemen, if you don't mind, I have an urgent meeting I must go to," the director said, and had the clerk usher them out.

"What the hell was that?" Henry sputtered.

"That's called the bums rush," Cain replied grumpily. "They're not interested in what went on in the Vercors. That's old news. They've moved on."

"So, the Maquis sacrifice doesn't matter in the big picture," Henry bemoaned. "Only to family and friends."

The two walked out of the building, hailed a cab, and went straight to the Victory Services Club pub, where they intended to drown their sorrows. Their thoughts had been so focused on the meeting that they hadn't opened the folders, thinking they just contained orders back to some Special Operations school for more training.

Henry opened his first. "*Mon Dieu*," he exclaimed. "I've been ordered to join the French 2nd Armored Division and take command of the *1er Bataillon du Régiment de Marche du Tchad!*"

"What the hell is that?" Cain asked.

"It's a battalion of mechanized infantry," Henry replied. "I'm back in the war!"

After congratulating him, Cain opened his folder and found several stapled sheets of paper stamped:

ORIGINAL ORDERS

FROM: Commandant of the Marine Corps

TO: Captain James Cain 027192 USMC

SUBJ: Termination of Temporary Additional Duty

REF: (a) Marine Corps Special Order 10-77 of 1 July 42

1. In accordance with Ref: A, your TAD orders are hereby cancelled. You are directed to proceed and report by first available transportation to 2nd Raider Battalion for duty.
2. Your priority for transportation is: AAAA
3. Leave is not authorized

By Direction of: Commandant of the Marine Corps

"Jesus Christ, Henry," Cain exclaimed. "We're going back to the war!"

The men adjourned in a huff to the Victory Services Club where they drowned out their sorrows. In fact, they drowned them so well that they almost missed their train the next morning. Hung over and downcast, they split up at the train station. With all they had gone through together, they had formed a bond that transcended mere friendship. They were, in Shakespeare's immortal words, "a band of brothers," forged in combat.

Author's note

The Maquis du Vercors never received the promised reinforcement and were defeated by the Germans at the end of July 1944. It was estimated that 639 Maquisards were killed during the battle. German casualties numbered 216 (65 killed, 133 wounded, and 18 missing). The German victors committed terrible reprisals against the local population, massacring over 200 civilians. The area was liberated by American forces in August, shortly after the battle.

My fictional characters, Captain Jim Cain and Gunnery Sergeant Leland Montgomery (who feature in the previous book, *Commandos*), joined the 2nd Marine Raider Battalion and we may see them again "raising hell in the South Pacific."

Josephine recovered from her injuries and subsequently returned to France with another Jedburgh team and served with distinction. Her exploits may be documented but they are currently still rattling around in my brain waiting for the right moment.

Henry went on to serve with distinction with the French 2nd Division, including the liberation of Paris. Perhaps we'll see him again, also.

Pool and his air crew made it safely back to England after an exhausting two-month trek across France to Spain. After a short survivor's leave, they resumed flight status.